THORN

THORN

Michael Dean

Bluemoose

First published in 2011 by
Bluemoose Books Ltd
25 Sackville Street
Hebden Bridge
West Yorkshire
HX7 7DJ

www.bluemoosebooks.com

British Library Cataloguing-in-Publication data
A catalogue record for this book is available from the-British-Library

Paperback ISBN 978-0-9566876-4-7
Hardback   ISBN 978-0-9566876-5-4

Printed and bound in the UK by Henry Ling Ltd, Dorchester

For Alan

And lest I should be exalted above measure...
there was given to me a thorn in the flesh.

II Corinthians 12:7.

Amsterdam, in the year of Our Lord, 1665

One

The mind and the body are one and the same thing.

Spinoza
Treatise on the Emendation of the Intellect

The other night I was convinced I saw Descartes. He was leaning his shoulder against a linden tree, relieving himself into the Lindengracht. I saw his face quite clearly. But how did I know it was him? The painter Rembrandt had painted him. But where had I seen the painting? At that point, I had not yet visited the painter's studio, let alone become the friend I was later to be.

I took a step toward the philosopher then stopped, pondering how I knew with such certainty it was him.

Descartes, meanwhile, had voided his waste. He hoisted up his breeches and caught sight of me watching him. It was him all right: the head considerably too large for the body; long hair, thin lips, big nose; that sly, superior look. An expression of alarm crossed his face as he caught sight of me; he glanced away, plotting his escape. It is often like this when two philosophers meet.

Some weeks later, the reason for his behaviour occurred to me: Descartes had impregnated a serving girl at the place of his lodging, here in Amsterdam. Some say she was one of many, both here and where he was enrolled to study, at Leiden. Dressed as I was in my threadbare cloak and worn breeches, he doubtless mistook me for a relative of the wronged girl, perhaps her brother. The light here was poor, the canal illuminated only by the stars and a gibbous moon.

Descartes turned away from me and fled, his lengthening springy footsteps making faint slapping sounds on the towpath.

'Descartes!' I cried out, as I ran.

He had heard me all right. He half turned as he increased speed, his huge head bobbing as if about to fall off altogether, his grey face like a creased sail, deflating as the wind went out of it.

I wallowed in his wake. 'Descartes,' I puffed, wheezing. 'The world is one. Descartes, wait! Mind and body cannot be of different substances because—' I stopped for a second, gasping, assailed by a painful stitch in my side. '—because there is only one substance. There is only one substance,' I shouted again, indignantly, with what wind I had left. 'Descartes, the world is not two. It is one. That is the meaning of life. The world is one.'

The philosopher paid me no heed. I began to run again, clutching my side, croaking out 'the world is one.' Descartes slowed his pace, perhaps having heard me, perhaps engaged by my argument, or perhaps just running out of puff, as I was. But at that moment, the flapping sole of my shoe caught in a tuft of grass, causing me to overbalance. I fell sideways into the canal.

And that was the last I saw of the philosopher that night. He made no attempt to rescue me, whether from indifference to my fate or lack of interest in my argument I cannot say.

* * *

Back in my chamber, I lit the battered copper lamp which hangs above my oak table, breathing in the blubbery smell of the oil. I had by now missed the meeting where I had been heading when I saw Descartes. It was a meeting of Waterlanders, as the freethinking *libertijnen* were called.

I pulled off my sodden clothes, all three layers of them, and dried myself on my drawers. I tossed the grey ball of wet garments on the bed, then sat down beside it, staring at it.

After a long while motionless, I dressed in dry clothes and lay full-length on the bed, clutching the wet shirt to my cheek.

The bed was all I had taken from my father's estate when he died. It was hugely elaborate, boasting a heavy, solid canopy, red velvet curtains and a red coverlet undulating over two big feather-filled bags. It filled my modest chamber. Every time I passed from the entrance door to the oak table, I was obliged to squeeze past the bed, scraping my thigh while my shoulder banged against the wall.

I was conceived in this bed. Both my parents died in it – my mother, Hana Debora, when I was six; my father two years ago.

My father was Michael de Espinosa, the merchant. No, make that the Portuguese merchant. No, make that the Portuguese *Jewish* merchant. Now we have it! I don't know whether it was his idea or Hana Debora's to name me Baruch, which means 'blessing' in Hebrew. As does Bento, my name in vulgate Dutch, and Benedictus, the Latin version. And as the family name, commonly shortened to Spinoza, means thorn, I go through life as a blessing and a thorn. Make of that what you will.

My father, my mother, my sisters and brothers, along with my present bed, inhabited a large house in the Houtgracht. It was a few doors down from the *Esnoga* – the synagogue – where my father was a *parnas*, a synagogue elder.

My great-uncle Abraham, one of the first Jews in Amsterdam, had been a founder of the original synagogue. So when my father died there was quite a party. Synagogue elders, merchants, neighbours. Creditors.

Father's body was loaded onto one of those flat lumbering funeral barges you can see wallowing along the Amstel any day. It was decked out in black, pulled by two horses plodding the towpath, one black one grey. We had ordered two black horses. There was a furious row with the funeral director when my brother Gabriel noticed the pallid substitute. Life so often evades symmetry, I have found. Indeed, one could say that the task of philosophy is to impose – or superimpose – a symmetry on life. But I digress.

The weeping mourners filled the barge for the two-hour journey to the body's final resting place. Others met the cortege at the Jewish cemetery. It's on land in front of the deconsecrated *Oude Kerk*. The cemetery had been given to great-uncle Abraham's generation of Jews by the Amsterdam city elders, at the time of the founding of the *Esnoga*.

The Jews were admitted as citizens of Amsterdam, though barred from the Guilds, at the very moment of my conception, in 1632.

Why? Because I was on the way?

No.

Because they liked Jews – traditionally a popular race?

No.

No – right of residence was granted because the Jews' knowledge of Spain and Portugal, where they had come from, coupled with their trading ability, was a huge advantage to the Republic.

Jews in boats, or at least organising boats, but not rocking boats. That was the deal.

The Jews were to blend in. Indeed the Republic (not the city of Amsterdam) forbade Jews to wear distinctive clothing which marked them out as Jews. Elsewhere, in some Germanic states, for example, Jews were required to wear distinctive yellow caps or patches. Not here. Here they were banned.

But there were conditions to the Jews being citizens. Oh indeed, there were conditions. The conditions were listed in a solemn document, a copy of which was kept under lock and key in the *Esnoga*. Great-uncle Abraham was one of its signatories, from the Jewish side. This is what he signed up to, in gratitude for being allowed to walk the streets of Amsterdam, looking like everybody else:

Jews must not have sexual relations with Gentiles.

Jews must refrain from criticising the Christian religion.

Jews must keep to Judaism.

I remember saying to my father that the Republic was the only country in the world where Jews were legally required to be Jews. Everywhere else they were legally burned for it. Like Portugal! I added gleefully. Like the old country! I was ten at the time. My father beat me so hard I stood to eat meals for a week.

And there he was, dead and waxy, floating down the Amstel on a barge, unable to beat me any more. I still miss him.

* * *

At the cemetery, the massive green-mould masonry of the long-ruined *Oude Kerk* cast its shadow over the mounds of grass running down to the river. The scattering of Jewish graves in front of it were all relatively new; gravestones still white and in good order. I looked at the names and dates of the dead. The oldest I could find was one Duarte Rodregues, who died in 1615, not even a full forty years before my father. The Jews living and dying in Amsterdam was all a new experience, all very tenuous. We had a foothold here, no more.

The rabbi appeared. This was Saul Levi Morteira, known as 'the burning brand of the synagogue'. His hooded eyes glowed, embedded close to the bold nose which pointed down to his bushy beard. The beard was a wondrous object, deserving of its own category in botany. By now it was pure white, with unkempt bristles sprouting in tufts, down past his clavicle. His hair was still thick, though: oily, mainly black, shot through with grey.

He had been a middle-aged man when I first knew him as my Hebrew teacher at *Keter Torah* – the Crown of the Law – when I was eight. Now, with me in my twenties, he looked as ancient and wise as an Old Testament prophet. As ancient as Moses, in fact, the prophet we had fought over so bitterly.

During our quarrels on the subject, I always visualized Moses as looking like Morteira, which made arguing with Morteira about Moses a strangely personal experience. I would see

Morteira, in my mind, coming down from Sinai carrying two tablets, as it says in the Old Testament – ten commandments being too many to fit on one.

As father's coffin was carried shoulder-high to its grave, Morteira came over to me and gave me his usual greeting: he pinched my right cheek between his index and middle fingers, then wrenched a chunk of my face-flesh 90° to the right. My eyes started to water. I knew from experience that past a peak of pain the cheek would go numb, but until then it took all my resolve not to whimper, scream or plead. He was waiting for that, his eyes never leaving my face. That or my gesture of surrender.

But I did not give him what he wanted. This time, for the first time, I fought back. I gripped his wrist in my hand and dug my nail into the layers of soft white skin. With a grunt of surprise, he let go.

He smiled at me. 'How are you, renegade?'

'Well, Ashkenaz, well. And yourself?' Morteira gasped at my audacity, then snarled. Although he hails from the Venice ghetto, and speaks Italian, Portuguese and Spanish like a native, Morteira is indeed an Ashkenaz – a Germanic Jew, originally from Vienna. They are the uneducated underclass of the tribe; the pedlars and tinkers, the tavern violinists; still in long dark coats, funny caps and untrimmed beards. Not Morteira himself, of course – apart from the untrimmed beard – but he is tainted by association.

When sufficient Sephardic Jews have escaped from Spain and Portugal to build the New Jerusalem in Amsterdam, the Ashkenazim will be their servants – or should that be *our* servants? The Sephardic Jews will rebuild the Temple – conquered and lost in Judea in 70AD – here, here in the rich Dutch soil of Amsterdam. The Ashkenazim can sweep the floor, polish the gold treasures and keep the lamps filled with oil.

'*Mijnheer Spinozie*,' Morteira said, with a sneer. It was a pun on my family name. *Spinozie* – spinach – makes you clever. 'Too

6

clever,' said the rabbi. 'Too much spinach. Always too clever for your own good.'

Morteira turned his back on me and swept, gown flowing, to the head of the open grave. There he stood, towering over the fresh mounds of earth, his skullcap pinned to his hair in case the strong wind over the flat land should leave him bareheaded – a crime against God.

The ruins of the Old Church formed a flat-looking backdrop, like those painted scenes they have in the theatre. Morteira's black rabbinic gown fluttered in the warm spring wind. So did untamed strands and tufts of his beard – renegades breaking away, going their own way, heretics like me. I heard Morteira's voice in my head – *ketter, ketter, ketter* – heretic. *Ketter, ketter, ketter* – pitter-pat – like falling rain.

* * *

My sisters, Ribca and Miriam, were at the family home with the women, preparing the funeral feast. My younger brother, Gabriel, came to stand next me as Rabbi Morteira intoned the blessing for the dead. I watched, my head up, as the mourners bowed their heads, rocked from the waist, ululated the ancient Hebrew sounds of mourning. I could feel Gabriel's eyes on me. He wasn't saying the words either.

Gabriel kept touching my arm, as if willing me to do what he wanted. He was always trying to get me to do something or other. I smiled at him. He was smaller than me but better-looking, with his regular features and compact build.

He looks more Dutch than I do. I'm exotic, with my olive complexion, oval face broken by a faint little moustache, dreamy brown eyes and strong nose. He's not. It's almost as if the family's efforts to blend in as Dutch had borne fruit in the time between my birth and Gabriel's.

'I need to speak to you,' he hissed, as father was being lowered into his grave. I shrugged. Gabriel always needed to speak to me. The family firm, now called *Bento y Gabriel D'Espinoza*, was in trouble. Like many others, we had lost ships to the war with the English. I had told Gabriel, and my father in his last years, that I wanted nothing to do with the company, elder son or not. I simply wanted to write my philosophy. I could cover my modest living costs from grinding lenses for microscopes, and now for these remarkable new double-lensed telescopes Drebbel has designed. But of course they would not leave me alone.

Gabriel did not want complete control of the company. I think it frightened him. He wanted me there, next to him. Father's will left more debts than assets, but I signed over all the assets to Gabriel, keeping only the family bed for myself. But that left Gabriel dissatisfied. Gabriel was always dissatisfied. And restless. Even as our father left this earth, or settled more deeply into it, according to your viewpoint, Gabriel was shifting his little limbs about, like a man with the St Vitus' disease.

When the ceremony finished, Gabriel and I were naturally the focus of attention as mourners crowded round us to express their condolences and pay tribute to my father. When that was over and it was time to make our way back to the river, where the barge waited, two youths approached us. They were not in mourning garb and they looked angry, even menacing.

'Creditors,' Gabriel murmured, in a resigned manner.

I knew who they were. Abraham and Adriaen Alvarez were suppliers of ours. They had supplied a ship where we were especially heavily involved; I think we owned a twenty-fifth share. But they had supplied certain commodities exclusively to us. The ship had been captured by the English, towed to London and looted. Nevertheless, my recollection was that we had still managed to pay them, when another ship got through from Brazil, carrying sugar, a few weeks later.

'We paid them, didn't we?' I said to Gabriel.

He touched my arm again, as if it were a talisman. 'What do you think?'

'We want a word with you,' said the younger of the two brothers, Abraham.

'In due course,' Gabriel said. 'As you see, our beloved father has just been laid to rest.'

'No, now,' Abraham said. 'Before the rest of the creditors get you.'

Gabriel sighed. He had already told me that some of our creditors intended to make their case over the funeral sweetmeats that our sisters were even now laying out.

'Face to face,' Adriaen Alvarez said. 'Behind the church.'

The Alvarez brothers glared at the Spinoza brothers, breathing hard, with no little belligerence.

'We intend to pay you,' I said, with a show of mildness. 'I assure you, you will get every *stuiver* you are owed.'

'Too right,' said the older Alvarez brother. 'Now you come with us to a quiet spot. You don't want to cause an outrage, I'm sure.'

So we accompanied them to a knoll behind the deconsecrated church, which turned out to be the spot where they had hidden their cudgels. Before they set about us, I suggested they at least refresh my memory as to the details of their grievance.

The Alvarez brothers, it seemed, had supplied some of our part of the cargo on the *Hoorn,* the ship captured by the English. They had – eventually – been paid for the sail cloth, bricks and beer they had supplied, even before the ship's intended return with southern fruits from Portugal. But they claimed they had also supplied, via the firm of *D'Espinoza*, all the beer for the sailors on the voyage. Gabriel did not try to deny it.

The Alvarez brothers had not been paid for this item. Gabriel did not deny that, either.

Though we made some effort to defend ourselves, the louts set about us vigorously with their cudgels. My attempt to reason with them, to point out the illogicality of their actions, met with no success. They said there would be further beatings until payment ensued, which I suppose was a refutation, of sorts, of my argument.

They left us on the ground, bruised and bleeding. And so it was in that condition that we attended the mourning feast for our dearly beloved father.

* * *

The association between mind and body – being of *one* substance, Descartes please note – caused me to touch my cheek at the place where the younger Alvarez had felled me, some two years ago. I do believe that the mind makes a picture of its own body, this picture enabling it to tell the body what to do and what to feel.

Had we retaliated with any success at all, Gabriel and I? I could remember only their blows on us, not ours on them, if there were any.

I rolled off the capacious soft bed, scraped my way along the wall and sat down at my table. Sighing with contentment, I packed my little Gouda clay pipe with the tobacco I favour – heavy with Latakia – and puffed away. The smell of the Latakia overcame the smell of blubber from the lamp oil – for now. The trusty little pipe, brown with use, grew satisfyingly hot in my hand. I cleared my mind of the clutter of the day, before preparing to go to work.

There were three books on my table, along with a pamphlet by the heretic Herman van Rijswijck who had been burned to death, along with his books, for his views. What? In the Dutch Republic? In the tolerant Dutch Republic? Yes! I'll tell you about the tolerant Dutch republic, shall I? The Dutch themselves have a phrase for it: *Een schijn van verdraagzaamheid* – an appearance of tolerance.

But here is the interesting part: when I left my little room to go to the meeting of the Waterlanders, the pamphlet was propped between the three books: Isaac La Peyrere's *Prae Adamitae*, about inaccuracies in the Bible; Cornelis Petersz's *The Light of the Truth,* and Robbert Robbertsz's *Short Summary of the Predestination Between Father and Son.* Now, the pamphlet is no longer propped between the three books. It is lying at some distance from them, at a corner of the table.

Whoever had searched the room had not even bothered to try to recreate the relative position of the books and the pamphlet. My, my, they were getting careless. Or did they no longer care whether I knew they had been in my room or not? Perhaps they were showing me I was being watched. Did they, indeed, want me to know?

As if I *didn't* know. For months now, I had painstakingly measured the angles between books when I left the room, then memorised the result. I had left a black ink smudge at a precise distance and angle from the corner of a book. Or I had left a tiny feather from the bed inside a book, to see if they would open it, to check the contents. At the beginning, some effort had been made to restore my signs. But no longer. They knew I knew.

Access to my little chamber was not especially difficult. My room was on the ground floor in the house of the linen weaver, Jan Teunissen, just a few doors down from the family home in the Houtgracht.

Teunissen is a Waterlander: he believes Christ to be a human, not a God. Like me, he believes the Bible stories are not reliable as truth. It was my landlord who had first asked me to address the Waterlanders on the subject of the bible stories, and I had quickly found friends there.

Teunissen would not have admitted my watchers to my room, but his servants were another matter. A few *penningen* pressed into a receptive hand would do the trick. As to the identity of those interested in me, there were two main possibilities:

Either they were among those watching the Waterlanders meetings – in which case they could have been sent by the Calvinist Church or the city authorities. Or they were in the service of Saul Levi Morteira. I inclined to the latter theory, as the man who has been following me is most certainly, from his appearance, a Sephardic Jew.

11

But the matter of my watchers was of secondary interest to me. I put it out of my mind and opened Robbert Robbertsz's book, lovingly caressing the frontispiece. Robbertsz is interesting. He was a freethinker, like the Waterlanders, and a mocker, like me. He mocked all forms of religion and religious observance, but did not mock the true service of God and man.

He once offered a competition to resolve that great theological dispute as to which came first, the seeds or the tree. He then entered his own competition and claimed the first prize for his solution. This was that the tree bears the seeds and the seeds create the tree. It is predestined.

It is in this sense, nature following nature's laws, that I myself believe in predestination. The idea is much misrepresented. It does not mean that if you stand in the doorway of the new Town Hall, a mysterious force will tell you whether to go in or not. I'm a determinist, for God's sake, not a fatalist.

Anyway, Robbertsz was excommunicated over fifty years ago, in 1591, and had to leave Amsterdam. He escaped with his life, which is more than Oldenbarnevelt did when he opposed Prins Maurits in matters of worship. Yes, in the liberal Dutch Republic!

Feeling that familiar tightening of excitement in my belly as my thoughts gathered in my mind, I eased my way along the wall, halfway along the bed. Lifting the counterpane, I dropped down on my belly and wriggled under the bed. At this point I was obliged to pause, as the considerable thickness of dust under the bed, not to mention the mouse droppings and the corpses and skeletons of the mice themselves, set me off on a coughing fit.

When this had finally subsided I used a blade, kept under the bed for the purpose, to raise a loosened floorboard. My manuscript lay where I had left it. The vellum embodiment of my heretical thought was untouched. They had not found it. At least, not yet.

Two

... *those who look to a supernatural light to understand the*
meaning of the prophets and the apostles are sadly in need
of the natural light, and so I can hardly think that
such men possess a divine supernatural gift.

Spinoza
Theological Political Treatise

I t is a myth that philosophers are necessarily solitary creatures.
Like anyone else, I welcome the company of men of the
same stamp. I even welcome interruptions in my tiny chamber.
I know I can always call up my thoughts again, and resume
exactly where I was before the interruption.

But I must confess I cannot recall who it was I had arranged
to meet on the day Rembrandt the painter became my friend.
It was probably one of the *libertijnen* from whose circle I
increasingly drew companionship. Was it the painter Ruisdael?
It may have been my brother-in-law, Samuel de Caseres –
married to Miriam.

At any rate, the day began unremarkably enough. I awoke,
as ever, as the first pearls of the dawn light gleamed through
the cracks in my shutters. The ideas of the night were turning
in my mind. I completed the chore of dressing: three layers of
clothes to keep out the Amsterdam winter. Then I opened the
shutters to let in the now-gleaming light.

Then the second chore: food. Eating to me is a necessary
bodily function, like its concomitant, defecation. I take no more

and no less pleasure in the one than the other. If anything, the satisfaction in the production of a perfect stool usually outweighs any joy I may have had in the consumption of it in its original form.

No doubt on that day I consumed a bowl of gruel, perhaps with raisins and butter. The bowl and a wooden spoon were among a few artefacts I had taken from the family house when I moved out. I had chosen a shallow bowl which I could lick clean, to save the use of a cloth. I do confess to some enjoyment of a glass of small beer, to chase down the gruel.

And so to work! Happiness filled my mind and body from bottom to top like water being poured into a bath.

The centring spindle and lathe next to the oak table were now bathed in the finest roseate light. The wooden seat of the lathe was worn to my contours. I had removed the vice which holds the lens to the grinding stone, preferring to hold the glass with my hands, for the greater degree of control this gives.

I took up the lens I was working on, pressing the treadle with my foot to set the lathe in motion. I hardly noticed the coughing which immediately ensued.

The lens I was grinding will eventually achieve a magnification of around 500, when it is finished off with carborundum and polishing powder. Soon we will achieve sufficient magnification to identify the one substance of all life.

The ancient Greeks, Epicurus and others, knew that life consists of matter in motion. Large elements consist of swimming small ones. But the subsequent lapses into obscurantism, mystification and superstition are the result of, or sometimes caused by, a misunderstanding of the nature of light. It is through sight, the queen of the senses, that we will eventually achieve understanding.

Take the rainbow. To the theologian, the rainbow is the glorious sign of the Covenant, while the physicist judges it in accordance with the basic laws imparted to create things by the

Lord God. The laws discovered by natural science are divine laws and *vice versa*. This rules out miracles.

Take Joshua: according to the Bible, Joshua asked God for an extension of daylight, so he could finish his battle against the Amorites in the light. 'Sun, stand thou still upon Gibeon.' And he got it. So, clearly, Joshua believed the sun revolved round the earth with a diurnal motion and on that day it stood still for a short time.

Ridiculous! Total superstitious rubbish! There was excessive coldness of the atmosphere on that day – hence the hailstones, see Joshua 10:11 – and that led to unusually great refraction of light.

See? All you have to do is increase the power of sight to increase the power of understanding of the working of God's laws – or nature's laws, it's the same thing. And banish all this superstitious gibberish that religion peddles.

* * *

It was time for my meeting with whoever it was. I wrapped my thick brown wool cloak around me and stepped outside into Houtgracht, blinking, shielding my eyes from the sudden crystalline light.

The north wind was cold as a blade, carrying the stink of the rendering works out at Marken. I was wearing so many layers of clothes I couldn't get my arms down to my sides, and still I was chilled to the blood. The canal was mostly frozen, cracking in the distance as bits of it thawed. Ducks were circling desperately, trying to maintain and extend their tiny circles of icy water.

I made my way carefully along the frozen towpath to the hump-backed bridge over the canal. Some ragamuffins were skimming stones across the ice and cheering when one reached the other side. I caught myself smiling at their simple pleasure.

On the near side of the canal there is a tiny run-down cottage, so close to the edge that it appears to be about to fall.

In the window of the cottage is a plaster representation of Saint Adrian, with his emblem, an anvil. This artefact is supposed to protect the inhabitants of the cottage against the plague.

As ever when I passed this way, I imagined myself knocking on the door of the cottage to bring enlightenment. The door would be answered by an ignorant peasant.

'Good morning, ignorant peasant,' I would cry out cheerfully, for I am at heart a cheerful fellow. 'Can you suggest to me please a single link in the chain of causality – just the one will do – between your possession of a statue of Saint Adrian and you not succumbing to the plague?'

In the theatre of my mind the peasant would confess himself unable to suggest a single causal link. The teleological cupboard, so to speak, would be declared bare. I would then offer to smash the peasant's statue for him, as a first step toward clearing the clutter of superstition from his dull mind and establishing of the beauty of logical thought in its place.

I would explain who Saint Adrian was, perhaps while I was smashing his statue in the peasant's parlour. The conversation would run like this:

Me: Saint Adrian is the patron saint of soldiers and butchers. Any idea how he came to be associated with plague protection?

Dull peasant: No idea.

Me (smashing the peasant's statue): Me neither, actually. A totally random and meaningless association. Do you know Adrian's story?

Dull peasant: Er, no.

Me: Adrian was a Roman officer who converted to Christianity. He was executed for it and his head and hands cut off. His wife, Natalia, took one of his hands as a memento. Any idea why?'

Dull peasant: Can't say I have.

Me: Any thoughts as to what a wife would actually do with her late husband's hand? I mean, where would she keep it? In the cold room, with the butter and cheese? Or maybe she'd wave it at passers-by. Well?'

Dull peasant: Beats me.

But as usual I passed by the peasant's cottage with this dialogue of the mind unsaid.

Just as well. I am widely criticised as sarcastic. No doubt the peasant would have added his voice to the chorus, as he was cleaning up the shards of his statue, mourning his lost plague-protection.

The point, however, is this: if the bible trains the multitude to give credence to fairy stories which are easily disprovable – like the Joshua fable, like the Moses fable – their minds are clogged with superstition. They are then not open to the beauty of clear reason which would lead them to God-in-Nature, Nature in God.

Never mind. It was a lovely day. So for now, at least, I left the multitude to its fate.

Having crossed the canal at the hump-backed bridge I turned right, away from the flower and vegetable market, into Breestraat.

This was the heart of the Jewish Quarter. Uncle Abraham's generation had settled on the island of Vlooienburg when they first arrived from Spain and Portugal, but immigrants always move on when they grow richer. So now the Jews are here, in Breestraat.

The Jews and Rembrandt. Even at this point, I knew Rembrandt to greet in the street. He comes to meetings of the Waterlanders now and again. I've no idea why he lives in the Jewish Quarter. Rembrandt has the only intact foreskin round here for miles. He's even got Jews in his basement. The Pereira brothers – Samuel and Jacob – rent storage space. They are Sephardi merchants, of course. What would you expect, pork butchers?

Over there, to the right, is the house of the merchant Daniel Pinto. Three-storey, redbrick, step-gabled. We know him well.

He is especially skilled at putting consortia together when we send a ship out to the old country with Dutch goods, then back with goods from Portugal or Brazil. Pinto's huge house is seven-to-nine Breestraat.

The house over there is occupied by Isaac Montalto, son of the court physician to Maria de Medici. Over there is Bento, or Baruch, Osorio. They say he has fifty thousand guilders in the Bank of Amsterdam. And then, all in the same street, there is Rodrigues, there is da Costa, there is Bueno, Lopes de Leon and so on and so on and so on. If they got out of Portugal in one piece, they're in Breestraat. I'm sure you get the picture.

And just across the Sint-Anthonisluis, within sight of Daniel Pinto's massive house, there is the house of that bastard Chacham Saul Levi Morteira. (*Chacham* means 'wise man', by the way. It's an alternative title to rabbi.) And he *is* a wise man. And very learned and exceptionally well-read. And he's still a bastard.

I must have dropped into a brown study. I do that quite a lot. When I came to, I realised I'd stopped in the middle of Breestraat. I saw old man Rembrandt himself. Rembrandt van Rijn. How long had he been there? He was outside Lopes de Leon's place, diagonally opposite his own house. He was carrying sketching materials and a light easel. I assumed he was about to walk down to the Diemerdijk, to do one of his landscape drawings. In fact, I think he told me later that that was his intention.

But as I watched him from across the road, he stopped and hailed a rough looking fellow. Even from this distance, I could hear his voice. Our ships a-sail in the Narrow Sea could hear him too, I reckon. He booms like a ventriloquist from out of that rounded barrel of a belly.

He was obviously hailing the ruffian. I watched the tableau – Rembrandt waving where he wanted the ruffian posed. Rembrandt listening. The ruffian obviously asking for money, because Rembrandt laughed and gestured at his purse. The ruffian striking a melodramatic pose, flexing his muscles. As the wind changed in my direction, I could hear Rembrandt's booming laugh at that.

Rembrandt was wearing the thigh-length belted coat he habitually wore to meetings of the Waterlanders. That and his stovepipe hat with the battered brim. To my surprise, given the winter cold, he took the coat off and lay it on the ground. I assumed this was the better to sketch. But, as he set up his easel, the ruffian ran towards him with, I feared, the intention to strike him down or do him some other harm. But no. The ruffian seized the coat and made off with it.

'Hey!' I called out and ran after the ruffian.

I have always been fleet of foot. If I had not fallen into the canal that night, I assure you I would have caught up with Descartes. I would have persuaded him to my view. You would never have heard of the mind-body dichotomy, believe me. But I digress.

I gained on the ruffian, who appeared to be trying to put the coat on as he ran, perhaps the better to make his escape. Behind me, I heard an inchoate rumble from Rembrandt. I seized the ruffian, still handicapped by his struggles with Rembrandt's coat.

'Hah!' I cried, having wind left only for monosyllables.

I held fast to the ruffian's arm. I heard Rembrandt calling behind me. 'Spinoza! Baruch, is that you?'

I had not the wind to reply that it was indeed me.

'Baruch, let him go,' the painter cried as he waddled up to us.

Now, it has always been a characteristic of mine to do the exact opposite of whatever I am told to do. I held the ruffian fast by one arm, as he wheezed stale wine fumes in my face.

Rembrandt began to remonstrate with the thief. 'What did you do that for, you dolt? Opportunity makes the thief, I suppose.'

I winced. I detest proverbs and set phrases, they are the enemies of original thought.

In wincing, however, I may have loosened my grip on the thief. At any rate, he broke free and landed a hefty blow which caught me on the shoulder. I gasped. Steadying himself, he threw a vigorous punch to my belly, doubling me up and winding me.

As I folded over, I caught sight of another figure coming running toward us. He was younger than me, for sure – by more than five years it later transpired, though you would not have guessed it from his appearance. And he was fairer, as befits a Christian.

This newcomer caught the escaping ruffian, who was half in and half out of Rembrandt's coat, and bent his arm behind his back, forcing the arm nearly as high as the fellow's neck, making him roar with pain.

'Titus!' Rembrandt cried. It was astonishing how much love the old man conveyed, saying that name, even in those circumstances.

'I am Benedictus Spinoza, the philosopher,' I said.

'And I am Titus van Rijn,' said the boy, with complete composure. 'Rembrandt's son. Pleased to meet you, sir.'

No handshake between us was possible, as Titus was pinning a struggling thief, nor even an exchange of kisses on the cheek, but the ruffian roared as if to complete the round of introductions.

'What shall we do with him?' Titus said. His control over the ruffian was now complete. The brute suddenly stopped struggling.

'Oh, let him go,' Rembrandt said, pulling his coat from the ruffian's arm and putting it on. 'I'll go and draw a windmill instead.'

'I think not, Papa,' Titus said with quiet authority. 'I fear we would see him again if we let him loose.' The ruffian glared at Titus but said nothing.

'Take him to the police,' I suggested.

Titus nodded, as if considering. But he already had a solution, clearly calculated. 'There's never anybody there, *Mijnheer*

Spinoza. At the police office I mean. Or the magistracy. They're always drunk or marching round the town. I'll take him straight to the *Tugthuis* in the Heiligeweg and tell them to lock him up.'

'Good idea,' I said. 'Cut out the middle man. My father was a trader. He would have approved.'

With a charming smile for myself and his father, the youth frogmarched the ruffian away, before Rembrandt or I had time to say another word.

'Well,' I said to Rembrandt, 'I hope we meet again soon, sir, under happier and more placid circumstances. Perhaps at the Waterlanders'...'

I stopped speaking. Rembrandt was facing me squarely, hands on his ample hips, elbows out, staring at my face, squinting slightly.

'What?' I said. My stomach was aching from the blows I had taken and I feared that the ruffian had somehow damaged my face. I touched my nose, a trifle self-consciously.

'I *must* draw you,' Rembrandt boomed. 'That face! I *must* draw that face. Now!'

'I'm afraid I am on my way to lunch with—'

'Now, I say! I'll make you immortal. Bugger lunch!'

Three

Lighting a candle creates more light in a room, but so does opening a shutter, which does not, of itself, create more light, only more light in the room.

Spinoza
Short Treatise on God, Man and His Well-Being

'A microscope,' Rembrandt was saying, or rather shouting. 'I'll do you with a microscope.'

'Why?'

'It's your emblem. Like Veronica and her handkerchief. St Luke and his cow. John and his book. Peter and his keys. It's what the viewer will recognise you by.'

The painter stank of turpentine, beer and stale sweat. He was scoffing herring and washing it down with Amsterdam beer in the *sael*, the room where he ate and slept. The bed was unmade, the sheets a yellowy-grey. I tried to keep my eyes off the stains, which even my innocent eyes realised were the product of his lovemaking with his mistress, Hendrickje. She had brought the food and drink in.

Averting my gaze, I sipped at my beer and rubbed my stomach as it went down. It still ached from the ruffian's blows. I had refused herring.

'I haven't got a microscope,' I said, eventually.

'What?' He boomed so loudly the glass rattled in the window panes. He glared indignantly at my lack of a microscope. 'I thought that's what you did all day? You look at lice through a microscope. Don't you?'

The painter jutted his chin at me, as if suspecting some trick – the possession of a microscope being concealed from him in some underhand way, perhaps for nefarious purposes.

'You're thinking of Hooke,' I said. 'Robert Hooke in England. I write to him. And Boyle. Hooke looks at insects through a—'

'No, I'm not! How the hell can I be thinking of Hooke? I can't be thinking of Hooke, in England or anywhere else, 'cos I've never bloody heard of him!'

Rembrandt roared with laughter and slapped his thighs.

'I just grind lenses. I then sell them to people who—'

'A lens!' Rembrandt bellowed. 'Oh yes! That would be a challenge. With the light shining through it. God, it would be like depicting water. Your hands prominent, of course. Holding the lens. The second most expressive part of a man, the hands. The eyes, naturally, tell you the most.'

'I—'

'Yours are marvellous. There's all the suffering of your tribe in those eyes. It's marvellous painting Jews. Like painting old people. They're all old, Jews. Born old. Centuries old. And the suffering! You've really got something to get hold of. Just look at the pain in your eyes!'

'Well, that's partly because I've just been hit in the—'

'Hendrickje!' Rembrandt stood, the better to bellow. 'Hendrickje, come here!'

Hendrickje Stoffels appeared within seconds, walking into the room quickly but without appearing to hurry. She wore the apron and white linen cap of a servant.

'Yes, Rembrandt?' she said, softly.

My poor battered stomach constricted at the sight of her, my breath all but ceasing. Hendrickje was round-faced, sweetly pretty, gentle and buxom. I felt my face flushing.

It hardly helped that I was sure both Rembrandt and Hendrickje herself were aware of my reaction to her.

23

Rembrandt threw me an amused, almost complicitous glance, but spoke to his mistress. 'Hendrickje, bring us some Leiden cheese, please. And join us. I'm sure our guest will tolerate your company.'

Now they were laughing at me, in my agony at her presence!

Hendrickje shot me a kind, almost tender, look. 'I'll bring you the cheese,' she said. 'But I have no time to join the gentleman, for I have work to do.' She had a soft country accent, which went well with the curiously formal, almost old-fashioned way she spoke.

I sat in a state of suspended animation until she returned, as I think Rembrandt did. The cheese was on a pewter plate, cut into squares. I tried not to look at her as she put it down on the small carved oriental table near us, but it was impossible. My eyes drank in her full, undulating figure. It took all my strength not to follow with my gaze every step her dainty little slippered feet took out of the room.

'Leiden cheese,' Rembrandt said, at almost normal volume. 'With kumin. Try some.'

I did, picking out a square and then another. It was delicious. 'It's delicious,' I said.

'Yes,' Rembrandt said, absently. His mood had changed completely, suddenly quieter. 'It is all I have taken with me from my home. Except the memories of my mother.' He stopped, suddenly heavy and pensive. 'I am a local man you see. East, west, home is best. I was local in Leiden. I would never have left if it hadn't been necessary for my success as a painter. And now I am a local Amsterdammer. I'll never go further than a mile from here. The world can come to me, every tree and every face.'

'I'm sure it will,' I said, sincerely.

'My patron, Huygens, wanted me to travel,' Rembrandt went on, still in that musing, absent mood. 'He was a powerful man; he was looking for a Protestant Rubens. Go to Rome to learn, he said. But I said no. Didn't go to London, either. Though my friend Lievens asked me to go with him. Have you heard of Lievens? Jan Lievens?'

'No.'

'Good!' Rembrandt said, with something of his old manner returning. He grinned, showing rotten gappy teeth. 'He was my contemporary and my companion in Leiden, but he was no good. Not skilled enough as a painter; too pettily competitive as a man.'

'Did—?'

'I do a Saint Jerome, he has to do a Saint Jerome. That's Lievens for you! And then he botched it. Totally botched his Saint Jerome. An etching, it was. Gloomy bloody thing. He should have called it St Jerome on a moonless night. Look, there are two sorts of painters, Baruch.'

'Are—?'

'Two sorts. the rough and the smooth. Guess which I am?'

'The rough,' I said, with some confidence.

'Correct, philosopher. Correct. I come from a rough family. My father was a miller, heaved sacks of barley malt around all day. We made beer, not flour. Beer is more important than bread. You know what Lievens' father was?'

'Well, as I've never heard of him, I can't —'

'An embroiderer! A bloody embroiderer! Women's work. Very smooth. You know what they call me, these fashionable painters?'

'I—'

'They call me *ketter.*'

'*Geen ketter sonder letter* – No heretic without a text,' I said, managing to get the proverb out while he was drawing breath, realising only later that I was dropping into Rembrandt's style of speech. 'What are you a heretic against?'

'Good question, philosopher! I am a heretic because I put paint on thickly. Plaster it on, like a whore covering up her smallpox. The fashion these days is smooth. Smooth and mild, like bloody Jan Lievens. Smooth and mild and milky. Mind you, it's all right if Anthonis van Dyke does it, because he's a genius, but not that second-rate bugger Lievens.'

He broke wind, then fell into brooding silence. I, too, said nothing. We sat there without speaking for a while, not at all ill-at-ease. Eventually, I reached for another piece of Leiden cheese. It really was delicious, even apart from the kumin, quite the creamiest I've ever tasted. And that seemed to break the spell.

'You know why I'm rough? You know why I'm not a smoothie, Baruch? I'll tell you. Because of this.' He put his tough stubby hand round his bulbous, bulging strawberry of a nose and squeezed it. Then he let go and roared with laughter – the earlier bellowing Rembrandt again.

'I call it my hooter!' he roared. ' I'm ugly, Baruch. That's why my painting is rough. How you look is how you are. Lievens is pretty as a girl. Skin like fresh cream. Member of the Guild of St Luke, of course.'

I smiled. 'And you're not?'

'Of course not. They're as alike as peas, that lot, and so are their paintings.'

'We should form our own guild, you and I. The Guild of Heretics.'

Rembrandt thundered laughter. 'Yes, you're right. The Calvinists call me a heretic, too. In their case, it's because I paint scenes from the Apocrypha. They don't like that.'

'What—?'

'Especially the story of old blind Tobit. I've always been fascinated by how we see. My father had an eye disease, you know. He squinted, like me,' Rembrandt comically emphasised his squint. 'Then he went blind, like old Tobit. I paint my old papa as Tobit. I paint my dear mother as Anna, Tobit's wife.'

Rembrandt had tears in his eyes. I nodded. I knew the Calvinists had preached against him. They were highly organised. Once they had chosen an enemy, he would be damned from every pulpit in Amsterdam, on the same Sunday. In chorus, he would be vilified, abused, hectored. Many had not been able to withstand it and had left the city, which of course was precisely what the Calvinists wanted.

'To hell with the lot of them' Rembrandt said. 'All I need is Titus, my boy. And Hendrickje, who I think you noticed!'

'No, I—'

'Shapely, isn't she? Here, I'll give you a treat. Come with me.'

Rembrandt got to his feet and pulled me out of my chair. He took a key from a chain around his waist and unlocked a door in the *sael*. We went into a small secret chamber, with Rembrandt locking the door behind us.

He just stood there.

Most of the paintings round the walls were Waterlanders. You could see that by their clothes, black fustian with white linen ruffs. But there was one... It was a drawing of Hendrickje sitting on a chair. She wore a skirt. Just a skirt, nothing else. My mouth went dry.

Rembrandt put an arm round my shoulder. 'Come,' he said, gently. 'I'll walk back to your lodgings with you and we'll collect the lens. Then I'll draw you. That's the look I want. Exactly that.'

* * *

When we returned from my chamber, Rembrandt took me up to his small *kunstkaemer*, where he did his drawings, where the winter light was so bright I had to shield my eyes.

He opened a huge, battered sailor's chest, painted with flowers which were flaking off. It was chock-full of a jumble of clothes and objects. The painter pulled at a tangle of cloaks, robes, armour-breastplates, crowns and the Lord alone knows what else.

Leaving all these unwanted bits of clothing scattered on the floor, he pounced triumphantly on an ancient, faded, red brocade robe with flounced sleeves, the like of which I have not seen before or since. It stank of dust and camphor. When Rembrandt gleefully shook it out, hundreds of insects, alive

27

and dead, fell from it. Enough to keep brother Robert Hooke studying for a decade.

The painter sat me in a hard chair and wrapped the noisome robe round me. The dust on it, and no doubt the moths, fleas and lice, set me to coughing. Ignoring this, the painter rolled his tubby frame back to the clothes box and burrowed in it again. He surfaced triumphantly, bearing an ancient black wig of extraordinary length.

I finally mastered my coughing. Rembrandt regarded me with some impatience. 'Finished?'

'I believe so. May I have a glass of small beer? Just for my ailing chest.'

'No. I want to get going.' He plonked the ancient wig roughly on my head. It bunched on my shoulders, it was so long.

'Was this originally a rug?'

'Shut up! Turn your head to look at me. That's it.'

'I've never been painted before.'

'You're not going to be painted now.'

'What?'

'This, my boy, will be an etching. I prefer them to paintings, at least at the moment.

You can alter them *ad infinitum*. You can make three hundred prints before the plate gets worn. Sometimes four. You can sell them and sell them and sell them. Hundreds of people are going to see you, Baruch. Hundreds.'

I was indifferent to this but smiled politely.

Rembrandt took a sheet of brown paper from his workbench and caressed it lovingly with the flat of his rough hand. 'Japanese,' he said. 'It costs a king's ransom, but it's the best. And the best deserves the best, eh?' He belched, as if in agreement with himself. 'Shouldn't really use it just for sketching. But what the hell.' He was murmuring to himself, though squinting at me. 'The first step is always the hardest.'

He took a quill pen which looked to me no different from the one I wrote heresies with, rested the paper on a block of wood, dipped the pen in a pot of black ink and made a few strokes without looking at me. He was breathing hard now, the old man. How old was he, exactly? He must be well over fifty.

'Here,' he said, walking over to me with the sketch. 'What do you think of that?'

He spoke casually, but his battered face with its tuberous nose was contorted with tension and what looked uncommonly like fear.

I glanced at his few spare lines. And there I was. My soul opened for the world to see: my gaucheness, my arrogance, my gentleness, my poor hidden inner kindness, my thwarted loving nature, my blocked anger seeping out in bile as sarcasm. My painful brains. All in less than a dozen lines.

'You are a genius,' I blurted out.

'Thank you,' said the poor wounded man.

A solitary tear ran down his right cheek; he made no attempt to hide it from me. He lay his rough paw for a second on my shoulder, with that gesture binding us for life. And we both knew it. Still speechless with emotion he bade me follow him. In the corner of the *kunstkaemer* he reached for the keys around his waist and unlocked another door. The motion to follow him was this time more impatient.

'I don't allow the apprentices in here at all. Nobody is allowed in here. Except me. And now you.'

The tiny chamber thus revealed had less clutter than the rest of Rembrandt's house. There was a small cabinet full of dusty Venetian glass, but the centre of the chamber was dominated by a strange device. It had four wooden struts rising out from a huge central cog, like a miniature windmill. It looked rather as I had pictured the instruments of torture used by the Inquisition in Spain and Portugal.

Rembrandt noticed my bewilderment and laughed. 'That is the device that will make your face famous, Baruch,' he said. 'Sit down sit down,' he added, suddenly impatient. 'I shall change things as I make prints, I always do.'

As I sat, he gushed forth a stream of speech. It was my impression that he needed to share what he was saying. It occurred to me that although he so obviously loved Titus and Hendrickje, he could share his innermost thoughts with neither of them.

'I've had no new commissions for... for a long while now.'

I nodded sympathetically, sitting there in my strange brocade gown and the longest wig in the known world, with my soul recently bared on paper.

'And then there was this business with Amsterdam Town Hall.' He spoke casually, but once more his porridge of a face hardened into cratered lines and lumps of pain. 'Have you heard about that?'

I was proud of myself that I had the wit to say 'no.' Rembrandt being passed over was the talk of Amsterdam, but at least I could spare him the knowledge that I knew. The old Town Hall had burned down. The pompous nonentities who make up our City Council had commissioned artists to paint friezes for the new building, on Dam Square.

As I recalled this, Rembrandt took a plate and started to cover it with what I later discovered was etching ground, from a pot on a low shelf. It was pungent; Rembrandt caught me sniffing at it.

He smiled. 'It's made of pine-tree resin, that's what you can smell. I get it fresh from the apothecary. Expensive stuff, but you must have the best materials, my boy. Nobody ever made a silk purse from a sow's ear.'

The movements of his art clearly soothed the painter as he talked. He was entering a trance.

'The burgomaster,' Rembrandt said, in that strangely absent voice, 'Cornelis de Graeff, who chose Pickenoy to do his portrait, also chose Govert Flinck to do the paintings for the new Town Hall. Among others. Jan Lievens was asked, too. But not me.'

I was silent. This was, indeed, new to me. Rembrandt started to draw on the ground-covered plate with a burin – an etching needle. He was working from the sketch he had made, but he constantly checked my face as he worked.

'Flinck was my pupil,' Rembrandt rolled each word round his mouth as if it caused him pain. 'My pupil... A journeyman painter who will never master light even when he lives in the light of heaven. But—' The anger was coming back; he was beginning to boom. I was glad. '—a journeyman painter who now has a mansion on Lauriergracht, with a grand showroom for his art. If you can call it that.'

I nodded.

'Keep still!'

'Sorry.'

'And do you know what Flinck did? Keep still! Don't react, just listen. I'll tell you. Flinck, out of pity, got the old man, his master, a commission by giving up one of the eight – *eight* – commissions he had been given by Cornelis de Graeff. So I did the commission. I did what they said. I did them an *Oath of Claudius Civilis*, a patriotic painting. And do you know what happened? Eh? Keep still. You know what happened? They sent it back.'

'Oh Rembrandt!'

'Maintain the pose! They said, to spare what little pride the old has-been has got left, they *said* they wanted alterations. Make it smaller, for God's sake. But really they've sent it back. Do you know why?'

'Why?'

'Claudius Civilis, our great Batavian hero, had one eye. So I painted him with one eye. I told the truth. If I'd wanted to paint two eyes I could have done it. I was chalking pairs of eyes on the fronts of houses in Lokhorststraat in Leiden when I was seven. But Claudius Civilis didn't have two eyes. He had one bloody eye. *They*, however – Cornelis de Graeff and his crowd – don't want the truth.'

I sighed. 'I can imagine. A freedom fighter who fought against the Spanish for Dutch freedoms must be shown with two eyes. I —'

'Shut up! I need to concentrate. Move your head slightly to the right. And think of Hendrickje's *titten* again. I want you dreamy.'

* * *

When he was satisfied with what he had etched, Rembrandt immersed the plate in an acid bath. I sensed I could relax, and moved my aching neck around. I felt – I *knew* I could talk to him without constraint, now.

'What about the *libertijnen*?' I remembered the paintings I had already seen downstairs, men and women in severe black and white. Rembrandt himself was thought to be a Mennonite, so the Waterlanders, always the loosest of confederations of anti-Calvinist protestants, would surely provide him with a source of commissions? Some of them – women as well as men – were rich and many well-connected.

Rembrandt sighed, windily and theatrically. 'Whatever it is that makes heretics heretics also makes them unable to get on with other heretics.'

'True. That's the problem with the Jews. You know the old joke? Take two Jews and how many individualists have you got?'

'Two?'

'Three.'

Rembrandt laughed. He was now removing the ground from the plate, leaving the scored drawing clear. I thought I could move now, so stood to watch him.

'Sit down!'

'Sorry.'

'Resume pose! Please.'

The engraver carefully dampened a piece of brown-tinted Japanese paper with a rag and laid it tenderly over the plate.

'So what happened with the Waterlanders?' I said, sensing that something specific had occurred. Sensing, also, that I could say anything to Rembrandt.

'Just a moment and I'll tell you. But first... we put the bun in the oven.'

Rembrandt peeled the damp paper from the plate and put it on the press, as I now realised the strange machine to be. He then seized one of the four spokes and leaned on it with all his weight. He grew red in the face but the paper was carried though the press.

As it popped out, a picture came into my mind of my stepmother, Esther, giving birth to Gabriel. They had tried to shut me out of our parlour, where Esther was lying on the bed I sleep on now. But I was determined, even as a toddler. I made my way into the room unseen and peeped round my father's legs at Esther's white thighs, open on a bloody mess. And Gabriel being pulled from who knows what depths, still tied to the life which nourished him.

Rembrandt waved the etching triumphantly, holding it carefully, for all the world as if it were my new-born brother Gabriel. But the face that appeared to me on the paper, in obverse, was mine. I gazed at it greedily, knowing I could understand myself better by studying it.

My eyes were depths. I cupped the half-ground, unpolished lens in what appeared, on the etching, to be my left hand. My moustache looked fluffy and immature. The light was coming from the right, casting shadow, which Rembrandt had achieved by hatching with the burin.

'There you are!' Rembrandt said, softly. 'There you are.'

'Yes, there I am. Left to right and right to left.' I stared at myself in silence a while. 'Shadow, too,' I mused. 'You really are amazing.'

Rembrandt grinned, showing old brown teeth. 'Right! Who needs mezzotint, eh?'

I continued to stare, fascinated, at my true self rendered onto the medium of paper for all to see. 'It even looks three-dimensional,' I murmured. 'Like a bas-relief, or something. Good heavens, man, how do you do it?'

Rembrandt tried to sound casual, but I could see how pleased he was. 'Oh, the grounds are porous. That's what gives that rough effect. I'll make a few more like this. Then I'll change it a bit.'

'Why?'

I half expected him not to answer, but he did. 'I always try to capture what the sitter is thinking. In your case, I am trying to capture the *ingenium*. But it's not quite...'

Rembrandt stopped. I had blushed scarlet in my shame at not knowing the Latin term. In how many more ways was I to be laid bare in the house of this painter?

'*Ingenium*,' Rembrandt said, quite kindly. 'It means the moment of discovery. You know no Latin?'

'To my shame, only a little,' I replied. 'And that self-taught. At the *Keter Torah* we read books in either Spanish or Hebrew. They didn't teach us Latin at all.'

'I learned it at school,' Rembrandt said, shrugging as if school was irrelevant, which it no doubt was.

'But anyway,' I said, belligerently, 'there is no *ingenium*. No single moment of discovery. The truth is arrived at by a journey of logic, step by step. You can no more take a short cut than you can jump over the canal to get from my house to yours.'

But Rembrandt had lost interest. He was leaning all his weight on a strut of the printing press, which turned and gave birth to more copies. I made to get up and go over to him.

'Maintain pose!' he yelled.

I slumped back in my chair.

'I'll alter it now. Then we'll make more copies.'

'Well, while I'm sitting here,' I grumbled. 'why don't you continue your story of your commissions. Or the lack of them. You were about to tell me about the Waterlanders.'

34

'Oh, yes,' Rembrandt replied easily, apparently more than willing to unburden himself of his worries. 'I was married, you know, a long time ago.' He stopped and went back to the plate, darting glances at my face the whole time. He took up the burin and began to jab and scratch directly onto the plate. *'Ingenium,'* he murmured to himself. 'The moment of discovery. Baruch, will you please think of Hendrickje's *titten* again. Bare.'

'No!' I shouted. I imagined myself besting the chemist Boyle in an argument about Glauber's salts instead. 'Oh all right,' I said. 'How's that?'

'Hmm.' Rembrandt lost himself in his alterations.

When he was ready, he continued his story. 'Yes, I was married. My wife was called Saskia. She... Baruch, you remember I told you I would never have left Leiden unless it had been practically forced upon me?'

'Yes.'

'Well, I would never have left Saskia unless...'

To my amazement, old man Rembrandt started to cry, his plump body heaving, pearly tears rolling either side of that extraordinary nose.

'My dear, dear Rembrandt! Come, let us take a break.'

'Maintain pose! I can work through anything. She died, Baruch. She died. The lovely darling girl. Oh, I loved her so much... But now I love Hendrickje. I truly do. It's like, I love Amsterdam now. Amsterdam is my home. Saskia was my Leiden, Baruch. Hendrickje is my Amsterdam.'

'I understand,' I said. And I did.

But what I understood, at that moment, was not Rembrandt's experience, but my own process of understanding. I had not shared any of Rembrandt's experiences – nothing remotely comparable to them. And yet I understood them and felt fellow feeling for them, by intuition. And it was at *that* moment, that precise moment of *ingenium* – even though *ingenium* does not exist – that I discovered the primacy of intuition over logic.

So I am not the cold logician I have so often been painted. Logic is only a burin, a sharp-edged needle we scrape at life with, to make a picture of how it works. Intuition is a magnifying glass, using the light to find a higher knowledge of God in Nature, Nature in God. And I am the Man With The Magnifying Glass, angling it this way and that. And that's the truth.

But Rembrandt was in the middle of his story. I stopped philosophising and started listening again.

'Saskia's uncle, van Uylenburgh, was an art dealer. I lent him money. I became a Mennonite, at that time, to fit in with him. Although... Oh, I don't know whether I believe in it or not. It has many merits... I don't know what I believe.'

'That's a healthier state than many.'

Rembrandt nodded, absently. He completed his alterations and began his assault on the printing press, talking as he worked. 'After Saskia died, we fell out. He had influenced Saskia's will, somehow. If I marry again – Hendrickje, anybody – I will lose Saskia's money. So I left van Uylenburgh's house and his company, forever.'

'Understandable.'

'Yes, but he replaced me, with Ferdinand Bol. Not quite an apprentice, like Flinck, but he was one of my assistants.'

I nodded.

'Bol is a lot better than Lievens, or Flinck. His etchings are imitations of mine, especially his *Holy Family*. But basically he is another mediocrity and always will be. You can't pass off apples for lemons, Baruch. Van Uylenburgh promoted Bol to the Waterlanders, whispered against me... Oh, you know the sort of thing. The women were less influenced by it than the men. Catrina Hoogsaet came to me to be painted, but she's separated from her husband. She doesn't care what anybody thinks. There have been few others of late. Very few.'

I nodded, sympathetically. 'I think I get the picture.'

'Maintain pose!'

Four

The law revealed to Moses was simply the laws of the Hebrew state alone, and was therefore binding on none but the Hebrews, and not even on them except while their state stood.

Spinoza
Theological Political Treatise

After Rembrandt had finished his etching, I felt I had taken a worse beating than I had at the hands of the ruffian. My back was stiff, my neck refusing all but the smallest lateral movement, my buttocks abandoning all feeling. Also, my scalp was itching; I suspected I was playing host to visitors from Rembrandt's wig.

As Rembrandt carefully locked the door to the printing room, I looked round the *kunstkaemer*. There were a few paintings on the walls, but most of them were stacked five or six deep on the floor, with the canvas side facing out. I had no intention of looking at anything, having, to be frank, had my fill of art for one day. But Rembrandt put his arm round my shoulder, reaching up as I am a head taller. He led me to one of the paintings, hanging near his easel.

'Tell me what you think of that. Tell me honestly.'

I stood squarely in front of the picture. As soon as I saw it was historical my heart sank. To me, Rembrandt's genius is grasping and capturing the human soul. He can do that only, it seems to me, when the sitter is in front of him – as indeed I had just witnessed for myself.

His histories feel stiff and contrived to me, even when he uses models. Unlike me, Rembrandt actually believes the biblical stories he is painting, but still their inherent artificiality defeats him. He has not painted a worthy bible story that I know of. Indeed, Rembrandt's landscapes are far preferable to his histories, because he can find the essence of a place, as well as a person, provided it is in front of him and provided it is, as he puts it, 'local.'

I stared miserably at the painting. It was a scene depicting the Pontius Pilate fable. The narrative was clever. Christ was shown in the far distance under an arch, being led away. Pilate was washing his hands.

'That soldier is good,' I said. 'The one between Pilate and the serving boy. He has one auspicious eye and one drooping eye. Clever.'

'I asked you what you thought,' Rembrandt said.

I sighed. 'Oh all right. We're all entitled to an off day, aren't we?'

Rembrandt laughed.

'The figures at the front are too big. Poor group composition. And too much stuff, stuff, stuff. Are you trying to show a ship's entire wares from the Baltic, or something? Look, we've got metal, silk, fur. Why not a few piles of timber while you're at it? The Pilate tale is muddled enough as it is, and this makes an even bigger mess of it.'

'Finished?'

'Well, you asked me. I suppose you want me to go now. When did you paint it? At the start of your apprenticeship? Or while you were being suckled?'

Rembrandt roared with laughter. 'No!' he boomed. 'I didn't paint it at all. It's by Jan Lievens. Look at the bloody paint, boy! You can practically see the canvas through it.'

Rembrandt bashed me affectionately on the shoulder, causing a bruise that took a week to heal.

'I'm glad I spoke the truth to you,' I said.

'So am I, Baruch. So am I.' And, dropping his voice, 'I will always believe you now.'

And then, as if we had wandered into one of the Old Testament tales, I heard the voice of Saul Levi Morteira, even though he wasn't in the room. The voice said 'Where is Spinoza?'

* * *

Chacham Saul Levi Morteira was never a bigot. He is a logical man who believes in disputation to reach the truth. As long as I have known him, he has actively opposed those who taught that we must blindly obey this text or that credo.

And he always set himself against the mystics, whether messiah-followers or kabbalists. This, indeed, was the basis of his acrimonious disputes with Rabbi Menassah ben Israel, who also lives down the road, off Breestraat. I've never met two men who hated each other more.

Among my first memories of him... I remember the sunlight streaming in through the high leaded windows of the *Keter Torah*. I remember dust motes swimming, as if they, too, were trying to find a way. I had just read the Pentateuch in Hebrew, straight through, for the first time. The Pentateuch – the book Jews believe was revealed to Moses by God. The book which forms the basis of Sabbath prayer and indeed of all Jewish belief.

I stood behind my school desk. There was a sense of expectancy among the eight other boys; a hushed respectful silence. There always was when I spoke. I loved it – I still do.

'It's ridiculous,' I said.

There was a collective gasp, then the air seemed sucked from the room.

'What is?' said Morteira, seated behind his desk, raised on a dais at the front.

'The whole idea that Moses wrote the Pentateuch, also known as the Books of Moses, also known as the *Torah*. For a start, he not only describes his own death but the events following his death. Pretty tricky that!'

I laughed and looked round, seeking support from the other boys in my derision. There were some furtive small smiles, but mainly black holes of round eyes and open mouths. I plunged on: 'Some places bear names they were not given until decades after the death of Moses.' I paused. 'I have the details. They make it clear beyond a shadow of doubt that the authorship of Moses is bogus. And in any case, if Moses wrote it, why does he use the third person when talking about himself?'

I paused for effect, looking round. 'I've had a look at Joshua, Judges, Samuel and Kings as well,' I said. 'The same applies. They could not possibly have been written by the person whose name they bear. It's all bogus. We're wasting our time here.'

Some years later I discovered that, on the very day of our dispute, Saul Levi Morteira had been working on what he regarded as his life's work – the Treatise on the Truth of the Law of Moses.

The *chacham* stood, tented in his black rabbinical gown. He spoke calmly and reasonably. He steered clear of disputing with me on matters of text, falling back instead on 'the need for faith' and 'the word of God' and 'the limits of our ability and duty to question.'

I could tell that his sonorous voice, his appearance and his authority – apparently embodying the very religion he defended – were winning over the other students. I sat down, defeated. I was eleven at the time, destined, so everybody had thought until then, for the rabbinate.

I don't remember exactly when Chacham Morteira abandoned that plan for me. His very last attempt to turn my feet to his own path was an offer to become a rabbi on his own first patch, the ghetto in Venice. He thought I might conform, away from Amsterdam. I didn't even consider it.

But, as a heretic, I at least found out who did write the Five Books of Moses, although it took me two full years. Moses actually did do some of it, though not much. The books are a mish-mash, written by many hands. The bulk was written centuries later by Ibn Ezra.

I remember sharing this discovery – which excited me greatly – with all the *parnassim* at the *Esnoga*. We get tourists at the synagogue – the Stadholder himself had come to watch us worship, we were such an exotic curiosity. And I told them, too. I told anybody who would listen.

I also added that if the Books of Moses were not given to Moses by God, then the Jews' claim to be the chosen of God, which is grounded in the *Torah*, is null and void. There is nothing special, I informed my audience at the synagogue, about the Jews. I had plenty of attention that day, probably because it was the day of my barmitzvah.

* * *

So what was Saul Levi Morteira doing here? Here in Rembrandt's house. I did not believe then, and I do not believe now, that his appearance in the house of the painter while I was there was coincidence.

I have already said that I believe I was being followed, and surely Morteira knew I was there. He knew of Rembrandt's Mennonite background and his attendance at Waterlander meetings. In suddenly appearing like that, he was investigating the nature of my heresies, the better to prepare himself to act against them. I had no doubt of that at all.

Rembrandt had not reacted to the sound of Morteira's voice. He led me downstairs to the *sydelkaemer*, where he conducted his business. On the stairs there were books, some piled, some open; a few gourds, gathering dust; a plant in a glass cabinet.

The *sydelkaemer* was hung with paintings, one of which I thought to be the work of van Eyck. Another, I could see, was a Raphael and yet another by Michelangelo. Assuming all three were originals, it occurred to me to wonder how Rembrandt could afford them.

Thrown against the walls of the *sydelkaemer* were piles of artefacts, thick with dust: a miniature cannon caught my eye; piles of armour – shields, cuirasses; some exotic stringed instruments I could not have named; an ancient uniform from some long-forgotten army; a jumble of casts of hands and heads.

I eyed them curiously, but my mind was pulled back to Morteira. I looked round for him. And there he was, as if I had summoned him by my thoughts, ushered into the *sydelkaemer* by Hendrickje. I froze. The turbulent conflicting emotions Morteira always aroused in me bubbled up below the surface.

Morteira, at first, ignored me and addressed Rembrandt.

'My dear Rembrandt, forgive the intrusion,' gushed the *chacham*. 'But I bring news of a commission, which I trust will be welcome.'

Rembrandt reacted with dignity, adjusting his hat as it slipped forward, wiping his hands on his coat before shaking hands with the rabbi. 'How interesting,' he boomed. 'And what is the nature of this commission?'

'The synagogue elders wish to honour me with a portrait, three-quarter length,' Morteira specified with his usual precision. 'I myself suggested you as the painter. I saw the illustrations you did for my friend Menassah ben Israel's fascinating mystical book *Piedra Gloriosa*.'

I snorted at Morteira's hypocrisy, and the subtle insult of implying that this book illustration was the only work of Rembrandt's he knew. The rabbi favoured me with a quizzical look, one eyebrow raised. It was a look I knew well. Rembrandt looked shamefaced and shuffled about, as if there were pressure on his bladder.

'The fee would be fifty guilders,' Morteira added, smoothly.

I knew this to be a standard amount for a painter of Rembrandt's renown. Again, he reacted with dignity, concealing how welcome the work must be to him.

'An interesting commission Chacham Morteira,' the painter said. 'You have a noble face. It will be both a pleasure and an honour to render the experience and wisdom of your life for all to see.'

Morteira bowed at Rembrandt's attempt at smooth and polished courtliness. He finally deigned to turn to me. 'Good day, Baruch. How are you faring? How is your work?'

'I am well, Chacham Morteira,' I replied. 'But unfortunately the demands of the family business leave me little time for the higher works of the mind, as we know it.'

The rabbi favoured this with a glacial smile and silence.

'May I pose you now, Chacham?' Rembrandt said. 'Perhaps even make some preliminary sketches? After some refreshment, naturally. Baruch, you will join us?'

The rabbi indicated gracious acceptance by inclining his head. I indicated clumsy refusal by telling Rembrandt I had work to do. Rembrandt led the rabbi back upstairs, to his *kunstkaemer*, bidding me a warm enough goodbye as he did so.

As the rabbi's broad, slightly-stooped back departed, it was all I could do not to seize his hand and pull him back. 'Please, please stay with me. Talk to me.' As ever, all I wanted, all I have ever wanted, was for Chacham Rabbi Saul Levi Morteira to love me.

꙰ ꙰ ꙰

I was about to slouch miserably to the entrance hall and then out, when Hendrickje Stoffels touched me lightly on the arm. I jumped.

'Oh, excuse me, *Mijnheer*,' she said. Was that innocence in her wide open eyes and dimpling pout? Or insolence? 'I wonder if you would mind waiting a moment, before you leave? It's just that master Titus wishes to speak with you.'

Hendrickje's round pretty face had dimples, like a dumpling with currants pushed into it. Even swathed in her stiff white

43

servant's apron, her buxom person, of which I had seen such ample evidence in Rembrandt's drawing, was clear in outline.

I realised I was staring at her, and not at her face. I blushed, then had a brief coughing fit. 'Titus?' I assumed the youth had returned from depositing the ruffian at the *Tugthuis* and had some information for me about the matter.

'Yes, sir.'

Hendrickje turned on her heel, having intimated that I should follow. I did. She led me to a tiny ante-room off the *sydelkaemer* which was no doubt used for closing deals. It boasted a couple of high-backed wooden prattler's chairs, black with polish, and a plain round table, much cheaper, in a corner away from the chairs. The table had a bust of Socrates and a conch shell on it. There were weapons – javelins, swords, sabres, a halberd – mounted on the walls. At Hendrickje's bidding, I sat on one of the uncomfortable chairs.

I am impatient by nature. Indeed, I find impatience solidifies to inner anger quite easily and quickly in me. But on this occasion I did not have long to wait.

Hendrickje ushered Titus in, her body showing the ambiguity of her position in the household. She was behind him, like a servant, but closer than any servant would stand to the young master of the house. Her arm floated, as if of its own accord, just behind his shoulder in a protective, almost motherly gesture. Her gaze never left his head, her eyes wide and softening.

'*Mijnheer* Spinoza!' The youth advanced with his hand outstretched. He carried what would have been immense natural authority in a man twice his age. For someone of his tender years it was remarkable.

I found myself on my feet, having jumped up as if the Stadholder himself had entered the room. 'Please,' I heard myself blurting out, 'Call me Baruch, as your father does. After all, I am not so very much older than you are yourself...' I blathered on in this manner a while longer, feeling not at all older than Titus but considerably younger.

'Very well, Baruch,' Titus said, gravely, rolling the strange name round his mouth as if seeing if it would fit or fall out.

'How is our thief?' I asked him.

Titus grinned. 'Safely under lock and key. He is one Joris Fonteijn of Diest, or so I have been told. A hardened criminal. It does not look good for him.'

The youth then effortlessly lifted one of the mahogany high-backed chairs, one-handed, and placed it opposite mine. Hendrickje made to leave, but Titus restrained her with the lightest of touches on the arm.

There was one more chair in the room, a much rougher and cheaper one. Titus took that for himself, waving Hendrickje to sit on the grand prattler's chair. She threw him a glance that was at once both tender and reproachful but sat with us, a servant no longer.

Titus came straight to the point – by no means the last time he was to do this in our acquaintance. He looked me straight in the eye.

'Hendrickje and I have concerns about Papa; two related concerns, in fact. We have discussed the matter, the two of us, and we want to share these concerns with you.'

'Why?' I said

'My father respects you,' said Titus. 'He always tells me if you were at a meeting of the Waterlanders. He often quotes what you said, even though, to be frank, I'm not sure he always understands it.'

I shrugged modestly.

'The first problem that we face, here in this household, is the number of powerful enemies my father is making. This is often not his fault, though he is certainly neither the most tactful nor the most circumspect of men.'

'Yes. He did indicate to me earlier... Uylenburgh...'

Hendrickje grimaced at the name, in a girlish manner. Titus threw her a faint smile.

'Yes, him,' said the youth. 'Though I'm afraid some of them are even more powerful. There is the burgomaster, Cornelis de Graeff.'

'Yes, your father mentioned...'

'Papa will have told you about the Town Hall commissions,' the youth asserted confidently, and of course correctly. 'He will not have told you the original cause of the enmity. His painting of Andries de Graeff.'

'No, you're right. He didn't. I've heard of the painting, though.'

Titus grimaced. 'Most people have, though not for the right reasons. Andries is Cornelis's younger brother. He didn't like Papa's portrait of him and refused to pay for it. Papa sued him.'

I winced. 'I didn't know that!'

Titus gave a wan smile. 'And what's worse, Papa won. Andries had to pay for the painting. The de Graeffs were humiliated. Papa hasn't had a commission from a notable family in Amsterdam since.'

'I see.'

'Andries and Cornelis are bad enemies to have. But Claes Pieterszoon is even worse.'

'Who's he?'

'You probably know him by that silly name he gives himself: Doctor Tulip. Dr Nikolaes Tulp. He was at the *Tugthuis* when I took the thief in. He took charge of everything. He's a magistrate as well as a City Councillor.'

'But Tulp, this Dr Nikolaes Tulp, isn't he...?'

Titus smiled. 'Yes, the very same. The man father painted dissecting a corpse. Tulp's still in the Surgeons' Guild, though Jan Diejman is running it now.'

'Tulp,' I muttered to myself. 'Tulp is *against* Rembrandt?'

I lapsed into silence with neither Hendrickje nor Titus disturbing my reverie.

As I mentioned before, at the moment of my conception the Jews became citizens of Amsterdam. Well, at the moment of my birth Rembrandt van Rijn was putting the finishing touches to the painting which made him famous far beyond the fluid and watery borders of the Republic. The painting was *The Anatomy Lesson of Dr Nikolaes Tulp*. It showed the good surgeon demonstrating his art at a public dissection of a criminal corpse.

'Tulp...' I said again, digesting the strange turn of events.

'Tulp the hypocrite,' Titus said angrily. 'Have you heard of the law he passed last year, banning luxury?'

'No,' I said. 'I don't suppose I would be directly affected.'

'He lives in a palace on the Keizersgracht, Tulp does. From which he sallies forth in a coach pulled by four greys, with his coat of arms painted on the door, to pass laws limiting luxury. He tells us how many guests we may have at wedding feasts, and what we may eat.' He laughed. 'He also had a bust of himself as a Roman emperor commissioned by Artus Quellijn. It's in Carrara marble and very pompous, according to Papa. Anyway, all this luxury led him to—'

'— a guilty conscience,' I completed the sentence for Titus. I saw Hendrickje was looking amused, which pleased me.

'Precisely,' said Titus. 'And the guilty conscience led him to—'

'Calvinism!'

'Actually, extreme Calvinism. Not that there is any other sort. Tulp is a real hardliner. At his instigation, and those of his ilk, every Calvinist church has been stripped of its paintings and whitewashed.'

'The second commandment,' I murmured. 'You shall not make for yourself an idol.'

'Precisely. And my father has had to hide certain paintings. Anything from the Apocrypha, of course. But also certain portraits of Mennonite preachers – Laszlo and the rest of them.'

'*Hide* them?' I remembered the drawing of Hendrickje. I bet that had to be hidden, too.

'Yes, they came here. The Church Elders. They searched the place, more than once.'

'Whaaat!'

Titus shot a look at Hendrickje.

'*Mijnheer* Spinoza —' she began.

I waved a protesting hand. 'Baruch, please. Call me Baruch.'

'Very well. Baruch. I was summoned to the Court of the Church for living in sin with Rembrandt. I was pregnant with Cornelia at the time.' She spoke softly and without rancour, as if recounting her daily purchase of vegetables at the market.

'They were savage to her,' Titus said, angrily. He reached across and squeezed Hendrickje's hand. 'Papa would marry her tomorrow, but he can't, because of the terms of Mama's will. We would lose everything.'

Hendrickje darted him a grateful look, putting her hand over Titus's for a second. They were like a loving brother and sister.

Titus was shaking his head, speaking musingly, as if to himself. 'But the living in sin is only part of it. What really exercises them is paintings like *Bathsheba*, where Papa shows Hendrickje naked.'

'They branded me a whore,' Hendrickje said, flatly. 'They denounced me in every pulpit in Amsterdam. They forbade me Holy Communion and put up posters declaring my Cornelia a bastard.'

Titus again squeezed her hand. 'I would like to have whipped them, every last one of them,' he ground out.

'Do you mean... they continue to come here?' I asked. 'Even after the verdict?'

'Oh yes! They will never stop looking for "evidence" as they call it.'

'My God!'

Titus looked me in the eye, willing me to understand. 'All this of course has meant that my father has a certain reputation. Tulp won't let the scandal die down. So not only have we lost the sitters, thanks to the de Graeffs, we have now lost the apprentices, too. At least those from good homes, who could pay well. So that's a hundred guilders a year per apprentice we're no longer getting.'

I nodded, sad at the plight of these worthy people.

Titus continued. 'I would be the last to claim that Papa is blameless in all this, dearly though I love him. He has harebrained schemes. He tried to buy back all his own prints. He bought some of them from as far away as Italy, at stupendous prices.'

Hendrickje gave a pout of rebuke. 'Titus! His works are like his children. He loves to have them around him.'

Titus sighed. 'And there is his independence, his fierce independence. He refuses to indenture himself, which stops his powerful friends, like Huygens, helping him as much as they could.'

'So, how bad is his situation?'

'We will have to sell this house soon,' Titus waved a hand up and down, indicating the elegant three-storey town house. Hendrickje's face was drawn and pasty. There were tears in her eyes. 'We owe... How much is it again, Titus?'

'It's complicated,' the youth said gravely, for all the world like a merchant with twenty years experience. 'My father paid far too much for the house in the first place, thirteen thousand guilders. We cannot meet the instalments. There are new loans to cover the old loans. The interest charges are steeper and steeper. My father is months from bankruptcy. Perhaps weeks. The house would be repossessed. He would likely have to leave Amsterdam. And us with him. I am too young to be anything but an apprentice and that would mean more costs, not less.'

'How can I help?'

'Just stop him spending,' Titus said. 'It would help a little. It's a comedy, Baruch. We put some of his possessions up for sale and he bought them back himself. Go to the auctions with him. Restrain him, at least. He listens to you.'

'He lives frugally, Baruch.' Poor Hendrickje was pleading. 'He wears poor clothes. I have to remind him to eat sometimes. And it's always just herring and beer and cheese.'

'At the auctions,' Titus said, 'if he sees something he wants, he just bids for it and buys it. No matter what the price. The auctioneers know him and put the prices up. They see him coming.'

'I'll go with him, certainly,' I said. 'If you think...'

'Look after him, sir, please,' Hendrickje said. She was a servant again, forgetting to call me Baruch. 'For he is a good man, and undeserving of all the bad feeling he attracts.'

Her eyes were moist. It was not difficult to see that she blamed herself for some of the enmity which had attached itself to Rembrandt. I resolved with all my heart to help if I could. 'If there is anything that is in my power to do, I will do it.'

'Oh, thank you, sir!' Hendrickje blurted out.

They saw me out together. The *voorhuis* was piled with animal skins. There was a length of fur, lousy with vermin; a clutter of grubby oriental chairs, at odd angles to each other; more piles of books. It was musty and malodorous. Hendrickje helped me pull my woollen cloak around me. I caught sight of myself in a strange octagonal-framed mirror on the wall: I looked like a mendicant Jewish friar in a fairy story.

As I walked off along the canal, the bells of the Zuider Kerck rang in my ears. I caught a glimpse of the Sephardic Jew I had seen before, the one who was following me. I stopped, considering what best course of action to take. But when I looked back he was gone.

Five

*Our mind acts at times and at times suffers; in so far as it
has adequate ideas, it necessarily acts; and in so far as it
has inadequate ideas, it necessarily suffers.*

Spinoza
Ethics

My method, when deriving my philosophy, is to let my
ideas simmer and stew in my mind. Then, when a certain
degree of solidification has taken place, I commit the essence
of the thought to paper. Then, and this is the hard part, I set
about designing an incontrovertible proof of my deductions.

I sharpened a quill, mused a while longer, then finally dipped
quill into inkpot. My musings were centring on the mind and
the body. And how the images formed in the one provoke action
in the other.

'The mind,' I wrote, 'as much as it can, endeavours to imagine
those things which increase or help its powers of acting.'

There came a thunderous knock on the door of my chamber.
I froze. What should I do? My landlord, Teunissen, would
normally greet all visitors in the vestibule and then admit
them. But supposing he were out? Or, more likely, still asleep.
It was early in the morning, the first glow of the pearly light
just touching the ice on the canal. The thunderous knock came
again.

There was a housekeeper and a maid in the establishment
– Teunissen was a widower, his wife having died in the plague

last year. But they were lax in their duties, especially with no woman to supervise them. There was the knock again.

It would take me some time to crawl under the bed with my writing, restore it to its hiding place and then open the door. Such a course of action would require quick movement and thought. I sucked the end of the quill. Then coughed. One more knock, authoritative, I thought, almost peremptory, on my chamber door. Oh, why had I not considered this eventuality before? My thoughts could fall into the hands of my enemies. O Socrates, bring me my hemlock now! I opened the door.

Titus van Rijn was twinkling with mischief, like a distant star on a frosty night. 'I hope I didn't disturb you,' he said, breaking into a smile which melted my anger. In any case, I was awash with relief that it was him.

'Why didn't you call out?' I said.

'I didn't want to alarm you.'

'You alarmed me a great deal more by remaining silent!'

This only widened Titus's grin. He pushed past me and slid along the narrow gap between the bed and the wall. 'What are you writing?' he said, looking down at my work on the desk.

'A treatise on philosophy.'

He smothered a yawn. 'Shouldn't it be in Latin?'

I felt myself blushing. 'It will be. These are just preliminary notes.'

Titus glanced at my work again. 'What strange language is this?'

'Spanish.'

'Is that what you speak with, er, with the...'

'With the Jews,' I finished it for him. 'No, we speak Portuguese but read and write in Spanish. Would you like some refreshment? Beer? I can call the girl and get you some food.'

'No, thank you.' Titus sat on the bed, at ease with himself and the world. I sat on the only chair, at my writing table.

'I can't stop long. I've come to bring you some news.' He crossed one booted leg over the other, the epitome of youthful charm. 'You remember the thief, Joris Fonteijn? The man who tried to steal Papa's coat?'

'Yes.'

'They hanged him yesterday.'

I thought of my bruised stomach at the hands, or rather fist, of Joris Fonteijn, but it seemed churlish to bear grudges. 'Oh dear!'

'It's excellent news. There is to be a public dissection tomorrow. It's the talk of Amsterdam. Everybody wants to come. There have been fights over tickets.'

'A dissection? Fascinating! I see parallels with my own work with the microscope. Uncovering what lies hidden, at the physical level. At the philosophical, too, the search for truth, the —'

'Baruch, the reason I said it's excellent news is that Papa has received a commission from the Surgeons' Guild to paint the dissection.'

'Titus!' I slapped my knee. 'I'm delighted for Rembrandt. I —'

'Papa is naturally delighted, too. He sees it as a chance to regain the standing he had after he painted the first Anatomy Lesson.'

'Ah, but you told me yourself that Tulp is —'

'— an enemy, yes. But fortunately Jan Deijman, the new president of the Surgeons' Guild, is a much quieter and more modest fellow.'

'Excellent!'

'It will be a group portrait. Deijman dissecting our thief, poor Joris. Assembled surgeons looking on admiringly. Papa wants you in the portrait.'

'Me? But I'm not a surgeon.'

'That doesn't matter. Papa says less than half these worthies turn up for sittings, so he has to use stand-ins. He has been known to keep the stand-in's face in the finished version.'

'Doesn't anybody mind? They pay to be in these pictures, don't they?'

'Most certainly. Papa says nobody ever notices. But, just between ourselves, he often takes the painting back for improvement even after the money has been paid. He is quite capable of altering the face back to the stand-in's, at that point.'

'But that's shocking! So if you take a painting like that militia painting. The Company of —'

'Yes, I remember that one. The face of Banning Cocq is actually a baker who had just died of the pox. Papa really hated him. Banning Cocq, not the baker. He kept calling him a jumped-up little popinjay.'

'But doesn't he mind? This...'

'Banning Cocq. He doesn't know. If Papa got wind that he wanted to see the painting again, he would change it back for a while. Then, knowing Papa, he would find a way to restore the dead baker.'

'But that's appalling. Is nothing as it seems to be? How can one ever establish the truth if —' I stopped, struck by a suspicion. 'So why does he want to paint me? Paint me in a group among whom I have no business?'

'He likes you.'

'He what?'

'I told you before, when you visited our house. He likes you.'

'That's impossible. Nobody likes me.'

Titus ignored that. 'He said he will meet you at the place of dissection. Ten o' clock tomorrow.'

Titus rose to leave, clapping me on the back, which started me coughing.

I waved at the youth, in protest. 'Titus! No! I have reached a crucial point in my investigations. I cannot possibly spare the time. It's out of the question.'

* * *

The Surgeons' Guild had their premises in the St Anthony's Weigh House, just across the canal from Rembrandt, a few doors down from Rabbi Morteira's house. They had quite recently had a Dissecting Theatre built there. Its amphitheatre shape and light-timber construction is an imitation of the much grander one at Leiden.

I had heard from my landlord that advance tickets for the dissection of Joris Fonteijn had sold out in hours, though some entrance tickets were always sold at the door. Dissections were still quite a rarity, despite the demand for them from the paying public – much the same people who would go to see a play at the Schouwburg theatre. But of course the theatre could continue in the summer, whereas dissections could only be done in the coldest months, or the putrefaction of the body would be too much to bear, for surgeons and audience alike.

And cold it was! I remember the snow being calf-high on the ground as I made my way to the Weigh House. My breath was coming in gasps, forming puffs of cloud in front of me, as I laboriously pulled first one leg then the other out of the clinging wet snow.

At the inner door of the Weigh House, a scrofulous fellow in torn clothes sat at a makeshift table.

'Eight *penningen*,' he demanded.

'I'm being painted, by Rembrandt the painter. Let me through.'

'I don't care if you're being buggered by de Ruyter's navy. Eight *penningen*.'

'I don't need to pay, I tell you.'

'Pay up or piss off. There's others waiting.'

The scrofulous doorkeeper indicated the queue. I do not usually carry money, for the very good reason that I do not possess any. I was not sure if I had even brought my purse with me. I struggled for it under layers of clothes. The people behind me grew restive, anxious as they were to gain admittance.

'Hurry up, you poltroon,' somebody shouted. 'You're holding everybody up!'

I pulled my purse into the light, pulled at the drawstring and searched inside. Nothing. No! Coins. I fished out six *penningen*.

'Here you are.'

'That's two *penningen* short.'

'So what? You couldn't even buy a tankard of small beer for two *penningen*.'

Somebody behind me shouted 'Get out of the way.' Somebody else shoved me in the back.

I turned to the crowd. 'I am Benedictus de Spinoza the merchant,' I began.

'In that case why haven't you got two *penningen*?' asked a woman in the queue.

'What a lousy merchant,' someone else quipped.

Everybody started to laugh.

'I am being painted by the painter Rembrandt. I had not expected to have to pay.'

I was shouting, being no friend of the malodorous *hoi polloi* at the best of times. 'Can anybody lend me two *penningen*?'

'Lend?' said the fellow who had shoved me in the back. He was a huge fellow with the forearms of a blacksmith.

'All right. Give. Please. Anybody among you good people...'

'Good people, is it now?' said one. But the mob's anger was laced with humour, albeit at my expense.

'Oh, I'll pay it,' said a woman, about three back in the queue. 'Let him through, or the corpse will be in pieces before we get in.'

I thanked my benefactress, handed over the six *penningen* I did possess, and made my way into the Dissection Theatre. As I expected, it was packed. I hadn't been here before. There were seven or so rows of curved wooden benches, after the classical pattern of a Roman amphitheatre.

All the seats were taken, people were standing at the back, crowded into the aisles, thronging at the front. I estimated the number of spectators at well over two hundred. But the din, trapped by the wooden roof, made it sound as though every human who had ever been born since the beginning of time were loudly demanding entertainment.

My brother-in-law, Samuel de Caseres, was there with my brother Gabriel. We were putting a consortium together for a ship to Portugal. I hoped that Gabriel was, for once, talking about something other than the venality of chandlers, the exorbitance of borrowing rates, the unfairness of scurvy and all the rest of it.

I picked out other friends and acquaintances in the throng: the painter Ruisdael, in his filthy, shabby clothes; my acquaintances from the Waterlanders, Franciscus van den Enden and Pieter Balling. Over there was Simon de Vries, a jolly fellow.

Descartes had been present at the first Anatomy painting, the dissection at the hands of Tulp. He was still writing his *Treatise on Man*, claiming that motion and substance alone can explain the world's phenomena. He had hidden his writing when Galileo was brought before the Inquisition. And now a second Anatomy would discover more about what I was convinced was the single substance of life. We were digging into nature; digging into God.

My gaze was drawn to the scene at the front of the theatre. Between the dais and the first row of benches, some ragamuffins had set up an impromptu game of korfball. Some had sticks, some didn't. The ball was a pig's bladder. As I watched, one of them struck the bladder a mighty blow into the air. It bounced off the corpse and rolled off the dais. Some attendants chased the ragamuffins away.

Joris Fonteijn of Diest was looking much the worse for wear, since I last saw him, as well he might. He was the colour of mature Gouda cheese, lying with his mouth wide open on a wooden table. A grubby linen sheet was draped over his privates, but otherwise his body was bare.

I made my way towards him, fascinated. What was the nature of that which had left him, or been taken from him? That was the question. Know that and we know everything. It must be of substance, because everything is of substance – one substance, with many variations. I had seen bodies before, of course. Plague victims. Who hadn't? There had been plague in the house where I lodged. But Joris Fonteijn was so complete. So untouched, except for the lack of life.

At the front, up on the dais, Rembrandt emerged from a crowd of surgeons and administrators of the Surgeons' Guild. He was wearing the same hat as the last time I had seen him. Also the same coat, the one Joris Fonteijn had tried to steal – ill-advisedly, as it turned out.

'I'm very pleased to see you!' Rembrandt looked a little harassed, but his battered features were animated – like a soldier going into battle. 'There's nine people in this bloody picture and only six have shown up. At least the damned corpse can't go anywhere.'

'Maybe you should specialise in cadavers?'

Rembrandt put his hands on his ample hips and bellowed laughter. 'Good idea. They wouldn't move once you've posed them either.'

'No. Except to go to heaven, of course.'

Rembrandt shook his head in mock reproach. 'Baruch, my boy. You need a... I dunno... a bodyguard or something. Here, come and help me get old Joris in position.'

At Rembrandt's direction, I helped him turn the heavy table so the feet of the dead Fonteijn were pointing toward the audience. Naturally, none of the eminent surgeons lifted a finger to help us. But there were whoops, catcalls and sarcastic advice from the *hoi polloi* throughout. At this point I had not perceived Rembrandt's intentions with regard to the positioning of the corpse, which, in view of what happened later, was just as well.

'Right,' Rembrandt said to me. 'You're standing in for Gijsbert Calkoen. He's about your age. Just passed his exams. He got married two days ago, so he's at home fucking his bride and having a better time than any of us here.'

Rembrandt took my upper arm in a vice-like grip and steered me to a place behind Joris Fonteijn's right shoulder. He then turned me, three-quarter face. 'Good,' he said. 'Now, don't move.'

He placed a black cloth over my right arm, as if I were a waiter at a tavern, and pressed part of a skull, the cranium, into my right hand. 'You might have to catch some bits of the deceased in that, once the dissection gets going.'

'Oh, good.'

'Maintain pose!'

'You haven't started yet!'

'Just practising.' Rembrandt's belly heaved with silent laughter.

I nodded and maintained my pose, wrinkling my nose a little at the strong smell emanating from Joris – a blend of the pickling brine we use for herrings at sea, mixed with the remorseless putrefaction it was designed to slow.

Rembrandt, meanwhile, broke into the tight knot of surgeons and emerged with a nondescript middle-aged man, well below my height, with a ginger beard over his weak chin, and a ginger moustache. This, it turned out, was Dr Jan Deijman. Rembrandt courteously introduced us.

'What? Spinoza the philosopher?' said the President of the Surgeons' Guild.

'Yes indeed, sir,' I replied, genuinely surprised. 'I was not aware my fame had spread so far.'

'Too modest, sir,' Deijman murmured.

I found this reply fascinating. Rembrandt has a saying – he always has a saying – that the painter always paints himself. It was not *I* who was 'too modest' but Deijman himself. As I stood there, the focal point of half Amsterdam, in a din that could wake the dead, I lost myself in the development of this thought.

Meanwhile, Rembrandt was bustling about. He stood Deijman on an upturned linen chest, so he was a head above me. He then grouped three more surgeons slightly behind me, in a triangle, with the one at the back also standing on some sort of box or chest the painter had apparently brought with him. The remaining two guild members he placed to the corpse's left, with the taller outermost.

The painter had now run out of surgeons. Titus appeared from nowhere, evidently knowing what was required. He plunged into the crowd and emerged with two merchants. Their families and friends, some by now obviously drunk, were roaring them on. One of them even took a mock bow as he prepared to be shown his place in the tableau.

Rembrandt put them on the corpse's left, in a second tier, diagonally behind the two genuine surgeons. That made four men to the left, forming a rhomboid, and four to the corpse's right – three in a triangle and one, me, in front. Deijman was directly behind the corpse's head.

Even as part of the tableau myself, I could see it was a daring composition – revolutionary even. But at this stage, I still missed the import of what Rembrandt was suggesting by the positioning. This was partly because the import depended so much on the corpse, and partly because I was still developing the idea of the centrality of the self and its struggle for survival in the group.

'Titus, how many hats have we got?' Rembrandt was shouting, irritable and rude. His mind was clearly on many things.

'Um... Three, papa.'

'Three! Why...? Oh, never mind. Give them to me.'

Rembrandt seized the three hats. One was given to Jan Deijman. It made him look taller. The other two went to surgeons, or stand-ins, at the back of the composition, for balance.

While Rembrandt was busying himself with hats, something in the nature of the noise from the auditorium alerted me to a change in the audience's mood. There was a buzz of interest, indignation and some anger coming from the front, where the merchants and the educated people were.

Rembrandt had by now gone to the front himself, taking up his position to start sketching the grouping of figures. I believe this made the import of the positioning clearer.

At any rate, a roaring voice cut through the din: 'You cannot possibly place the figures like that. It is a blasphemy against God.'

I recognised the man striding along where the ragamuffins had been playing korfball: Dr Nikolaes Tulp. Tulp had aged considerably since the painting of his anatomy lesson by Rembrandt. The number of years elapsed was the same as the difference between my age and Rembrandt's – twenty-four. In that time, Tulp had grown grey and portly, but that only added to his massive authority.

The issue dawned on me: Carracci's painting of the dead Christ had itself caused heated controversy because Christ's feet were facing the viewer, which was held to be disrespectful. However, engravings of it were widespread. It was all over Amsterdam. I was sure that Franciscus van den Enden had it in the window of his art shop.

By placing the dead Joris Fonteijn as he had, Rembrandt was reflecting Carracci's composition, obliquely comparing the deceased criminal to Jesus Christ. Had Rembrandt done this deliberately? I do not believe he knew the answer to that himself. Creative artists do not think, they intuit. But I feared he may provoke a riot.

Jan Diejman immediately left his posed position and descended the dais to his predecessor as President of the Surgeons' Guild, Nikolaes Tulp. Two senior surgeons followed, as did I. Rembrandt and Titus joined the knot around Tulp.

Tulp, I noticed, was dressed from head to toe in Calvinist black, without even a touch of white at neck or wrist – no lace, no linen. But the material of his doublet and hose was of the finest Chinese silk, the richest and shiniest I have ever seen.

The clothes were Tulp's reconciliation: he was both a Regent – a rare political rank for a surgeon – and one of the *vromen*, the extreme religious wing of the Calvinists. The eyes are the windows of the soul, the face shows the man, but the clothes... the clothes show what the man thinks of himself.

Deijman's entire manner, even the way he stood, deferred to Tulp. Tulp himself had adopted a dandified old-fashioned Mannerist pose, one toe pointing down onto the ground, heel-raised. He made the comparison with the Carracci painting, angrily repeating the charge of blasphemy.

'Why was I not consulted on the choice of artist?' Tulp shouted, jutting his pointed beard at Deijman. 'We have already had occasion to charge this fellow with more sins than I care to name. He is entirely unsuitable.'

Nothing could have better encapsulated poor Rembrandt's fall from grace than the central figure of the painting which had propelled him to fame denouncing him, and demanding that he not be allowed to paint its successor.

'Rubbish,' I said.

Everybody ignored me, which was probably just as well.

'We can ask Rembrandt to adjust the composition, so the comparison with Carracci is less obvious,' Deijman said. He spoke as if every word cost him physical effort.

One of the two other surgeons muttered, 'Yes, that's what we'll do.'

Tulp glared round the group. I could sense him calculating that it was too late to bring proceedings to a halt now. 'I insist on power of approval of the finished painting,' Tulp said. 'I insist on a veto, at a full meeting of Convocation. If I turn it down, we burn it as a work of blasphemy.'

There was a generalised murmur of disagreement, with the young element, myself and Titus, the loudest. Rembrandt himself cut through it, anxious to resume the first group portrait commission he had had in over a decade, apparently fearless in the face of possibly having it burned.

'I accept Dr Tulp's condition,' he said. 'Can we please now get on with it?'

* * *

Lanterns were brought and placed at the points of the compass, lighting the tableau, making poor decomposing Joris Fonteijn look even more yellow.

Above the din, I heard one of the surgeons ask Dr Deijman *sotto voce* if he wished to say a few words to the multitude, before the dissection began. The speaker was a fellow with a greying beard, receding hairline and red ears. He had been placed immediately behind me – or immediately behind Gijsbert Calkoen, which was who I was supposed to be. Like the other surgeons, he was dressed in black with a white linen ruff at his neck.

To say that Deijman was startled at the idea of addressing the multitude hardly does his reaction justice. His nondescript face registered shock, laced with horror and disbelief, as if the virtue of his mother had just been called into question. I do believe he actually went into spasm. Then he stared at the scalpel he would soon be wielding, fear and dread chasing each other across the bland scenery of his features.

'You do it, Abraham,' Deijman croaked. 'You're the rhetorician.'

I looked at Deijman, fascinated. He was now staring down, wide-eyed with terror, at his predecessor as President of the Surgeons' Guild, Tulp. Tulp had seated himself in the front row, in prime position among the places reserved for *praelectors* over fifty.

The surgeon addressed as Abraham left his place in the tableau, much to Rembrandt's all-too-audible fury, and stood at the front of the dais. He adopted a rhetorician's pose, feet apart, one slightly in front of the other, right arm extended.

I guessed him to be a member of the Rhetoricians' Club. Funnily enough, the Club used to share premises with the Surgeons' Guild, but the rhetoric made too much noise, so the surgeons moved. Who among us does not have problems with the neighbours?

'From the light comes life,' the surgeon began, in a reedy but clear voice, waving at the four lanterns illuminating Joris.

This was an extremely clever opening. I applauded, as well as the skull in my hand and the cloth over my arm allowed. The majority understood it as irony, which indeed it was, as Joris was so unequivocally and irredeemably dead. But those of greater refinement gained a deeper meaning, namely that once this investigation had been carried out, we would indeed know more of life and how it worked.

I resolved then and there, skull in hand, up there on the dais, to divide my own explanation of life – for that is what philosophy is – into that which can be comprehended by the multitude and that which is reachable only by those of discernment. Such as myself. And a few others.

But the surgeon was continuing: 'My name is Abraham de Hondecoeter...' The man was a natural orator; the audience fell quiet.

However, at that moment two dogs which had entered the auditorium began to copulate, right in front of the tableau on the dais. This, not unnaturally, distracted the crowd, who howled with laughter and made ribald comments, cheering the male dog on. The scrofulous fellow who had taken the entrance fee ran up to the dogs and started beating them with a stick. This had no effect on their activity, so he seized the bitch by the ears. The bitch bit him.

The scrofulous fellow retired from the fray, waving his bleeding hand indignantly. Two attendants appeared with a sack, into which they finally drove the conjoined animals. Between them, they lifted the sack and carried it, heaving and struggling, away.

'My name is Abraham de Hondecoeter,' the surgeon repeated, to establish order once again. 'We are here today to witness a dissection. This, in the presence of a distinguished retired professor of this Guild, Dr Nikolaes Tulp.'

There was a murmur of appreciation at Tulp's name, even a scattering of applause, though this was mainly from the *praelectors* at the front. Tulp stood, gravely took a bow, then resumed his seat.

'Dr Tulp,' continued de Hondecoeter, 'once said that the anatomist is the true eye of medicine. And what we shall discover today, when we cut open this corpse, is what made him a thief. We shall see if this man —' de Hondecoeter indicated the decomposing Joris Fonteijn with a flourish '—*has a mortal soul.*' de Hondecoeter waved his right arm with rhetorical vigour. The multitude applauded and cheered.

'Or not.' There was a dramatic pause. The theatre fell silent. 'We shall indeed see today the nature of the soul. You see a bird flying by in the sky...' de Hondecoeter shaded his eyes, twisting his whole body to follow the flight of imaginary birds. There was a ripple of applause at the rhetorician's skill.

'That bird, those birds, fly we know not where. And then they die.' De Hondecoeter clutched his chest and groaned – the birds having evidently expired from a thoracic complaint, possibly heart failure.

'Their immortal souls reconstitute in the body of another bird which comes back to life...' De Hondecoeter rendered this resurrection by putting his hands together in praying mode, then laying his head on the back of one hand, eyes shut. He then 'awoke' with a startled jerk, opening his eyes wide and staggering about on the dais in imitation of a bird new to the business of being alive and unsure of precisely how to go about it.

This brought a storm of applause, which increased and was joined by foot-stamping as the surgeon, still in the guise of newly-alive bird, tentatively flapped both arms.

'And so they come back to us in spring,' de Hondecoeter said. 'New birds with new souls. And *this*, ladies and gentlemen —' (There were indeed a few ladies but not, I estimated, above nine or ten.) De Hondecoeter's rhetorical right arm pumped like a piston. '*This* is what you are about to witness today!'

The applause was thunderous. The rhetorician de Hondecoeter resumed his position; the painter Rembrandt began to paint.

Looking back on that day, it seems to me hardly credible that I had not realised until now that Deijman intended to dissect Joris Fonteijn's brain. I realised it only when the surgeon made the first saw-cut to remove the top of the skull – the part I was already supposed to be holding, the better for Rembrandt to paint it.

De Hondecoeter, flushed with the success of his speech, his ears glowing, appointed himself my guide and started whispering into my wig. 'Now watch Tulp. Just you watch Tulp when he realises what Deijman is doing.'

I looked at the surgeon, sitting his with his legs splayed wide apart in the first row. His thin lips were pursed in disapproval; the face, behind the pomaded beard, registering a plethora of dark emotions.

I gave a slight shrug, conscious of the need to maintain pose for Rembrandt. De Hondecoeter was whispering in my ear: 'When Tulp did his dissection of Aris Kindt, the first one Rembrandt painted. You know? The one illustrating the mind giving instruction to the arm, enabling the arm to move? Tulp took his information for that lecture from Book One of Vesalius. Vesalius deals with the brain, the seat of the soul, in Book Seven. So —'

I leaned back slightly, the better to complete the surgeon's thought '— so Deijman is saying "I can do more advanced work than you. I am further ahead, I am better."'

'Precisely!' De Hondecoeter clapped me on the shoulder for my perception.

'Maintain position, you two,' came the familiar yell from Rembrandt.

I fell to wondering, yet again, at the savagery of man. Deijman and Tulp were like Rabbi Aboab and Rabbi Morteira, sworn enemies, even without the excuse of ideology. Tearing into each other, wishing to best and beat each other.

Why is man so savage? We are jungle animals beneath our elegant clothes. As I said before, I am no hermit, but I limit my contact with my fellow man to letters and the occasional glass of beer or shared meal at a tavern. Any closer contact seems to engender these savage rivalries. Why? I wonder. Why?

My musings were broken into by de Hondecoeter, resuming his delighted murmuring of gossip in my ear. 'Deijman's quite new to the job,' he said. 'Only been head boy for three years. Hardly done any dissections. And of course he lacks all Tulp's flair. Solid, that's what he is.'

I nodded, hoping he was also deaf, as he was standing more or less right next to us.

He was sawing away at the top part of Joris Fonteijn's skull. As the circle was completed, the top of Joris's head came off and was passed to me before I could wave it away. This, unfortunately, left me with two skull tops, one in each hand, as if this were some new-fangled percussion instrument.

Apparently oblivious to my plight, de Hondecoeter continued to pour a stream of gossip into my wig. 'Six silver spoons, that's what's Deijman's getting for doing this. To the value of thirty-one *guilders*. It's too much.'

I nodded again, increasingly unsure of what was required of me as recipient of this information. To this day, I don't know if Deijman could hear it and was ignoring it, or whether the general hubbub was drowning the gossip. But at any rate, Deijman suddenly turned his head and spoke to de Hondecoeter.

'Abraham, I'm about to start the dissection proper. Tell the audience what's going to happen, please. And warn them against theft.'

De Hondecoeter, to Rembrandt's loud exasperation, again made his way to the front of the dais, breaking the aesthetically pleasing tableau on one side.

'Ladies and gentleman,' he began, again in rhetorician's pose. 'What you are about to witness is the removal of the membranes from the brain.' There was an appreciative gasp at this.

'The two halves of the brain will then be separated from each other,' de Hondecoeter continued. 'You will see a part of the brain called "the sickle" removed for the very first time in human history, here, today in Amsterdam.' That got vigorous applause and foot-stamping. 'Now, this part of the brain will be passed round among you, for your perusal. But Dr Deijman has asked me to remind you that the fine for the theft of body parts from the Anatomy Theatre is six *stuivers*. Thank you.'

de Hondecoeter resumed his place in the tableau. I peered into the bloody mess of Joris's head. His membranes were being pulled out like red strips of whip leather.

Deijman was rather nervously lifting the *falx celebri*, which he pulled away from the rest of the bloody mess as if he were lifting a leek from a clod of earth. He waved it in timid triumph, spattering us all with bits of brain. It was taken down into the audience, then passed from hand to hand.

* * *

The demonstration was finished, the multitude making their way from the theatre, most of them no doubt heading for taverns or who-knows- what places of ill-repute. I thankfully abandoned both my skull tops on the table, next to the bloodied mess of Joris Fonteijn of Diest, whose brain membranes were now splayed out all over his face.

From out of nowhere, Nikolaes Tulp apprehended me, placing a commanding hand on my shoulder. 'I hear you have no knowledge of Latin, Spinoza.'

'Where in heaven's name did you hear that?'

'We make it our business to know about the Waterlanders.'

'Who is "we"?'

'The brotherhood of Calvinists.'

'But I'm not a —'

'We make it our business to know about all who attend meetings of apostates. I am aware that you are a Jew. One could hardly be in doubt of it.'

'It depends what you mean by —'

'Will you answer my question, boy? Do you or do you not have a mastery of the Latin tongue.'

'A mastery, certainly not. I have some but not —'

'*Qui vivi nocuere, mali, post funera prosunt. Excuvaie sine voce docent.* What does that mean?'

'Um... Something about evildoers... Of benefit...'

Tulp's face – it was aged close up, the skin leathery – cracked into a sneer. He imitated my voice and my accent. '"Something about evildoers..."' he minced. 'It means "Evildoers who, while living, have done damage are of benefit after their death. Their skins teach us this even though they have no voice." Do you know who said that, boy?'

'Caspar Barlaeus.' I was furious with myself. It was the motto of the Surgeons' Guild, carved into the wall in gold lettering behind my head. I knew *that* much Latin. Tulp had made me lose my composure, so I forgot it.

'Correct. My friend Barlaeus, with whom I investigate the wonders of God's creativity, made manifest in the body. At least you got that much right. But how do you expect to write philosophy, boy, with minimal Latin? Surely not in vulgate Dutch?'

'No!' I spoke with some force. It would be even more dangerous to put my thoughts down in a form accessible to all. 'I intend to master Latin. Sooner rather than —'

'I see! Intend to master Latin. Good. Good. Did you know that I write poetry in Latin?'

'No. Congratulations. Excuse me. I have to...'

The bully went as far as to restrain me by gripping my arm. 'I am a member of a circle. We meet to compose Latin poetics. Much of it is published.'

'Splendid. Well done! I —'

'I also had a career as scientist and surgeon that makes me famous beyond the bounds of the Republic. And my name will live forever. Do you know why, boy?'

'Rembrandt's painting?' I hazarded.

'No!' thundered the surgeon. 'What do I care about that heretic, his daubs and his whore. There is a part of your body, Spinoza, a part of every human body, that *I* discovered and named. The *vulvula ileo-coecalis*. Known now as the *valvula tulpii*, after me.'

I was impressed, despite the man's relentless hounding of me. 'Really, I didn't know. Where...?'

'Here.' Tulp pulled my doublet and woollen shirt up with practised skill and grabbed a handful of my middle portion, seizing the area he had named.

I broke his grip and made my way to Rembrandt's easel, curious to know what the painter had made of the day's events. I was aware of Tulp following me, but gave my attention to Rembrandt's work.

Rembrandt had brought off the daring composition masterfully: the two groups, one either side of Deijman, the light shining onto the all-too-Christlike figure of what had once been Joris Fonteijn and was now... what, exactly?

'Change that figure, Rembrandt.' Tulp was now standing behind me. He spoke softly, but with great menace. 'If you leave it like that, I promise you, you won't be paid a *stuiver* and the painting will burn, like the blasphemous object it is. God is not mocked.'

Rembrandt, in his shabby coat, evaded the grandee's eye, but he spoke firmly enough. 'I won't change a thing,' he said.

'Very well,' said Tulp. 'Then you might as well pack your bags and go. Because you are finished in Amsterdam.' Rembrandt turned his back on him. He busied himself with packing away his drawing materials and paints.

Tulp turned his attention to me. 'And as for you, Spinoza. Remember this: *quin cassa caduci, fundamenta tui circumspice corporis.* Oh, but you can't understand that, can you?'

Tulp made to walk off. I caught him by the arm. 'It means that one day we will all relinquish our bodies and our houses,' I said. 'It's from Petrarch.'

The surgeon gave me a long stare.

Much later, I added an ending to this scene, in my mind. It didn't really happen, because my Latin wasn't up to it yet – it had not yet received the kind attentions of Clara Maria van den Enden. But its place in my mind is real enough, to me.

'*Tandem omnia librans*,' I said to Dr Tulp. '*Rideo meque simul mortali quidquid in orbe est*. As I'm sure you are aware, Dr Tulp, that is also from Petrarch. And it means "And yet, while I am pondering all this, I feel like smiling. Smiling at myself and at whatever is mortal in this world." '

Six

*Each thing, in so far as it is in itself, endeavours
to persevere in its being.*

Spinoza
Ethics

Franciscus van den Enden was a creature of extremes, a man of great volatility. He had begun his journey of belief, so I heard tell, as an ultramontane Catholic. Although subject to bouts of atheism, he was currently among the more extreme of the anti-Calvinist Protestant sects who met as Waterlanders.

So if belief may be imagined as taverns along a road, he had travelled far, stopping infrequently. However, with men like van den Enden, it is more convenient to see belief as a circle, like beads on a necklace. In which case he had slid along the necklace from one point of intolerance to the nearest adjacent point of intolerance, so not travelling far at all, and returning close to where he had started.

I stopped outside his shop, sniffing at the smell of baker's yeast which hung over the whole area. It was at a good address in the Nes, the sort of place that had caryatids on the house-fronts. However, my brother, Gabriel, my informant on the practicalities of life, had told me van den Enden was struggling with his finances and may even have to sell up soon. To make ends meet, he was giving Latin lessons, which is what I was doing there.

In his shop window there was a print by Jan Lievens, the friend of Rembrandt's youth. It depicted Mercury and Argus. There was one by Rembrandt himself, showing the raising of Lazarus. I felt that my friend's assertion of supremacy over his contemporaries, as an artist, was fully warranted.

I then looked for a print of Rembrandt's engraving of me, holding a lens. Vanity! Vanity, Spinoza, it will be your undoing yet. There was no engraving of me. However, among the higgledy-piggledy jumble of prints, some framed some not, I did spot another one by Amsterdam's finest.

It depicted a rather cheerful-looking trussed hog, apparently unaware of his impending execution. For the father of the family, standing behind the hog, was holding an axe. I was reminded painfully of Rembrandt's defiance of Dr Tulp, fervently hoping the hog would not turn out to be another of his famous self-portraits.

I did not, at that time, make the connection between the threat to Rembrandt from Dr Tulp and the threat from Morteira to me, though in view of what happened later, I certainly should have. Such connections form the spirals woven by time. In fact, they are the main purpose of the concept of time, which, I have always thought, has little value in itself to the philosopher.

As I stood there, in the snow, I was filled from heart to mind with a sudden rushing of happiness – or *laetitia*, as I was soon to learn to call it. This happiness, I knew, was associated with what awaited me at van den Enden's. I was reminded of Terence's maxim 'Nothing human is alien to me.'

Afloat with this all-embracing elevation of the spirit, I made a note in my mind for transcription when I returned to my room: that joy is not a matter of the spirit alone. Joy is the affect by which the mind passes to greater perfection.

Just as I thought that, I was attacked by a mad dog. The cur came at me from out of a ditch between the van den Enden house and the street. It bounded at me, a great mangy black thing, frothing at the mouth. Still absorbed in my thoughts,

I was unable to defend myself as it seized my leg at the calf, shaking its head back and forth with my person in its jaws, for all the world as if it were trying to detach the leg from the rest of me. Indeed, if the beast can be said to have thought or conscious intention that, in summary, was it.

'Dogs have surrounded me,' I shouted at the mad dog. 'Like a lion my hands and my feet.'

The quotation from Psalms failed to influence the mad dog. A change of tactics, then: I bent to beat at the cur with my fists, but this also had no evident effect. I tried flapping at the hound with my cloak, seeking to mask its eyes, or even damage them. This had greater success. As I wrapped the brown wool of the garment round the mad beast's head, it desisted long enough for me to free my leg. It then raked my arm with its jaws through my cloak. I beat at it with the unwounded arm.

A passer-by appeared, a tall fairly-made youth of about my age, in an expensive-looking cape and high folded-down boots. He glanced with minimal curiosity at my plight, then knocked at the door of van den Enden's emporium. A maid in cap and apron opened the door to him – the shop being on the ground floor of van den Enden's house. She saw me battling with the now leaping dog and fortunately seemed more interested in my predicament than the young man had been.

'Just a moment, sir,' she called out to me. 'Help is at hand!'

'Hurry!' I called out in reply. 'Hurry, I cannot fend off the cur much longer.'

The maid thankfully reappeared quickly with a wooden carpet-beater, with which she assailed the cur, catching it with full-force in the side. She followed this with a lusty blow to its hind quarters, at which the cur slunk off, limping somewhat.

'Thank you,' I said, breathlessly. 'I am in fact expected at your establishment. Please be so good as to tell *Mijnheer* van den Enden that Master Spinoza has arrived.'

The maid, a middle-aged portly woman with a pronounced goitre, did not move.

'Please be so good —'

'I heard you. Is that it, then?' She shouldered the carpet beater like a musket. Then she stood there, staring at me.

'Please be so... Oh I see.' I felt in my worn purse. Nothing. I did not intend to spend any money that day. Ah, but at the corner of my purse there was a single mouldering *penning*, a sixteenth of a *stuiver*. I fished it out and presented it to my rescuer.

'That's all I've got,' I said.

She snatched the *penning*, sniffed it, bit it, then tucked it in her apron pocket. 'So, how're you going to pay for your lesson, if you've got no money? That's what you've come for, isn't it? Learn Latin? ' Her goitre quivered in outrage.

'Yes, indeed. I had assumed I would pay at the conclusion of a course of lessons. Say, five or —'

'I've heard some excuses in my time!' My rescuer glared at me. 'Wish I'd left you to the dog.' She appeared about to flounce off, then noticed something. 'The carpet beater's busted,' she said. 'Look at it! Won't work now.' She waved the implement in my face. 'You'll have to pay for a new one.'

I lost my temper. 'Pay for a new one? But you broke it, not me, ' I yelled.

'Don't you shout at me! You shout at me and I won't let you in. There'll be no Latin lessons for you, my lad!'

'All right. I apologise for shouting. Now, *please...*'

The servant stomped off, the wounded carpet beater at 'march' position over her shoulder. I stood there for a while, nonplussed, as the bells of Amsterdam's Niewe Kerk began to peal. Then I noticed the goitred one had left the door open. I made my way through the deserted shop, up a winding staircase inside, where I found myself, unannounced, in the van den Enden living quarters.

* * *

75

There were various rooms, all at different levels, some with the door open, some with the door shut. Nobody in sight. I stopped at a mezzanine between two floors. It had one room only on it. I peered in.

Seated at a table there was a young girl in a simple grey dress, with flaxen hair peeping out from under her cap. She was frail-looking but appeared intelligent, with a high white forehead. A book was open in front of her. She kept looking down at the book, then up again, as if she were thinking about what she was reading.

Looking at her, my breath shortened until I was panting. My view of her was three-quarter face. I could also see past her into what must be some sort of side-chamber. I moved a little so that I could see her face better. She had clear skin and a straight nose. Something of the happiness I had felt before the dog attacked me returned, but it was subtly different in nature, less tranquil, less meditative, more like excitement. It also, in a way I was at a loss to explain, carried a future element in it.

But then I realised the girl was not alone. A figure came into my somewhat oblique sightline. This was the well-made youth who had left me to my fate as the cur had me in its jaws.

The girl spoke to the well-made youth. '*Asinus Buridani*,' she said in a bell-like voice. 'Explain, please.'

'Genitive,' said the youth, now out of sight to me. 'Showing possession. The ass belongs to Buridan.'

'Correct,' said the girl. She moved on to some other phrase – *anima sensitiva*, I believe it was.

I was seething with anger. Correct! I clenched my fists. Correct, correct... The ass belongs to Buridan, but the ownership of the bloody ass is hardly the issue, is it? So-called problems like Buridan's Ass have cluttered philosophy for centuries.

The ridiculous postulate is of an ass who is starving *and* thirsty. All right? He hesitates between hay and water, this ass, until he expires from hunger and thirst, presumably simultaneously. Ludicrous! The choice is unreal. Philosophy should not concern itself with asses. More pertinently, no choice can *ever* be completely equal. One choice can *always* be *proven* to be better.

I was about to point this out to the girl in the grey dress when a voice above me called out 'Is that you, Spinoza? It's about time.'

I walked back to the spiral staircase, which evidently ran through the middle of the house, making my way toward the voice.

* * *

Franciscus van den Enden was closer to Rembrandt's age than mine. He stood there, tiny and splenetic, red-faced and dressed in brown from head to toe, for all the world like a choleric gnome.

'How do you account for this behaviour, Spinoza?' he greeted me. 'You arrive for your first Latin lesson late and unannounced. You break my household equipment, to wit one carpet beater, for which you refuse to pay. You are dishevelled and filthy.' He glanced down at my shredded breeches and now-visible drawers, muddied and bloodied. One arm of my doublet and part of my cloak was in a similar state. 'You creep around like a thief in the night...'

'I —'

'It shows a lack of respect for me, Spinoza. A fundamental lack of respect.'

'Hey, look here. Your maid —'

'No, no, never mind that your plans were well-laid.'

I remembered at this point that van den Enden was deaf. But as he never listened to anyone else, he had, in a sense, overcome the deficiency. Or at least rendered it irrelevant.

'Please, just —'

'I've never liked you, Spinoza. You are arrogant. Everybody says so. Just like the rest of your people. And you have wasted

77

my time.' He took a timepiece from his waistcoat pocket and opened the lid. 'What o' clock is it?'

Was he asking me? I peered at the strange thing, a mass of dials, hands, moons and peculiar symbols. 'Three something.'

'The king has nothing to do with it. You have missed your lesson.'

I felt a rush of excitement. 'Is there another teacher?' I bellowed into his ear. 'Free at this time?'

Van den Enden recoiled, but answered readily enough. 'There is someone else who teaches the basics. Stuff I have no time for. But that's not for you, surely? You are rude and have too high an opinion of yourself, but you are an educated man.'

'My Latin is at the first stages, sir.' I stooped, the better to roar into van den Enden's ear. 'Perhaps I might try this other teacher.'

'Don't take that tone with me, Spinoza! You come here late, in a state of filth, destroying my artefacts. You snoop round my house, as if trying to purloin something. And now you're impugning my methods. Typical! Chosen of God, you think yourself. Eh? You know best. You know everything.'

I had an idea. I said absolutely nothing. I assumed a seraphic smile, based on the one on my mother's face when she died. I waited, the rictus frozen in place. van den Enden jutted the point of his greying beard at me. There was silence. Eventually, as I had hoped, his spleen dissipated for lack of any opposition to feed it.

'My daughter will give you your Latin lesson,' he said, quietly.

'Thank you, sir,' I replied, with all the loudness I could muster. 'And what is her name?'

'Oh, I know you're to blame. You don't have to tell me that.' He waved his little brown arms at me, as if scaring crows from a field. 'She has another pupil with her at the moment. Go and clean yourself up, then return to the room below.' He indicated the room where I had so recently listened in. 'Her name is Clara Maria.'

* * *

'Hello?' she said, curious but unafraid, as I made my way tentatively into the mezzanine room, now free of the well-made youth, I was glad to see. 'Whatever happened to you?'

I had located a barrel of water in the courtyard outside the house and done my best to repair the ravages wrought on me by the hound. However, news of my impecuniousness had spread, so none of van den Enden's servants would help me, let alone offer a change of clothing. I fear that all I had achieved was to soak myself, so that blood and mud clung to me in a damp mess.

'I was attacked by a dog.'

'Oh really!' she turned in her chair, to face me squarely. Her grey eyes widened. Her face was animated, curious, interested. 'What made the dog attack you?'

'I fear it may have been mad,' I said. 'However, I am not entirely unused to such a reaction to my person, even before I have said anything. It increases in vigour, sometimes considerably, as soon as I give my thoughts utterance. This reaction to me extends, sad to say, throughout the animate kingdom of beings. Although I have yet to be assailed by a vegetable or plant.'

'Oh dear!' she said, nodding with every appearance of wisdom. 'How sad! Perhaps...' Her voice was lower than would be expected from such a slight frame, but melodious, even sing-song. 'Perhaps you could tell me who you are?'

I realised I had entered a lady's room entirely unannounced. 'My name is Benedictus Spinoza. I have been passed to you by your father, Franciscus van den Enden...'

'Yes, I know who my father is.'

'Indeed. For a Latin lesson.'

'Why do you sound so funny?'

'Ah! That is because I am not speaking in my mother tongue. We spoke Portuguese at home. It is still the language of my day-to-day thoughts. I learned Dutch... well, I can't remember how I learned Dutch. I just did.'

She was silent a moment, thinking about that, looking curiously at me all the time, with frank grey eyes.

'You don't look Dutch,' she said finally, judiciously.

I smiled. 'What do I look like?'

She put her head on one side, assessing. 'Like a magician. From the east.'

'Thank you!'

There was a silence.

'Good,' she said, finally. 'I like teaching Latin. So... you'd better sit down, then, Benedictus Spinoza. I can't sit here for an hour twisting my neck round to look at you.'

'Excuse me!'

I hastened to sit down. It was then, when I sat down, that I looked at the room properly for the first time. Because my senses were so sharpened and enhanced by Clara Maria, the picture of the room printed itself on my mind with a clarity and permanence I had not experienced before or since. Even now, writing this some months after the events I am describing, the room is more real to me, in my mind, than the room in Rijnsburg in which I presently write. More real and certainly more vivid.

Like nearly all of these so-called 'between rooms' there was no natural light. Clara Maria was lit by lamps in the darkest corners. The walls were of painted wood, the ceiling surprisingly high. The room was redolent of symmetry, of order, of calmness. I thought of it as a Christian calmness which spoke of safety. At any rate it consciously harked back to the style and motifs of the Greeks and the Romans.

The pattern in the coffered ceiling was repeated in the marble floor. The fireplace was counterbalanced by a walnut cupboard, built into the opposite wall. All the furniture was placed along the walls. Clara Maria and I sat opposite each other at a large console table, our shoulders practically touching one wall.

The paintings on the walls were hung in groups, as was customary in fine houses – a custom imitated in my own family house on the Houtgracht. I recognised a rather inferior portrait of van den Enden himself, grouped with what were presumably his forefathers from Antwerp. Like many families, the van den Endens had followed the trade from Antwerp to Amsterdam when Antwerp's harbour had silted up.

I recognised a landscape by Ruisdael, who knew van den Enden from the Waterlanders. Nothing by Rembrandt, I was fairly sure – for one thing it was all so second-rate.

In the group with the Ruisdael there was a piece by the younger Cuyp – Aelbert. You could tell it was by him because it showed cows. Cuyp was apparently obsessed by them, painting little else. I am sure even a church interior represented by Aelbert Cuyp would include a cow somewhere.

Opposite me, on the far wall, was the only feature of the room not matched by another – a large mirror in a heavy golden frame. I caught sight of myself as I sat down and hastily averted my gaze. That dog had a lot to answer for...

Clara Maria's teaching methods were ingenious. She began by explicating the grammar of Latin phrases, as I had heard her do with the well-made youth.

The first one she threw at me was *ab aeterno* – from eternity – coupled with *in aeternum* – to eternity, which allowed her to expound on the reason for the differences in the form of the words. But then she asked me my profession, the better, I believe, to match the content of the Latin phrases to my needs.

'I am a philosopher,' I said.

She burst out laughing.

I said nothing. I could feel my cheeks taut with beaming.

'Oh, I'm so sorry,' she said, dabbing at her eyes with a tiny linen handkerchief, pulled from the sleeve of her dress.

'That's all right,' I said. 'But philosophy is quite a serious matter, you know.'

'Oh yes!' said Clara Maria, her eyes wide. 'It was the way you said it that was funny. She adopted a basso voice: 'I am a philosopher.'

I laughed. 'I didn't mean to sound self-important.'

'Oh, but you must be!' she said, suddenly serious, even solemn. 'If you don't think you are important, nobody else will.'

I raised my eyebrows. Clara Maria's tiny frame appeared to hold an unlikely load of wisdom in it.

'What form does your philosophy take?' she said, her head on one side.

'I am writing a book,' I replied, proudly. And then as she started to laugh I tried, too late, to dilute the pride. 'At least I am trying to.'

'What is your book about?'

'I intend to explain life,' I said.

'What part of it?'

'All of it. What it is, how it works. A total explanation. Of Everything. Everything there is.'

'Not good enough.'

'Not good enough!' I stared at her.

'No. Too vague.'

'Vague! It's not vague at all! Nothing could be less vague. My method is to prove every single assertion I make. I shall prove them by the same style of geometric proof that Euclid the Greek used: Proposition – Proof – Corollary. And so on. My finished statements will be incontrovertible.'

'Are all these statements of equal weight?'

I stared at her. It was an astonishingly perceptive question. 'You are intelligent,' I blurted out.

'Of course I am,' she said, impatiently. 'The question is, are you? You've outlined a method, one which is overweeningly ambitious. You've mentioned – one can hardly say described – a goal, one which is grandiose and vague. Meat on the bones please, mister Baruch Spinoza, the philosopher. Meat-on-the-bones!'

'Meat on the... What do you mean, meat...?'

She put her elbow on the table, then cupped her chin in her hand. 'You *must* have a central core to all this. Summarise the essence of your philosophy while taking one breath only.'

'Very well.' I took a deep breath, started to cough, then began again. 'Everything in existence desires its own survival, well-being and development, and acts solely in order to promote it.'

She pealed laughter, her slender shoulders shaking. 'That is the most obvious statement I have ever heard.'

'Thank you!' I blundered on. 'Everything is *Deus sive natura* – God in nature. You see, I know *some* Latin. God is nature, nature is God. There is only one thing, one substance on earth. It is nature, it is also God.'

She screamed. She looked fearfully toward the door, then crossed herself. There were tears in her eyes, tears of concern.

'Benedictus —'

'Call me Baruch, it's my Jewish name. Or Bento. My family call me Bento. I think I'm in love with you, by the way.'

'Bento, you simply *cannot* go around saying things like that. It will put you in terrible danger.'

Her hand was now close to mine on the table. Emboldened by her emotion I dared to consider moving my hand so it touched hers, fleetingly, perhaps with the appearance of an accident? I considered all aspects of the question. Would such contact offend her? Would...

'Bento! Did you hear what I said?'

'Yes.' Something occurred to me. 'We are what we know. We constantly construct and reconstruct ourselves from inside, with our minds, redefining the little portion of God-in-Nature that is ourselves.' I was quite pleased with that. I wished I'd thought of it before.

Her eyes were wide with fear. 'Bento, you are mad. You cannot exalt Man like this. You have ended God; you are ending religion. You... They will kill you for this.'

'I know of the dangers if... if my ideas fell into the wrong hands. But —'

'The wrong hands!' she cried out. 'Any hands, Bento. You simply cannot think these things, let alone say them out loud.'

'I know.'

She held her head in her hands for a minute. Then she looked up and expelled a puff of air, visibly pulling herself together, and resumed the chin-on-cupped-hand pose. 'I have to ask this,' she said, 'though I fear the answer.'

'Ask away,' I said. 'I think you are perfect.'

She was ignoring these remarks. I was getting used to that.

'All right. *If* we are all one substance, even the Lord our... oh I can't bring myself to say it. *If...* No, I have a question. According to your ideas, what happens to the immortal soul, on death? Are you saying... When we die, are you saying God dies?'

She crossed herself.

'Not exactly,' I said, meeting her gaze for the first time. 'The soul is of the same substance as the body, and so dies with the body.'

'All right. But if there is no heaven...'

'There is no need to be good. Quite. But good and evil are relative, you see. Not absolute.'

'You can't say *that*. You've just abolished morality.'

'No, I haven't. I've just said it's more complex than people think. Is it wrong to kill dogs?'

She nodded. 'Oh I see. I see. Suppose the dog outside was about to kill you? Suppose the dog was mad —'

'— or was carrying a deadly disease.'

'So who judges the dog-killing issue? Religion, presumably.'

'No, absolutely not. Because religion is based on a random collection of bastardised texts, like the bible, encrusted with superstition and mumbo-jumbo —'

She put her hands over her ears. 'Stop!'

I stopped.

'Who then? Who judges?'

'The state, free of the fetters of religion. The state should be the guardian of freedom and liberty. The state should decide whether or not I was entitled to kill the dog, which I was unfortunately unable to do.'

Her lovely skin was pale and, if I am honest, slightly blotchy with her emotion. Her eyes were wide. The room was hot, even in winter, because there was no outer window. There were a couple of delicate, and very pretty, beads of perspiration on her brow.

'Do be careful, Bento.'

SHE CARES SHE CARES SHE CARES.

She thought for a moment. We were silent. A clock I had not noticed in the room before was suddenly audible, ticking.

'You should not write any of this down, you know.'

'I have to.'

'Why?'

'Because it is the truth.'

'But you don't intend to have it printed?'

I remembered that her father printed books among his many activities, which included writing plays in Latin and painting. 'No, no. At any rate not in my lifetime. I'm not a complete fool, Clara Maria. I'm a little unworldly perhaps—'

'A little!'

'But I'm not oblivious to the danger.' For a second I considered telling her of the searches being made of my room by Morteira's minions. But I didn't.

'What language do you write in?'

'Spanish.' A language Morteira spoke like a native! 'But I shall translate it into Latin when I have learned enough from you. Unless...' My heart sank. Had I frightened her away? Ended my Latin lessons when they had only just begun?

But she reassured me. 'No, don't worry. I'll continue to help you. At least, I'll continue to teach you Latin. If you want me to.'

'Of course I want you to!'

She stood, a little laboriously, and went over to the walnut cupboard. Blood rushed to my face. She was lame; one leg was withered. She practically dragged it behind her.

No matter! No matter! You blackguard, Spinoza! You unworthy moral pygmy to have even a second of doubt. I mentally begged her forgiveness.

She put two books on the table. 'Here,' she said. 'This is a Basic Latin primer, such as a teacher uses in Latin School. You can do much of the basic grammar yourself at home.'

I took the book. 'Thank you, Clara Maria.'

She nodded, as if to herself. 'Next time, we will work more on phrases for philosophy.' She gave a little laugh, to herself. '*Causa libera*,' she shot at me.

'Natural cause?'

She laughed delightedly, suddenly childlike. 'No, free cause. Natural cause is *causa naturalis*. You can explain the difference to me next time, Mr Philosopher.'

'I would like that very much.'

'Me too. Will you write something in my *Album Amicorum*, please?'

She passed the second book along the table. It was of expensive paper, no doubt supplied by her father's emporium, held together by strips of leather. Clara Maria untied two of them, so that I could open her album and write something.

'May I look through your album? Or is it...?'

'No, no. Please look if you would like to.'

And so I did. There were poems, some in Latin. Some very short scenes from dramas, also in Latin. There were messages from people, presumably her friends. There were improving mottos which had struck Clara Maria. One was 'What use are spectacles and a candle if the owl cannot see.' I was reminded of Rembrandt the painter, with his fondness for such aphorisms. Even as I thought of him I saw some drawings in the album. Some were landscapes, some were tronies of young men.

'Did you draw these? They are very good.'

She laughed. 'No. I do draw, from time to time. But not as well as that. My father knows many artists. Some are kind enough to...' She shrugged her slender shoulders to complete the sentence.

An idea struck me with great force. 'Do you know Rembrandt van Rijn, the painter?'

'I think my father has met him at religious meetings. But I'm afraid I don't know anybody as eminent as that myself.'

'I know him quite well,' I said casually. 'I'm sure he would be happy to do a drawing for your *Album Amicorum*.'

'Really? Oh, that would be...'

'I tell you what. I'm going to an auction with him soon. Why don't you come? Bring your *Album Amicorum*. And we'll ask him to draw something there, on the spot.'

'I don't think Papa would —'

'Don't tell him.' I was amazed at my own audacity. I was risking everything on one throw of the dice.

But she laughed. 'All right.'

'Your lips are like a crimson thread, your speech is lovely.'

'I beg your pardon?'

'I said "I'll see you at the auction, then."'

I was preparing to leave, clutching my Latin primer. We were both standing. I held out my hand to her. She curtsied, a little unsteadily because of her lame leg.

'Do you have many pupils?' I asked, partly to make conversation as I left, but I was thinking of the well-made youth, with a sudden rush of jealousy.

'Only a few,' she said. 'The main one is Theodor. Theodor Kerckrinck. He's a scientist, like you. Didn't you see him on the stairs? He's very handsome!' Clara Maria blushed.

'Is he... um... I mean he's not betrothed to you or anything?

She looked at the floor, hugely embarrassed. 'No, no. Well, not officially. One day perhaps, but not yet.' She giggled. 'I can't marry for another three years. I'm only thirteen!'

Seven

... desire is appetite with a consciousness of itself

Spinoza
Ethics

'Non ridere,' I said aloud as I sat at my table in my tiny chamber, by the butter-light of a single small lamp. 'Non lugere.' I paused. 'Neque detestare, sed intelligere.' I completed the aphorism. My Latin was bounding forward like a runaway horse. I translated, in my mind: not to laugh, not to lament, not to detest, but to understand.

To understand. To begin with ideas in the mind – not from empirical observation, which can be faulty and particular. Then to understand. To do that one must subordinate the passions, especially the lower passions, like licentiousness.

If only she were Jewish. Jewish girls can marry at twelve-and-a-half. Once again, I tore off my breeches and flung myself down on my bed, letting the red coverlet envelop me. My imaginings, as my hand reached between my legs, were necessarily vague regarding Clara Maria. But I did imagine her happy, albeit somewhat dishevelled.

* * *

The auction where I was to meet Rembrandt and Clara Maria was at the Keizerskroon Inn, on Kalverstraat, a spacious room on the third floor. As I took in the auctioneer's table at the front and the clutter of artefacts round the walls, I realised that these two people were the ones I loved most in the world – along with Rembrandt's son, Titus.

Rembrandt was beaming round the auction-room, like a man at his passion, which is what he was. As for myself, I suddenly felt faint. I was having to force myself to eat, of late. My work on the manuscript was proceeding, but it had slowed, not least because I was taking frequent breaks, of one sort or another. In short, I could think of little but Clara Maria.

I was watching the door, my breathing shallow, terrified she would not appear. I had spent hours rehearsing my first greeting to her, compiling spontaneous witty remarks, aphorisms and sayings to amuse her, and holding entire conversations with her in my mind. These conversations increasingly culminated in a proposal of marriage. I had taken to consuming small beer, the while, so her answer was always yes.

I had naturally asked the painter in advance if he would contribute to Clara Maria's *Album Amicorum*. His agreement was instant and in the warm tone and manner he was increasingly adopting toward me. Even if it was accompanied by a comradely wallop in the small of the back, which left me coughing and caused some bruising.

I was pleased that I did not possess a timepiece or it would never have left my hand.

'She's not here yet, then?' Rembrandt remarked, with exaggerated mock-innocence.

'Not yet,' I said, feigning nonchalance so poorly that Rembrandt roared with laughter.

'Never mind!' the painter said, touching my arm, then rubbing my back to soothe me – I swear Rembrandt is one of the most earthy, physical men I have ever met. His eyes were twinkling with merriment. He wore the same coat Joris Fonteijn had tried to steal, and the same hat. The only difference was in the tightness of the coat. The painter, I surmised, was consuming more beer, herring and Leiden cheese.

Eating and drinking to forget, perhaps. These were serious times. Leiden had suffered dreadfully in the plague, even worse than Amsterdam. According to Titus, one of Rembrandt's beloved brothers had died from the terrible, agonising affliction that comes to us for no known reason. Rembrandt himself never mentioned it.

Tired of the tension of waiting for Clara Maria, I looked round the room, hoping that distraction would provoke the appearance I desired so much. As I did so, I winced at my own fall into superstition – there being, naturally, no logical connection at all between the two events. Was love to render me superstitious? Was it to coddle my brain, like hot water round an egg?

I saw the unappetising figure of the painter Ruisdael. He was dressed, as ever, in clothes that looked as if they had been abandoned in disgust by someone considerably larger. His face was caked with grime. He gave me a ghastly, gap-toothed grin across the room, but mercifully did not come over.

Behind Ruisdael, appearing as if from steam, I saw the Sephardic Jew who had been following me around, and who was surely in the pay of Morteira.

'Back in a minute,' I murmured to Rembrandt.

I headed through the multitude toward the head of the Sephardi, bobbing on a thin neck above those around him – he was remarkably tall. The man's olive-skinned face contorted with alarm, a rich full mouth opening slightly. He fled toward the exit door, pushing past those in his way, muttering imprecations at them. As he left the auction room, I smiled to myself. I had taken action – effective action!

I made my way back to Rembrandt's side. As I did so, I caught sight of Clara Maria, before she was hidden by the crowd. She was smaller than I had remembered, tiny in fact. It was the first time I had seen her walk a distance, as she came through the crowd. Her limp was significantly more pronounced than I remembered. Her left leg had some sort of calliper strapped to it; she dragged the near immobile limb after her.

She was again wearing the grey-blue colour she favoured, with a modest white cap. She was carrying her *Album Amicorum*.

'Clara Maria,' I blurted out, then stood there like a lovelorn fool. She smiled, quite confident in what must surely be new surroundings.

'And you must be the famous Mr Rembrandt, the painter.' She spoke pertly, offering Rembrandt her cheek to kiss. 'I am Clara Maria van den Enden.'

Jealousy rose through my body that the cheek had not been offered to me, but I fought down the unworthy emotion. Rembrandt kissed her, right-left-right after the Amsterdam fashion.

'Pleased to meet you, young lady,' Rembrandt said.

He broke wind loudly, as the courtesy was completed. Clara Maria gave a peal of laughter.

'Too many herrings,' Rembrandt said with mock-solemnity. 'A small but great pleasure,' he added. 'I refer to the herrings, young lady, not your good self.' He looked down on her – even Rembrandt dwarfed her. 'Although on second thoughts...'

A tinkle of laughter was the painter's reward. Clara Maria held up her *Album Amicorum*. '*Mijnheer* Rembrandt, I would be deeply grateful if you would honour my *Album Amicorum* with a sketch. I would like to say, sir, that I consider you among the finest artists of our time, equalled perhaps only—'

'NO!' Rembrandt bellowed, so loudly that the crowd around us turned in amusement. 'Don't spoil it, young lady. You were doing beautifully. Let's leave out the bit about me being equalled, shall we?'

'I was about to say by Johannes Vermeer of Delft, sir,' Clara Maria said, firmly.

'Could have been worse.' Rembrandt pulled a morose face. 'The Bore of Delft at least has talent. Though if he paints just one more woman having a good think as she goes about her daily business, I will personally put my fist through it.'

Clara Maria laughed.

Rembrandt was encouraged. 'He paints too much, that man,' he boomed. 'That's why he can't sell anything. Did you know he's become a Catholic? With any luck it'll ruin his career.'

Clara Maria laughed again, one hand on her hip, like a man. Rembrandt had taken the *Album Amicorum* from her. They were ignoring me. Such, indeed, is frequently the fate of the philosopher. At any rate, it keeps happening to me.

Rembrandt produced a quite ordinary quill and a sealed pot of ink from the pocket of his coat. He made his way to a table at the side of the room. Some pieces for auction were on it – some armour, I recall, and a pistol – Rembrandt laid them aside. Clara Maria and I followed him. We watched as his face settled into concentration.

He found a clean page in the *Album Amicorum* and smoothed it with his forearm. He broke the seal on the pot of brown ink, dipped his pen into it and moved it backwards and forwards. I do believe I did not breathe while he was doing this. I intend no blasphemy for the sake of provocation – I never do, though nobody believes me – but I felt that the experience was what the world considers holy. For Rembrandt van Rijn created an evocation of life before our eyes, where before there had been nothing.

What he showed us, a matter of moments later, was a sketch of blind Homer reciting verses. There were thirteen or fourteen figures touched into life by lines in brown, in addition to the blind poet himself. We could see – we could feel – their experience of the master's verses. Their emotion entered us from its place down the centuries. He had resurrected them.

Clara Maria was openly crying, and I loved her for it. I had no shame for my own tears, either.

Rembrandt signed the drawing. 'There, young lady,' he said, bringing to those three words a monumental tenderness. He handed her the now precious *Album Amicorum*.

'This is the proudest moment of my life, sir,' Clara Maria said, with a natural dignity that excluded sycophancy.

'It's better this time,' Rembrandt mused. 'I did the same subject for a friend of mine. An ex-friend now, as so many of them are. A man called Jan Six. It was for his *Album Amicorum* too. But I wasn't happy with it. I'm never happy with them. But this one is definitely better.'

Rembrandt punched me on the upper arm with massive force. I was not clear exactly why he did this – to rid himself of some superfluity of emotion, perhaps. I will simply make the observation, without rancour or even complaint, that many people of my acquaintance find the solution to their problems in doing some sort of violence to my person. At any rate, I winced at the pain. Clara Maria laughed.

An auctioneer appeared at the table at the front of the room and the auction began.

* * *

I was conscious of my responsibilities to Rembrandt's somewhat unorthodox family. I was here to limit his expenditure, to stop him spending at all, if I could. I stiffened and gathered my determination.

To my amazement, Rembrandt was regarding me, hands on hips, with undisguised, though fond, amusement. I looked at him, then looked away. Then looked at Clara Maria. Then looked hastily away again, as I felt myself blushing. To my horror, Rembrandt was now openly chuckling at me.

'What is it?' I hissed. I feared he was making a spectacle of himself. The auctioneer had already solicited bids for some musical instrument or other, but Rembrandt's laughter had the people around us distracted and listening to our little party.

'You are thinking,' Rembrandt boomed, loud enough to be heard at the city gates, 'that I must not spend too much money.'

'How did you know that?' I said.

'Am I right?'

I shrugged. 'Not too far off.'

Rembrandt assaulted the other arm with a massive punch.

'Ouch!'

Clara Maria was smiling, clutching the *Album Amicorum* to her breast.

'Baruch, my dear friend,' boomed the painter, ' you have the most mobile face I have ever seen, bar none. It does not so much express your thoughts as shout them like a milkmaid on her rounds.'

I tried to express surprise without it showing on my face. 'I... er...'

'There you go again!'

I tried to move out of punching range but only succeeded in deflecting the blow onto my ribcage. How many other people end their visit to an auction black with bruises?

'I... Well, yes. Your problems are...'

'Money cannot satisfy desire,' said Rembrandt.

'No, but it comes in handy for paying off the mortgage and buying herring. Not to mention canvas and paint. You can't do that with bloody proverbs and sayings, you idiot!'

I recoiled at my own boldness. Here we go again! Sarcastic, Baruch. Hurtful, Baruch. Not a nice man, Baruch (except in my own heart and mind). But I needn't have worried. Rembrandt's heart is as big as his talent. I took another punch, then a bear-like embrace.

'I know Titus and Hendrickje spoke to you,' he said when he had finished hugging me.

'How?' I asked.

'Because they speak to everybody.'

'Oh!'

Clara Maria laughed. But before I could feel too hurt by the loss of exclusivity in my role as helper, an item came up for sale which clearly interested Rembrandt. It was an etching by someone I knew to be a favourite of his.

'A grisaille landscape by Hercules Seghers,' called out the auctioneer, looking straight at Rembrandt. The auctioneer, the painter had told me, was called Pieter Haringh. Obviously, he knew Rembrandt well enough to know what he was likely to bid for.

Just visible to us, on a sort of portable podium at the front of the room, the tall long-faced Pieter Haringh waved the tiny Seghers grisaille hopefully in the air. 'It shows a landscape with trees,' he added helpfully. 'What am I bid?'

'I'm going to open at twenty,' Rembrandt whispered to me. 'I love it, don't you? Twenty guilders!'

The auctioneer nodded in acknowledgement of the bid, a smile stretching his long moustache. He solicited a higher bid.

'No!' I shouted, clutching Rembrandt's arm. 'Twenty guilders? Are you completely insane. Have you forgotten...?'

Rembrandt was doubled up with laughter. Clara Maria, needless to say, was laughing, too. Fortunately another bid came in for the tiny print and Rembrandt did not respond.

The Hercules Seghers landscape sold for twenty-five guilders. Titus later told me that Rembrandt had noted the successful bidder, tracked him down and bought it from him at an even higher price. But at the time, I escaped with another punch on the arm and more fond laughter from the man and the woman I loved most in the world.

I was powerless – oh that word, sometimes I feel it sums up my entire state of being – powerless, I say, to prevent Rembrandt buying a plaster statue of Diana bathing, by one Adam van Vianen. (No, I hadn't heard of him, either.) A work which seemed to me totally devoid of merit, character or originality.

I didn't even try to stop him when a bust of Homer came up. I myself bid for the skin of a lion, hoping my brother Gabriel would pay from the company's funds if I got it.

But I succeeded only in driving the price up.

'How are you going to get that home?' I asked the painter, indicating Homer.

'Oh, Hendrickje will send a boy,' he replied airily.

Rembrandt also felt he could not lead a contented and fulfilled life without the following: a wooden trumpet; a sacredan wood linen press; a book by Albrecht Dürer on the art of proportion, in German, a language the painter has no knowledge of; a tric-trac board; a large plant of marine origin, unmistakeably deceased; a plaster mould of Prince Frederick Henry – I quote: 'I did an Ascension for the bugger for 1,200 guilders and he only paid me half. And that years later. I intend to throw darts at it.'; a book with outstanding examples of calligraphy; an illustrated book, again in German, about Flavius Josephus – I quote the full exchange between us: 'He was a Jew, wasn't he?' 'No, Rembrandt, the scribe of Jewish resistance to the Romans was a Catholic.' 'Well, you should know.' 'Oh go on, buy the bloody thing.'

There was more, but I can't remember it all. In short, I failed in my task to limit Rembrandt's spending.

* * *

'Spinoza!

I jumped and unfortunately emitted a rather undignified shriek. I have a delicate constitution and am easily startled. Clara Maria, needless to say, laughed fit to break out of her corsets.

I stared. What on earth was my landlord doing here? I could sense Clara Maria's wondrous grey eyes on me. Blood rushed to my head, drowning my judgement in swirling carmine hubris. Oh what a glorious, grandiose panic!

'Ah, my good man!' (I had never addressed my landlord like this before). 'Surprising to see you surrounded by art.' I waved at Rembrandt and Clara Maria, puffed up as any toad. 'This is my landlord, Jan Teunissen, linen weaver and industrious fellow. This is Rembrandt, the famous painter, and my friend Clara Maria van den Enden.'

Teunissen, a ferret-like fellow, red as Esau and even hairier, nodded curtly. Clearly not as impressed as I had hoped by my fine friends, he started to speak.

I cut across him. 'How's that brother of yours, Teunissen?' I said, jovially. 'I haven't seen him around for a while.'

'He died at Martinmas,' Teunissen said.

'Oh, I'm—'

'Your friend said you were here, so I—'

'What friend?'

'I don't know! He didn't give his name. He's *your* friend, not mine. He said he'd just spoken to you. Said you were at the auction.'

The blood drained from my face, and much of my hubris with it. 'But nobody knows I'm here.' The awful suspicion grew in me. 'What did he look like, this friend? Tall, thin neck? Dressed in black? Wearing a skull-cap?'

Teunissen nodded, impatiently. 'That's him. We both wanted to speak to you. He said you were here, at this auction, but you'd be back in a few minutes. We waited a while, then I left him to it.'

'You left him in my room?' I was aware of Rembrandt and Clara Maria looking at me. Rembrandt, bless him, looked concerned. It was impossible for me to read Clara Maria's thoughts from her face.

Teunissen shrugged with a mixture of impatience and boredom. 'I haven't got all day, Spinoza. I'm on my way to the dyer's. I need to speak to you. Urgently.'

'What...?' I had gone from carmine red to the palest white, as fear took hold of me.

'Spinoza, my maids are refusing to go near your bed linen. If you don't stop committing the sin of Onan on my premises, I'll throw you out.'

There was a deep silence in our little circle, while around us the auction room babble continued. I stared at Clara Maria. Did she know what the sin of Onan was? An educated young lady like her? Of course she did. Her face was grave.

My landlord continued his torture. 'Come on, Spinoza. I'm a busy man.' He glanced contemptuously round the auction room. 'Unlike you.' His beady ferret eyes fixed mine. 'I want an undertaking that you will stop stimulating your private parts and making a mess on the bed linen. I want it now.'

I nodded. 'Yes,' I croaked.

Teunissen nodded curtly. He turned on his heel and made for the door. Clara Maria followed him. Such was the crush in the auction room, they appeared to be leaving together.

* * *

Looking back on that day, I still find it difficult to credit that it could have got worse for me. But it did. Rembrandt showed his concern for me, as a friend, by a massive blow to the upper rib cage, which left me winded. Not that I wanted to say very much, at that point.

'Baruch,' said the painter, thoughtfully.

I rubbed at my side, wincing, but nodded to show he had my attention. At least if he was talking to me, he could not simultaneously bid, thus spending even more money.

'You know I love Titus as much as any father ever loved a son. As much as Abraham loved Isaac.'

'Abraham was ready to let Isaac be killed,' I pointed out. 'I know people call me over-critical, but it seems to me that if you are judging fatherhood that is a bit of a demerit.'

'All right, all right. I love Titus *more* than Abraham loved Isaac. But I'll tell you something about, Titus, Baruch. About my lovely boy.'

I nodded, indicating interest, my eyes never leaving his fists, in case he wanted to show renewed affection by assaulting me.

'Titus,' Rembrandt announced portentously, 'hasn't got the faintest idea about money. Unlike me.'

I nodded again, politely. Does genius actually exclude self-knowledge? Did Rembrandt understand the entire universe *except* himself, despite the immortal self-portraits? Was that actually *why* he painted the self-portraits, to grasp the last elusive problem?

'You didn't hear a word I've been saying, did you?'

I jumped, startled. 'Mmm, what? Oh no. I'm afraid I didn't. Could you say it again?'

'What were you thinking about? The painter said, gently, with avuncular tenderness.

I said the first thing that came into my head. 'I was thinking that there is no transcendence, only immanence. Everything is material.'

The painter shook his head in mock sadness. 'I didn't understand a bloody word of that. Are you listening to me?'

'Yes.'

Rembrandt looked into my eyes. 'Yes, I can see you are. Right! Titus, and Hendrickje, too, for that matter, both of them think about small sums of money all the time. Now, if you owe 8,500 guilders you're deep in the shit. Right?'

'Right.'

'And you're even deeper in the shit if you have no source of income.'

'Is it as bad as that?'

Unusually for him, Rembrandt looked sad for a moment – down, even defeated. Just for a second he looked like a very old man. 'Tulp...'

'Oh no! Don't tell me the surgeons turned down your wonderful portrait?'

'No, Tulp's too clever for that. And I've got too many supporters in the Guild. No, the bastard has blocked my payment. He claims there is a dispute, over the amount to be paid. They can string that out for years. It's standard stuff. It's what that arsehole Frederick Hendrick —*Prince* Frederick Hendrick— did over my Ascension. And my Resurrection, come to that.'

I shook my head, then touched Rembrandt lightly on the arm, to show my fellow-feeling.

The painter shook himself like a wet dog, visibly husbanding his strength. 'So, if your finances are that bad, you might as well buy—' He stopped as the auctioneer announced the next lot. '—thirteen Chinese bamboo flutes.'

This time I realised he was teasing me, though the auctioneer was looking hopefully in our direction, obviously seeing the painter as a possible purchaser of the absurd offering.

'What I need,' said Rembrandt slowly, 'is one big gain that will wipe out the whole debt. Put me back on a sound financial footing, once and for all.'

'And what might that be?'

'Buying into a shipping consortium. Like—'

'Oh no!'

'Like the big Jewish consortium the firm of *D'Espinoza* is putting together. The good ship *Den Prince*. Ring any bells? Sailing from Amsterdam to Lisbon?'

I saw Titus's face in my mind's eye. I was supposed to be stopping Rembrandt forking out for etchings, paintings and artefacts, not conniving at risking a fortune. Then relief flooded me: the painter could not have the huge sums needed to buy into a shipping consortium.

'You're thinking I haven't got the money.'

'How did you know that?'

'You suddenly looked smug.'

'Thank you.'

'But you're wrong.'

'I am?'

'Yes. As Titus's guardian, I have access to all Saskia's part of the van Uylenburgh fortune, which was left to him.'

I felt my eyes widen. 'You can't touch that!'

'I already have. I went to the *Weeskamer* – the Orphan's Chamber. I signed my name a few times. The money's at home, lying around somewhere.'

'You *have* told Titus about this? Rembrandt, please!'

The old man's small eyes twinkled. He squinted at me. 'I don't think it's come up, actually. No.'

I thought for a moment. 'No! Rembrandt, you're my friend. I... I love you like a brother. That's why I'm saying no. The *Den Prince* consortium – any consortium – it's just too risky. Even though the war's ended there are still English privateers. And the Spanish. It's... No!'

'Oh, I knew you'd say that. That's why I went to see your brother first. He's agreed. I'm the only Christian in the *Den Prince* consortium. The money's not really lying around at home. Your brother's got it.'

I took a step back. 'You went to see Gabriel? And he agreed?'

'Sharp, philosopher, sharp.'

'And you haven't told Titus and Hendrickje?'

'No. No point in worrying them. Like I said, they don't understand money. They aren't practical men of affairs like you and me.'

I looked at him. He looked back. I knew that look. 'Why are you telling me this, now?'

'Because I've got another deal. Your brother Gabriel's shilly-shallying and I want you to persuade him. Strike while the iron's hot.'

'Oh no!'

'The Pereira brothers rent my cellar. They store stuff there. They've sold me a half-share in some tobacco and some bricks. I want them on board, to be sold at the other end, at a handy profit. That's in addition to my percentage as part of the consortium. I'm getting used to this dealing lark. I reckon I'm pretty good it.'

'And you want me to speak to Gabriel? Help you risk everything, your future, Titus and Hendrickje's future, and on such a risky venture?'

'Got it in one. What was that stuff about immanence, again?'

'Oh, it doesn't matter!'

* * *

I hurried back to my room after the auction, anxious to see if the Sephardi 'friend' who had been left alone with all my possessions had found the book of my philosophy. Would I be able to tell if he had discovered my hiding place, under the bed? Would there be signs that he had read the book?

The answer, as happens so rarely in philosophy, was clearer and simpler than I had expected. The floorboard from under the bed had been flung in a corner of the room. My book was nowhere to be seen; evidently my 'friend' had taken it.

Eight

When we love a thing similar to ourselves, we endeavour as much as we can to bring it about that it also should love us.

Spinoza
Ethics

Tranquillity was a state of being now consigned to memory, banished from experience, since that dreadful day at the auction room. The fear that I may never see Clara Maria again was made even more painful by the likelihood that she must now view me with... what? Disgust? Contempt? Loathing?

But man is born in hope and lives in hope. So I fully intended to keep my appointment for my next Latin lesson, there to plead my cause as a man of at least *some* worth.

Also, a most welcome distraction had presented itself, an extension to my activities. In a shop near van den Enden's emporium, I saw and purchased a single-lens microscope. It was offered cheaply because the lens was scratched. But I was easily able to polish out the damage. The lens then offered a most impressive magnification.

Excited at the prospect of studying Life, I began by cutting myself to obtain samples of blood. I wanted to see the essential substance of myself in motion, and this I did.

I then remembered something Rembrandt had said about studying the louse. I trapped some of the insects and – a guess this – placed them in a bottle with the lid sealed tight. Lo and behold, they died! I studied their corpses, both whole and anatomised. As I did so, I did my best to look like Rembrandt's etching of me, holding my lens: The Man With The Microscope.

During my frequent trips to the neighbourhood of van den Enden's shop, and also in my wanderings about town, I kept a look out for the Sephardi – Morteira's creature. I did not see him again, doubtless because Morteira had obtained what he wanted.

However, I kept catching tantalising glimpses of Descartes, who always managed to elude me. I remained convinced that most of these sightings truly were Descartes, though one of the fellows I hailed, with an observation on the lack of any goal or purpose in Life, let alone a 'final' one, turned on me, and unfortunately attacked and robbed me. It probably was not Descartes, then.

Here is a footnote to the above: I recently received a letter from Boyle, in England, who informed me that Descartes is dead, and has been for some years. It is not always easy to keep in touch with events.

* * *

I was trembling with fear when the day finally came to visit Clara Maria for my Latin lesson, arranged, naturally, before the disaster at the auction room. I imagined many catastrophic outcomes.

For example: the van den Enden maid I had already offended would turn me away at the door, on her mistress's instructions – or even on her master's instructions, if Clara Maria had told her father what she had learned about me. 'You have committed the sin of Onan,' the maid would thunder, her goitre atremble with righteous rage. 'It is the talk of Amsterdam. Get you gone!'

Or... a tearful Clara Maria would voice her outrage, pointing to the door with an extended index finger quivering with violated rectitude.

Or... Clara Maria would set the well-made youth on me; the well-made youth would thrash me. Occasionally I imagined defeating the well-made youth in combat, before claiming an impressed Clara Maria as my prize. But that strained credulity so much, even as fantasy, that I abandoned it.

The truth —events, Life, call it what you will— as ever was more prosaic. The maid with the goitre did indeed open the door to me, but she had forgotten me so completely that she enquired my name and my business at the household.

I was required to wait, I thought past the appointed time for the lesson, though I carry no timepiece. And that made me fear the worst, naturally. But when I was finally shown into the mezzanine room, Clara Maria was sitting at the table by the wall, composed enough. She was wearing the same grey dress as last time, and gravely offered me her cheek to kiss.

I was delighted by that, naturally, but she cut through my effusions of joy at seeing her, proceeding to the lesson in a businesslike way. Neither of us mentioned our last meeting. Our time passed smoothly. I have an affinity for languages. I was making rapid progress in the dead tongue, we both knew it, and to my delight she took pleasure in it.

As the lesson came to an end, she said something which fired me with happiness.

'Bento,' she began, quite casually. 'Your Latin is coming on at such a pace I feel you might benefit from a part in my father's play in the Latin language.'

'I... That would be most pleasant. May I ask, are you in it?'

She ignored my question. 'My father's play is a version of the story of Philemon and Baucis, as told by Ovid. We can work on your part together.'

There was a small smile at this point, the first she had favoured me with during this second lesson.

'How wonderful! But please answer my question: Are you in it?'

'No. It will be performed in public, so only men are in it. And anyway, there's my leg.'

'Your...? Oh, the crippled leg, you mean? Yes, you wouldn't want to be dragging that around on stage, with people watching. That's understandable.'

'I shall be making the costumes.'

'Good! Good.'

'And Theodor is in it.'

She said that as if it were some consolation.

I nodded. 'Uh huh!'

'You remember Theodor?'

'Yes, I remember him.'

She stood, but I sensed she would not want to see me to the door, because of her leg. I wished her a tender goodbye, but she cut short further effusions from me. I made my way down the stairs, filled by my huge gain of the day: my appearance in the play would mean I would see her more often.

Outside, as I was hit by the steely cold, a voice said 'I want a word with you.'

I spun round, my fists clenched. It was the man I still thought of as 'the well-made youth', Theodor Kerckrinck. He looked me in the eyes. I am tall but he was even taller, and broad-shouldered with it, in bulging brown doublet.

'Two things, Spinoza. Two things I want you to be very clear about.'

'Oh yes?'

'About Clara Maria.'

'I thought it might be.'

'The way you talk to her. All this "I think I'm in love with you" stuff. It's got to stop. She's asked me to speak to you.'

That was exactly what I had said, not this time, the first time. He could have learned that only from her.

'I —'

'It's unseemly.'

'Look, please, I —'

'And it's also illegal. You are a Jew, Spinoza. You are not allowed to go near our Christian women. That was the agreement when we let your lot into Amsterdam.'

'Yes, I know.'

'Oh, you know! And here's something else.' Theodor Kerckrinck leaned close to my face. For a second I thought he was going to kiss me on the cheek, but he whispered into my ear. 'I've had her cherry, Spinoza. Her little flower. And she comes back for more, pretty much every week.'

Tears bulged my eyes.

'So keep your nose out of it, Spinoza! Keep away. All right?'

'All right.'

* * *

I had spoken to my brother, Gabriel, having met him by chance in the street, and mentioned that I did not think we should take Rembrandt into the *Den Prince* consortium, because he was risking Titus's money.

Gabriel is becoming more and more splenetic these days, possibly owing to the strain of running the *D'Espinoza* company. He's always been pompous. Chronologically he's younger than me, but the boy's natural age is forty and he went straight to it as soon as he abandoned his walking frame. He has called a 'family meeting', a 'meeting of the shareholders', which of course is the same thing. The windy old fart. I've got to go.

And so here we are, in the old family house in the Houtgracht. It was the first time I had been inside for months, even though I pass it nearly every day on my way into town. It looks just the same, except that Mama and Papa are dead.

The furniture had been bought in great uncle Abraham's time, with money from the sale of jewels smuggled out of Portugal. Now coming up to fifty years old, the heavy oak dining table and the twelve chairs were battered, reeking of lanolin from the daily polish to preserve them. The pewter plates had been given a buffing too, by the look of it.

My sisters, Miriam and Ribca (Rebecca is really my half sister, we had different mothers), had been prevailed on to make *de noen* – the massive midday meal. As usual, this was pea and prune soup, followed by *hutsepot*.

The *hutsepot* was served direct from its iron stew pot in the peasant manner, in an attempt at Dutch modesty, which was in turn an attempt to blend in. (Jews? Us? Surely not!) Although it featured mutton killed according to Jewish ritual – as if that made any difference to the sheep.

This deft bit of ritual throat-slitting had been carried out by our Ashkenazi butcher, Morteira's cousin. They had a deal going: the cousin gave Morteira free meat and Morteira told the butcher how to save his immortal soul. Morteira got the best of the deal, if you ask me. 'A bird in the hand...' as Rembrandt would say. But I digress.

In addition to Miriam, Ribca and Gabriel, Miriam's husband, Samuel de Caseres, was also there. He too worked for the company, keeping the accounts at Gabriel's direction.

The maid served us enough soup to put out a fire in a timber yard, from a horse-trough of a tureen in the middle of the table. The *hutsepot* was then served before anyone had finished the soup, after the Jewish custom of eating plenty and fast, before our latest persecutors could arrive to take it away. I got a plate heaped to the height of a small sand-dune with meat and four or five vegetables, about as much as I normally eat in a month.

'I'll never get through all this,' I moaned from my place at the foot of the table. 'Take it away.'

The maid looked questioningly at Gabriel, perched at the table-head on a cushion, to make himself look taller. The maid was Jewish. She had to be. Jews were forbidden to employ Christian servants. It was part of the conditions of entry to Amsterdam. These Jewish maids all came from good families, or said they did, so they had to be paid nearly double what Christian maids in the same street were getting.

She was called Esther, the maid was. Lots of Jewish women were called Esther. My father's third wife —Ribca's and Gabriel's mother— was also called Esther. So was Morteira's wife. This was because Jews were forbidden to have saints but secretly coveted them, like sneaking the occasional mouthful of pork. So Esther from the Purim story was given a kind of unofficial promotion to sainthood.

This Esther – the original Ur-Esther – had been married to Ahasuerus, king of Persia. When Ahasuerus's adviser, Haman, tried (as usual) to destroy the Jews, Esther helped save them. This is celebrated at Purim. But the point is, Esther was a *secret Jewess*.

She had hidden her Jewish faith from the king, her husband. She revealed it only when she and her cousin Mordecai thwarted Haman's plot. I don't know how she revealed it, maybe she gave him an enormous portion of kosher *hutsepot*.

It was this secrecy which appealed to all the Portuguese and Spanish Jews. They, too, had been secret Jews. They had pretended to be Catholics for decades, back in the old country, observing Judaism unseen by Christians, or so they hoped. If they were caught, they were tortured by the Inquisition.

Esther —back to Esther-the-maid, now, not Purim Esther— looked at Gabriel for instruction, still holding the hillock of food intended for me.

'Give it to him,' Gabriel commanded the maid. 'Eat it,' baby brother commanded me.

'Right!' I shouted, feeling the old mix of claustrophobic frustration, anger and helplessness that the family house, the family firm and indeed the bloody family itself engendered in me.

Esther-the-maid banged the pewter plate down, scraping the table and covering my lap in bits of white turnip drowning in gravy.

'Watch it!' I yelled at her.

'Watch it yourself.'

She was an ill-favoured lump, Esther-the-maid was, with the lowest slung breasts I have ever seen. It was a wonder she didn't tread on them.

I looked away from her, to indicate my disdain. The gravy was seeping through my thin breeches and my thinner drawers, but I was determined not to lose dignity by fishing vegetables from my private parts. I cut a hunk of mutton and stuffed it in my mouth, left-handed.

It caught in my throat. I choked and had a coughing fit.

'Get me some small beer,' I spluttered at Esther-the-maid. Wine had been served with the meal. I don't drink wine, it makes me vomit.

'No,' said Esther-the-maid. 'Not unless you ask nicely.'

Ribca, the one I had always been closest to, politely repeated my request to Esther-the-maid.

'He's got to say it,' Esther-the-maid said, sulkily, jerking her head at me.

'*Shalom bayis*, Esther,' Ribca murmured, gently. The Hebrew phrase means peace in the household.

'Yes. *Shalom bayis*, Esther,' I repeated to the recalcitrant servant. 'So do what you're bloody told!'

Esther-the-maid stomped out. Ribca fetched the small beer for me. I gulped it down, but was still unable to swallow any meat, which consisted almost entirely of gristle.

'Is this the best Morteira's cousin can do?' I said, indistinctly, still attempting to chomp my way through the meat. 'No wonder the high and mighty Sephardim are told it's a sin to buy from an Ashkenazi butcher. This lamb's a sin, all right. It's terrible.'

I took the mauled mess out of my mouth and, having nowhere else to put it, placed it by my plate.

'Oh dear!' Samuel de Caseres said, in effete reproach.

I lost my temper. 'Oh piss off! All right, all right. Sorry, Samuel. Sorry!'

Eventually, when Esther-the-maid had managed to serve everybody, aided by Ribca, Gabriel spoke again.

'Right,' he said, and then the knell of the tocsin, 'Let's get down to business. Point one on the *agenda...*' He paused, looking smug, hoping I wouldn't know the neologism, but I did. I nodded encouragingly and smiled. 'Point one is that our oldest brother, the head of the family now that our blessed father, may his soul rest in peace, resides among the angels, wishes to refuse the biggest contributor we have to the consortium. The biggest contributor by far.'

'How much does Rembrandt want to put in?' Miriam asked.

I realised I didn't know that myself. Judging by the expectant looks round the table, as everyone consumed enough meat and vegetables to withstand a siege, neither did anybody else. Except Gabriel.

Gabriel paused for dramatic effect. 'Ten thousand guilders,' he said. I winced. Everyone else round the table showed pleasurable amazement. I wondered if Rembrandt had cleared out all the money his wife had left in trust to Titus, who had been an infant when she died. Had the amount been calculated to free him from debt, once and for all? He could expect anything up to thirty percent profit, if nothing went wrong. I knew that much.

Gabriel's little features were contorted with tension. The way he was sitting rigid on his cushion reminded me of the days when he was in his high-chair.

'Without Rembrandt's money, the consortium will struggle to purchase enough goods to fill the ship for the outward journey. Times are hard. Trade has still not recovered from the war.'

'But Rembrandt should not be using Titus's money to —'

'That's his affair.'

'Titus doesn't know anything about it.'

Samuel de Caseres shook his head impatiently. 'Irrelevant!' he said, triumphantly, as if he'd just invented the word.

He was an empty vessel, this Samuel de Caseres. A man who had no discernible personality or characteristics of his own, but rather went through life as a *tabula rasa*, letting the nearest or strongest inscribe on him what they would. At the moment he was Gabriel's.

'I should make it clear,' Gabriel said, 'that I have discussed with the joint leaders of the consortium, Baruch's request that we turn down ten thousand guilders.'

'What joint leaders?' I said. I stopped eating. I have a delicate stomach and I was feeling sick. 'I thought we were putting the consortium together ourselves.'

Gabriel spoke quietly. 'The Alvarez brothers.'

'The Alvarez brothers?' I stared at him.

'Yes.'

'The Alvarez brothers are joint leaders? With us?'

'Yes.'

'The Alvarez brothers are thugs.'

'They have money and they get things done.'

'Most of their money is from extortion.'

'So? If you do what they want, they are good people to work with.'

'Yes, but if you don't do what they want, they roast you over a fire. Have you forgotten that it was the Alvarez brothers who beat us up on the day of father's funeral?'

'No, I haven't forgotten. But the relationship has changed since then. We laugh about it now, from time to time.'

'Oh, you laugh about it? Yes, what an enjoyable day Papa's funeral was. Ho-ho-ho! Getting beaten with cudgels behind the Oude Kerck. We must do it again, some time. You free on Saturday? Use pistol butts next time.' I paused for breath. 'And you told them I want to refuse Rembrandt's money?'

'Yes.'

'What did they say?'

Gabriel hesitated. 'They said they were going to roast you over a fire.'

'Well, thank you, Gabriel, brother of mine. You should have been there when they chucked Joseph in the pit. You'd have had his breeches off him as well as his coat.'

Ribca looked reproachfully at Gabriel. 'You shouldn't have told the Alvarez brothers about Baruch,' she said. 'He shouldn't have told them,' she repeated to me, in case there was any doubt. She has a big heart, Ribca. Not much brain, but a big heart.

'I think we should put it to the vote,' Gabriel said. I sighed. 'All those in favour of the proposal by our beloved Baruch, senior partner in the firm and *titular* head of the family, since the sad loss of our dear father. That proposal being that we should turn down the largest single contribution to the consortium, an amount of ten thousand guilders from the painter Rembrandt, thus almost certainly making it impossible for the *Den Prince* to sail to Portugal with a full load of Dutch produce, raise your right hand.'

I put my hand up. Nobody else did.

'Those against?'

Miriam, Samuel and Gabriel voted against.

'You haven't voted,' Gabriel said to Ribca.

Ribca looked cow-eyed at me. 'I'm not voting against Baruch.'

'Thank you.'

'Even though I think he's wrong.'

I sighed again. 'All right. If Rembrandt is to be included, then I might as well tell you this. He's bought some bricks from Samuel and Jacob Pereira. He wants them on board as part of a separate arrangement, as well as his consortium share.'

'He keeps full ownership of the bricks?' Gabriel said.

'Yes.'

'I said no to that originally. It's unusual. But all right. For such an important shareholder we can accommodate it, provided his bricks don't take up too much space. So, tell him yes.'

'Right. Thank you.'

I stood.

'Where are you going?' said Gabriel.

'Outside. I'm going to be sick.'

* * *

I left the family meal early, and gratefully. When I reached my room, I found Titus sitting on my bed, his face drawn, tense and angry.

'Titus! I'm delighted to... but what's wrong?'

'What's wrong!' the youth cried with some bitterness, twisting on the counterpane, the better to look me in the eye. 'How could you, Baruch? We trusted you, Hendrickje and I. How could you betray us so?'

'What have I done?'

'Baruch, we asked you to accompany Papa to the auction to *stop* him spending money. And instead you get him to invest in some hare-brained scheme involving your family firm.'

'No, no!' I said. I squeezed past him to sit at my table. 'Your father came upon this idea himself. I argued against it. I have just come from my own—'

'Oh, come on! Papa is the most impractical of God's creatures. He would not even know of such matters as consortia, ships—'

'But he did!'

'How?'

'Morteira,' I said. The name was out even before it formed in my mind. 'He has been painting a portrait of Chacham Saul Levi Morteira.' I glanced at the floorboard which had covered my now-stolen manuscript. It was lying across the lens-grinding machine, nails in the air.

Titus shook his head. 'Why would Morteira urge him to such a course?'

'I don't know,' I said. 'But I see Morteira's hand in this. I'm sure of it.'

'You see demons everywhere,' Titus said, softly. 'You see demons where there are none.'

It was a common view of me, and one I feared because it was difficult to refute.

'I am innocent,' I said. 'Your father went straight to Gabriel, my brother.'

'I know. But you could have stopped the investment because, as the elder son, you own seventy percent of your family's trading company. Gabriel has only twenty percent and your sisters the other ten.'

'How on earth do you know that?'

It was true, but I had entirely forgotten it, so small a part did the trading company play in my thoughts. I now realised why Gabriel had gone to the trouble of calling that absurd Family Meeting. And that I could have outvoted all the others. Too late!

Titus shrugged. For the first time, I thought him a little discomfited. 'Morteira told me.'

* * *

I remember sitting at my table, the victim of my thoughts, no longer their master. Had Kerckrinck been telling the truth when he said those terrible things about Clara Maria and his possession of her? Of course not! The man was a tavern boaster, up to no good. Then why could I not forget what he had said?

My landlord pushed open my door – he never knocked – and announced my 'friend', the Sephardi Jew who had stolen my manuscript.

'What took you so long?' I said

The Sephardi was unabashed. 'Chacham Morteira wanted to give your manuscript his full attention. But he has been busy.'

I was indignant. The rabbi goes to the trouble of stealing my philosophy and then he can't even get round to reading it.

'Busy?' I repeated, angrily.

'But he will see you now.' The Sephardi was speaking Dutch, but with a lisping Portuguese accent.

'He will see me now? That's bloody good of him.'

For a moment, it occurred to me to be awkward, like a rebellious child, to defy the *Chacham*, my surrogate father. But I didn't. Of course I didn't. I never do, when it comes to it.

'I'll get my cloak,' I said.

Outside, the bitterest of the chill had eased. There was a pearly grey sky, which looked low enough to touch. I trudged along with the man who had been following me – a man many would have dismissed as a figment of my imagination. Well, here he was. He even had a voice. Not to mention a rather irritating effeminate lisp. And presumably a name.

'What's your name?' I asked, as we passed the cottage of the peasant who had the statue of Saint Adrian.

'Miguel da Silva,' the Sephardi lisped.

'Same first name as my father,' I cried, delightedly, before I could stop myself. 'Are you from Portugal?'

The Sephardi's full lips narrowed in a sneer; he ignored my remark. We were approximately the same height, which is perhaps why we walked step for step, as we proceeded along Breestraat.

He, though, had a curious bobbing gait, as if he were steadying himself against the pitch and yaw of a ship. Many Iberians walk like that, I have no idea why. I changed rhythm to get out of step with the thief who had stolen my manuscript, but tripped over my own legs and fell heavily against him. I noticed he had a dagger in his belt.

'Oh, sorry!' I said, apologising for my clumsiness.

He did not reply.

As we passed the painter Rembrandt's house, I felt a fresh pang at Titus's newly low opinion of me. Did Hendrickje, too, not like me any more? Rembrandt, surely, would still be on my side.

Not far from the spot where Joris Fonteijn of Diest had tried to steal Rembrandt's coat, there was a dead body in the gulley in front of a house. Had the man been tossed there? It looked like it.

He was folded in rigid agony, his face grey, buboes and lesions visible on his face and neck. Miguel da Silva had seen him, too, but he averted his gaze, pretending the corpse was not there.

As I watched, a plague cart turned into the street, a great clopping dray-horse heading it toward the lifeless body. The deadly visitation had started yet again. It would turn men to religion, it always did.

First Joris Fonteijn, now the unknown plague victim... Life passes like smoke. We walked on, our footsteps echoing on the bridge over the Snoekjesgracht, to the home of the Ashkenazi sage, Chacham Rabbi Saul Levi Morteira. We strode in silence, keeping in step once again, enemies mindful of mortality.

Despite myself, I felt a surge of joy as the *chacham*'s familiar tall, thin house appeared. I had first been allowed into this holy of holies just after my barmitzvah, despite the furious row the joyous event had provoked, because of my remarks about the Jews being the same as everybody else. I and three other boys, just thirteen, newly elevated to manhood, had been chosen above all others to visit and dispute with the rabbi in his home. And I was the best of them, the cleverest, the most fluent, the best read. We all knew that. If anybody didn't know it, I told them quickly enough.

A maid admitted us to the familiar tiled entrance hall. We were asked to wait. Ignoring the maid, the Sephardi disappeared up the wide staircase. I sat down on a red upholstered chair. What did I feel, then? Certainly not fear. Boredom. I get bored easily.

Morteira left me waiting for what must have been thirty minutes, because I heard the faint tinny chimes of the Zuider Kerck twice. I did not dare leave; he knew I would not dare leave. I began to compose a letter in my mind to Boyle in England, about the degree to which all fluids are the same.

A maid appeared, making my heart beat faster at the prospect of seeing the *chacham*. I hoped she would show me to his inner sanctum, his library-cum-study on the third floor, where only the chosen few were allowed. And she did! She did!

The Smyrna rugs were so vivid in my mind I almost said hello to them. The vase on a stand in the corner was Ming,

Morteira had told me that himself. It had gained a chip since I was last here.

The *chacham* rose, huge from behind his desk. Even viewed objectively he was a big man, but to me he was the size of Sinai. His patriarchal white beard seemed, if anything, even longer than before, its point touching the first swellings of a paunch. He indicated my manuscript on his desk, but I had already noticed it.

'Baruch!' His huge arms opened wide, black rabbinical gown flapping, and for a moment I thought he was going to hug me. 'It has been too long since you have been here.'

'I am pleased to see you again, Chacham Morteira.'

The rabbi waved me to the round table in the middle of the study. I sat before a silver platter containing seed cake, sweetmeats of various kinds, brazil nuts and almonds, fruit cut into segments. I took it in at a glance, then looked away from it.

Morteira sat heavily opposite me with a voiced sigh of woe, the *kvetch* of ages. He gave a languid wave, commanding me to eat. My mind formed a polite refusal, asserting my independence from him, while my hand took most of the nuts at one go and stuffed them into my mouth.

The rabbi rang a beautiful small silver bell. A maid appeared instantly; not the maid who had showed me up to the study. She waited in silent enquiry. A clock ticked. I gazed round at the books and manuscripts on the shelves, for all the world as if I had never seen a book before, and munched my overlarge mouthful of nuts.

'China tea, please,' the *chacham* said. 'For two... unless... something else? Wine?'

He raised his bushy eyebrows whenever he asked a question. 'Tea has the greater medicinal property.'

I knew that. It was in Tulp's book, though pinched word-for-word from Piso. I tried to swallow the mouthful of nuts, but fell to coughing. Then I couldn't breathe.

The maid regarded me dispassionately.

'Tea will be fine,' I brought out finally, addressing the maid. 'And more nuts,' added the *chacham*, dryly.

'You are still a child, Spinoza,' the rabbi observed mildly, before the maid had even left the room. 'When are you going to grow up?'

'Oh, piss off!' I shouted.

The rabbi shook his head, emitting a another small reluctant sigh, as of suffering under burdens nobly borne.

'You always were foul-mouthed.' The *chacham* spoke as if talking to himself

He stood, and for a moment I thought he was walking out, perhaps at the manner of my speaking, but he gathered up my partial manuscript, the start of my *Ethics Demonstrated in Geometrical Order*, and placed it on the table next to what was left of the nuts.

'He who philosophises is evil,' the rabbi said, sitting heavily again. 'You should have joined the rabbinate, when you had the chance.'

'Why? Do they have evil people in the rabbinate?'

He laughed. 'Far too many, as it happens. It would have kept you out of trouble, you know. '

I took the remaining few nuts and stuffed them in my mouth, shaking my head as I did so. I hesitated. Oh, Spinoza don't ask him what he... 'What did you think of my book?'

The maid appeared with a tray, on it two patterned cups of China tea and a pisspot-sized bowl of mixed nuts. Morteira was the only person I knew rich enough to afford tea, the oldest natural medicine in the world. Tulp's book, which is irritatingly good, says it eases cramps and lifts sluggishness. I wouldn't know. I drink the cheapest small beer I can find.

The rabbi took his tea from the maid. I took mine. The maid put the nuts down on my manuscript and left.

The rabbi rubbed his hands together, as if trying to keep warm – which perhaps he was, it was bitterly cold in the room.

'You were asking what I thought of your manuscript, Baruch. I'll tell you. It's the work of a brilliant child. A child of genius.'

'Have you heard the idea that all Jews are children?'

The rabbi winced slightly. 'It's not new to me. Have your tea.'

I obediently gulped the strangely flavoured liquid. Then I took another huge handful of nuts. I was suddenly hungry. I craved nuts.

'You believe in the separation of all religions from the state?'

I nodded, furiously chewing.

'You believe the state and not religion should make men good?'

'Should be the guardian of all liberties... But, broadly, yes.'

The rabbi sipped tea in a manner so delicate it was almost effeminate, but his black eyes never left mine. 'But that is not the case, in the real world. It will not be so in our lifetimes or the lifetimes of our children or of our children's children.'

'But if we do not —'

'Be quiet, a moment Baruch, please. I want you to be calm.'

'I —'

'Have some more nuts.'

I took some more nuts.

'Baruch, your ideas are more dangerous than gunpowder. In fact your ideas are like gunpowder sprinkled over a child as he lights his way home with a burning brand.'

'Perhaps all ideas should be so. Or should be seen so. In their infancy.'

Morteira sighed. 'But yours more than most. Yours above all!'

'Any particular one of my ideas?'

'The central one.'

'What, that God and nature are one?'

'No, no, no. That is merely silly.'

'Thanks.'

'Baruch!'

He banged the table with his fist, his eyes blazing. Then he took a pair of eyeglasses from a pocket in his robe and held them in front of his eyes. He had marked a place in my manuscript with a strip of red thread. He opened it and read my own words back to me: '"The mind's highest good is the knowledge of God, and the mind's highest virtue is to know God."' He put the eyeglasses on the table, blinked, then stared at me. 'That is a sin and a blasphemy. You cannot say that God is intelligible to the intellect, that God can be understood.'

'Why?'

'Why? Because you will unleash chaos, that is why. People will no longer obey.'

'Obey what? You?'

'Obey *anything*. The world is not ready for this and may never be.'

I met his gaze for the first time since I had entered the room, perhaps for the first time ever. 'I know,' I said. 'But I believe it to be true. And I believe I can prove it. I will not write truths I cannot prove.'

'So,' Morteira said, putting his cup down. 'We come back to the real world. You know... when the Jews were admitted to the Dutch Republic. When no less a figure than Gropius spoke for us. Did you think it was forever?'

'I... I hadn't thought about it.'

'You hadn't thought about it. It is not only conditional, Baruch. It is *renewable*.' His old eyes were blazing now, with righteous fury. Or maybe madness.

'I —'

'I... I... I...' the rabbi mocked me. 'It's always "I" with you, isn't it Baruch? That's the problem. Jews obey God. To analyse God is to challenge Him. It makes us no longer Jews and therefore liable to expulsion. Again.'

There was a heavy silence in the room.

Morteira glared at me. 'And you, you don't even stop at that. This —' He smote the manuscript mightily with the flat of his massive hand. 'This will draw down the wrath of the Calvinists, too. Because it challenges them as much as it challenges us.

And we promised not to do that. As a condition for our admission.'

'What do you want me to do?' I said.

'Did you intend to get this printed?'

'One day perhaps but... not for years. Maybe not in my lifetime.'

'That's something at any rate.' Morteira shut his eyes for a while then opened them again. 'But you must stop writing it down.'

'That's impossible, I can't keep it all in my head.'

I took another huge handful of nuts.

'Baruch, this is how we will proceed. You will visit me every week in this room. We will dispute as we always used to. But we will dispute your ideas. You decide what we talk about. Nothing is out of bounds. But I take notes, Baruch. I and not you. You may look at my notes, which will reflect our discussion, but they do not leave this room.'

'Chacham Morteira, I —'

'Wait, I haven't finished. In order to leave your mind free for philosophy, the *parnassim* of the synagogue will pay you ten thousand guilders this year. Thereafter we will pay you a thousand guilders a year for life. Think about it. You don't have to answer now. But, Baruch, remember, he that is wise hearkeneth unto counsel.'

'Proverbs 12: 15. You misquoted it. It's "he that hearkeneth unto counsel is wise."'

Morteira shut his eyes. He muttered, just audibly, 'The boy could irritate a rock.'

'Why are you offering me ten thousand, Chacham Morteira? Not nine, not eleven.'

If Morteira had a weakness, it was that he could not resist showing how clever he was.

'If you don't want the money for yourself, which I'm sure you don't, you could buy Rembrandt's share in your family's consortium. He could pay back Titus's money. I think you may even find that the Surgeons' Guild will pay him for that painting quite soon, with perhaps a token minimal alteration. And after that, more commissions will come Rembrandt's way, I'm sure of that.'

'You've spoken to Tulp, obviously?'

'Yes. And to Cornelis de Graeff, our clever Calvinist burgomaster.'

'You cunning old bastard.'

Morteira inclined his head in acknowledgement. 'You will have some powerful men on your side, Baruch. You can continue to develop your thought, do your work, untroubled. Indeed, by opposing your arguments I shall be assisting you to refine them.'

Morteira waved a wide-sleeved arm, airily. 'Rembrandt avoids the risk of prison. He can move forward in prosperity. He will not have to sell his house and be reduced to penury.'

'Morteira... Morteira... So if I refuse... And if Rembrandt is made bankrupt and leaves his house...'

'Not if, when.'

'Then it will be my fault? You will have made it my fault?'

'Yes. But it won't happen, because you will do what I say. I shall have to destroy this manuscript.' He patted it with his hand. 'But it will be a small price to pay.'

'You are the devil incarnate.'

'You overstate my importance.'

'And you will burn in hell.'

Morteira smiled. 'The commentaries are ambivalent about the existence of hell, as I'm sure you know as well as I do. I take it your answer is "yes" then?'

'I'll let you know.'

Nine

Isaiah saw God clothed and sitting on a royal throne,
Ezekial saw him in the likeness of fire. Doubtless they
both saw God as they were wont to imagine him.

Spinoza
Theological-Political Treatise

I had resolved to declare my love for Clara Maria van den Enden. I composed drafts of this declaration in my mind, pacing my tiny chamber, as far as this was possible. I even made notes of my more felicitous phrases. As paper is extremely expensive, these notes competed for space with my philosophical jottings, which I had begun anew after my meeting with Morteira.

So a typical extract from the matter to be found on my table was: 'Bondage is man's lack of power to moderate and restrain the passions.' Followed by, 'Please accept my all too unworthy devotion, O chaste and lovely being. To thee I pledge my heart.'

As I wrote the word 'chaste' I recalled Theodor Kerckrinck's foul claims about Clara Maria, but again I rejected them with scorn. However, I found myself recalling and rejecting them with ever greater frequency, until I could think of little else.

Eventually, I postponed my philosophical activities altogether, to concentrate entirely on seeking a scientific proof as to whether Kerckrinck had... I can hardly bring myself to write it... whether Kerckrinck had had carnal knowledge of Clara Maria or not. Was a geometric proof after the manner of Euclid possible? I determined to attempt it.

I began naturally enough, with Vesalius, the acknowledged master in matters of the body. I scoured the bookshops of Amsterdam, including van den Enden's, for the seven volumes of his work, covering the skeletal system, the muscular system, matters vascular and circulatory, the heart, the brain, the abdomen...

Nothing. Eventually, I found the work I was looking for, written not by Vesalius but by none other than Nikolaes Tulp. The tome was entitled *The Arraignment of Urines*. It boasted a print of Tulp as frontispiece, round faced with an extravagant twirl of a moustache pointing upwards at both peaks – vain bastard – and a goatee beard.

Inside was the description of uroscopy – vulgarly known as *piskijkerdom* – that I had sought. Over three hundred learned pages, richly illustrated, Tulp left no one in any doubt as to the significance of the colour, texture, smell and taste of the subject's urine.

When a woman has been tampered with, Tulp describes and illustrates the changes that come to pass in the matter floating in the suspension – yellower; in the surface scum – firmer; and in the taste – sharper. I was entirely convinced. *Eureka!* A proof of geometric precision indeed.

So my course of action was clear: all I had to do was obtain some of Clara Maria's urine and analyse it according to Tulp's criteria. If her urine was pure as the driven snow – in a manner of speaking – I would confound the rascal Kerckrinck with it. He would slink away when faced with the incontrovertible proof of her purity. I, then, would propose marriage to Clara Maria. Who would accept.

* * *

It was the day of the first rehearsal of the play in Latin by Clara Maria's father, the deaf idiot Franciscus van den Enden. We met in a large, light room at the back of the house. It was behind the shop, on the ground floor, and gave out onto the garden.

The rascal Kerckrinck was among those present. He was in ridiculous fancy-dress, involving a doublet with slashed blue and white sleeves, white breeches and expensive-looking brown leather boots, extravagantly turned over just below the knee. The popinjay! The poltroon!

Clara Maria, demure and sweet as ever in a blue dress, was looking at him, but with a faint smile which I hoped indicated contempt. Van den Enden himself, apparently undeterred by either his deafness or his idiocy, had awarded himself a part in his own play, as I suppose he was entitled to do.

In addition to Kerckrinck, van den Enden and myself, the cast was completed by Jacob van Ruisdael, the unsavoury painter, who van den Enden knew from the Waterlanders, as did I.

The minute figure of van den Enden, dressed once again in brown from top to toe, was addressing the other three men in the cast plus his daughter, as we sat in a line on chairs provided for the purpose. His face was red as a cherry, from effort and triumph.

'My drama,' he squeaked, pacing up and down, 'is a re-working of the story of Philemon and Baucis. It is a story of the welcoming of strangers into our midst.' Was he looking at me? Or was I imagining it?

'An old couple dwell in a cottage. Two strangers knock on the door.' He paused dramatically, walked to a table against the wall and rapped on it. 'The strangers had approached a thousand houses. A thousand times had they been turned away.' The absurd elf mimed being turned away. 'But old Philemon and Baucis welcomed them. They were given wine and food. And as they were eating, the elderly couple noticed something wonderful.' Van den Enden paused. 'The clay dishes the strangers were eating from filled up as they ate, so no food was gone.'

Everybody except me gasped.

'That was handy,' I said. 'Saves you going to the market all the time.'

Kerckrinck made a shushing sound at me. I shot him a disdainful look. Clara Maria was looking beatifically ahead, waiting for her father to continue.

'I'll take questions later!' van den Enden snapped petulantly at me. 'The strangers were the gods Jupiter and Mercury, in disguise,' he continued. 'In gratitude, they asked Philemon and Baucis their desire. The old couple said they wished only to die together. The two gods granted them their wish. Then they made Philemon an oak and Baucis a linden tree. And as the old couple kissed, their branches were for ever intertwined.'

Everybody stood and applauded. I joined in. I can even clap sarcastically.

I had formed a detailed plan of campaign before the play-reading. In order to obtain a specimen of Clara Maria's urine, it would be necessary to ply her with liquid. I remembered the China tea Morteira served – it had diuretic properties.

'Let us take a rest before we go on,' I said to van den Enden, roaring through a bright smile. 'Perhaps a cup of China tea?' I suggested, at full bellow.

'Your fee?' Clearly my roaring and bellowing had been insufficient. 'Spinoza, I know you Jews are usurers and bloodsuckers to a man, but surely even you cannot expect a fee to perform a play in Latin?'

'A cup of tea, Papa,' Clara Maria trilled, quite softly. 'That's what Bento is suggesting. I think it's a good idea.'

'Then why didn't he say so?' Van den Enden apparently had no problem understanding his daughter. 'People speak so indistinctly. Why does he go on about money if all he wants is a drink?'

Eventually tea arrived, in a china tea set – teapot and cups – rather more functional than those at the Morteira establishment. The maid poured the tea and left. There was sporadic conversation.

Theodor Kerckrinck was standing, his fine manly figure towering over van den Enden. I could hear they were discussing the parlous state of van den Enden's finances. Then they talked about Kerckrinck's medical studies. I noticed that van den Enden appeared to understand everything Kerckrinck said, without too much difficulty.

The painter Ruisdael stood aside from the group, apparently in a universe of his own making. A fixed half-smile played around his lips, as he stared into the distance. His musty odour hung like a fetid low cloud over the room.

I chatted to Clara Maria about my philosophical discoveries. 'We suffer, in so far as we are a part of nature,' I said. She nodded gravely, opening her eyes wider. I saw that she had drunk a sip or so of tea and rushed to the table where the teapot stood, intending to fill her cup.

Kerckrinck made his excuses to van den Enden and joined me at the table.

'I told you to leave her alone,' he hissed in my ear. 'If you do not desist in this pestering of Clara Maria, I shall horsewhip you. And any court in the land would only praise me, because she is a Christian woman and out of bounds to Jews.'

'Do your worst!' I told him.

I seized the teapot and filled Clara Maria's cup. Every time she took a sip I tried to fill it again but she made me stop. Her eyes were looking a little glassy. I hoped that that might be a sign of her wanting to pass water. Indeed, my hopes rose as she stood – I was explicating the role of external cause, as I recall. But she simply went over to Kerckrinck.

At that moment van den Enden called us to order. 'The allocation of parts,' he cried. 'The God Jupiter, disguised as a mortal, will be played by myself.'

'Bloody effectively disguised as a mortal, then,' I muttered to myself, under my breath.

Van den Enden whirled round. 'I heard that, Spinoza. I'll thank you to keep your sarcastic remarks to yourself.'

'Sorry.'

'That's all very well. But you might at least apologise.' Van den Enden then continued as if nothing had happened. 'The God Mercury, the mighty descendant of Atlas—' Guess who that's going to be? '—will be played by Theodor Kerckrinck.'

Clara Maria gave delicate applause and a small smile up at Kerckrinck. Well, the Gods don't always get the girl, I thought. My knowledge of Greek and Roman mythology may not be great, but I know that much. We'll see!

'The part of Philemon will be played by the painter Ruisdael.' The unsavoury bundle took a bow. 'And Baucis by the Jew Spinoza.'

It shames me, looking back on it, but for a moment I was actually glad. Kerckrinck had got the role of a God, but Baucis was in the title, wasn't he? It was only when there was a titter of laughter that I remembered that the title characters were an old man and an old woman. These Roman names were unfamiliar to me, but it was dawning on me, all too slowly, that Baucis was the old woman of the pair.

Right on cue, appropriately enough for a play, two maids appeared bearing bundles of clothes.

'I have by no means finished the costumes,' Clara Maria announced to the gathering. 'In fact, I've hardly got started.' She giggled. 'But here's what I've done so far.' Dragging her lame leg, she made her way to the table, where the maids had laid the pile of clothes.

The maids had not left the room, I noticed, as one would expect them to. One of them was my goitred enemy, the one I had fallen out with when I was attacked by a mad dog. (Why do I have so many enemies? From my birth to the moment of writing this I have desired no man harm. Ah well!)

Clara Maria sorted through the pile, finally waving aloft a large pair of wings, made, it would seem, of goose feathers stuck to some sort of framework.

'These are for the mighty God Mercury,' she said, smiling at Kerckrinck.

Kerckrinck, smirking, went over to have his wings fixed on by Clara Maria. The intimacy of this contact was making her blush, I noticed. 'And these...' Clara Maria held some garments aloft, blushing even redder. 'Oh dear...'

Now I understood why my goitred enemy was still hanging around. They had brought me a woman's grey wool dress and white cap, for my role as Baucis. But there was also a pile of white linen. These, I surmised, were women's undergarments.

I realised bitterly that even the maids must have known of my role in the play in advance. But if I was to continue in the play at all, I had no choice but to don these items. My only consolation was that Clara Maria, perhaps out of embarrassment, had re-filled her cup with China tea from the pot and drained it. At least that part of my plan was working.

With as much dignity as I could muster, I struggled into the corset and shift, pulling them on over my clothes, then pulled the dress over my head on top of all that. I defiantly set the cap on my head and glared around me. Kerckrinck was doubled up with laughter, as was my goitred enemy. Ruisdael and van den Enden were laughing too. Even Clara Maria was simpering behind her hand.

While I had been absorbed in my struggles, Ruisdael had donned a forester's cap, which apparently completed his ensemble. Van den Enden had strapped on a breastplate to represent the discovered Jupiter. The maids finally left the room.

Clara Maria followed them, moving as quickly as her lame leg would allow. I suspected that my plying her with China tea was having the result I desired. Soon I would have proof of her virtue. I hitched my skirts up and followed her, catching sight of Kerckrinck's face angering as I left.

'Spinoza!' van den Enden called out. 'Come back here this instant!'

'Back in a minute,' I called over my shoulder, as I fled.

Did the household have a privy hole? I hadn't thought of that. Most large houses had one, as we did in the family home in the

Houtgracht. The night soil cart came to empty it once a week. Depending on when the last visit had been, my analysis could become rather problematic – difficult to isolate the sample.

I saw the narrow back of my beloved disappearing along the corridor ahead of me.

'Clara Maria,' I called out. 'Clara Maria, are you going to relieve yourself?'

She turned. 'What?'

'I ask only because I need you to do so, before I declare what is in my heart.'

'Bento... Bento please do not talk to me like this. I do not understand you. You are frightening me, a little.'

'Clara Maria... my darling.' I wiped my brow with my forearm; oh this damn corset! 'Do you have your chamber pot?' Ladies of Clara Maria's class use small, shaped china chamber pots, which they occasionally keep about them. 'Pass water, please. Then nothing will ever come between us.'

She screamed.

Kerckrinck appeared from nowhere and knocked me to the ground. Then everybody else came at a run, including my enemy, the goitred maid. As I lay in a heap on the floor, my dress round my ears, I explained, through swollen lips, that there had been a misunderstanding. Clara Maria, I must say, was gratifyingly concerned about my injuries, fussing over me. Van den Enden, however, simply wished to get rehearsals under way, which we did, once I had been rather roughly pulled to my feet by Kerckrinck. Clara Maria reappeared in the rehearsal room a while later. Something in her demure manner told me that the first stage, at least, of my experiment with the tea had been successful after all.

I resolved to try again as soon as possible.

* * *

It was around that time that I realised I was being followed again, and not by Miguel da Silva, Morteira's man. This one was shorter, broader and had reddish hair.

Could I have been mistaken? I smiled to myself, even as the question formed in my mind, one evening in my room. I spent most of my life not only establishing the truth but irrefutably proving it: my tools my microscope, my mind and my quill. But here was more uncertainty inserting itself into my life – into my life, and, more seriously, into my thoughts.

For I could not forget the man following me, any more than I could forget Clara Maria. I peered down the barrel of the microscope and saw, not the basic substance of blood, as I had hoped, but the face of a stranger and the smile of the girl I loved. How strange, how very strange.

My thoughts, and the thoughts about my thoughts, were assailed by the angry voices of my landlord, Jan Teunissen, and my brother, Gabriel. I gleaned that the one was going out and the other coming in, though Lord knows what they had found to quarrel about in that brief moment. Man is indeed a disputatious creature, more at ease with easy victories than uneventful peace, naturally given to hounding the weak.

My brother finally burst into my chamber, cloak swirling, hat askew, face hectic with thoughts gone out of control.

'Sit down,' I said. 'Calm down.'

'Don't tell me to calm down, Baruch,' Gabriel shouted. 'You are so smug, aren't you? Not to mention a walking disaster area.'

'Good evening,' I said.

'And cut out that bloody sarcasm!'

I turned in my chair, removing the slide with the blood smear from under the microscope. I faced Gabriel, who had sat heavily on the bed. 'A beer? Something to eat?'

Gabriel put his head in his hands. He spoke through a sob. 'Have you any idea what you've done?'

I sighed. 'Not at the moment, but I'm sure you'll tell me.' I poured myself a small beer from the jug kept in the corner, by my table.

'You didn't go and see Morteira, did you, Baruch? You didn't take up his offer.'

'How do you know that?'

'Because, you bloody poltroon, I've just come from his house.'

I sipped at my beer. I puffed at my Gouda clay pipe. 'What were you doing there? Do you want to take your cloak off.'

'No, I don't. It's freezing in here. What was I doing at Morteira's? I was trying to get him to rescind our expulsion from the synagogue.'

I was shaken by that. Stunned. 'What? We have been...? Who, exactly? Why?'

Gabriel shook his head, then straightened his hat, which nearly fell off. 'Oh Baruch, Baruch, Baruch. Never was a man more inaptly named. You are a curse, not a blessing. You are a curse on this family.'

'Thanks.'

'Baruch, we have all been expelled from the *Esnoga*. All the D'Espinoza family including Samuel, who only married in. Our dues have been returned. We have been expunged from synagogue records.'

'Whaat?'

'How many Jews, since the founding of the Temple, have managed to be excluded from the synagogue? Jews just don't do that. There isn't even an established procedure for it. It's an amazing achievement Baruch, even by your standards.'

I was inclined to agree. I still didn't understand it, though.

'So,' I struggled. 'This is some sort of revenge on Morteira's part, because I won't give up philosophy? Right? But why involve others? It's a bit petty, isn't it?'

Gabriel was close to tears. 'Oh Baruch, how can a man study so much and know so little of life? God save us and preserve us from the blundering of wise fools.'

I could feel my face colouring. 'All right. Explain it to me.'

Gabriel sighed, pulling his cloak round him as if to ward off evil. 'Baruch, I'll try to keep this really simple for you...'

'Thank you.'

'If we are no longer synagogue members, we are no longer proper Jews. That means the Jewish merchants will not trade with us.'

'Why ever not?'

Gabriel actually screamed, although softly – a sort of soft choking, sobbing sound I have never heard before or since. I was quite interested in how he did it, actually. I resolved to see what Vasalius had to say about the larynx and the vocal chords.

'Baruch, all the Jewish traders have to keep together. Trade together. That way we can quantify Jewish trade, in the areas we know, which is trade with the countries we had to leave – mainly Spain and Portugal. Our right to stay in Amsterdam is due for renewal *this* year. Did you know that?'

'I think Morteira mentioned it.'

'Our consortium, the *Den Prince* consortium, is no longer part of Jewish trade. Because we are no longer in the synagogue and they keep the records.'

'I see.'

'Baruch, we have lost over half of our consortium. We now have no chance of filling the ship with Dutch goods on the outward journey to Lisbon.'

'Can you...?'

'All I can do is limit the damage. I have brought forward the sailing date. The *Den Prince* sails next week, before we lose any more consortium members.'

I had a happy thought. I hoped Rembrandt had pulled out, returned Titus's money. I hoped Titus would be my friend again. But then why should he pull out? He was the only non-Jew in the consortium. Just as he was the only non-Jew in Breestraat.

'Rembrandt...' I said.

Gabriel nodded. He was beginning to regain command of himself. 'Yes. Good idea. I have spoken to Rembrandt. He is willing to increase the amount of bricks he is sending. That is some help to us.'

'Oh good...'

'The Alvarez brothers, our consortium partners, are still in, thank God.'

'Good-oh! At least the criminal element hasn't forsaken us.'

'But they are blaming you for the damage to the consortium.'

'Me?'

'Yes! Who else? It was you who antagonised Morteira. You who—'

'All right, all right. Look, I—'

'Oh shut up, Baruch!' Gabriel wiped his nose on the sleeve of his doublet, a surprisingly crude gesture I had not seen from him before. I wondered if he had got it from the Alvarez brothers. 'I came here to warn you.'

'Against the Alvarez brothers?'

'Yes!'

'As I recall, the last time we spoke, at the family home, they wanted to roast me over an open fire. Has there been any advance on that?'

'Actually, yes. They want to kill you.'

I swallowed hard. 'What would that achieve?'

'Quite a lot. If they can kill you before the ship sails, Morteira would let the family back in the synagogue, and the consortium members we have lost would rejoin.'

I scratched my head, under the tasselled cap I wore indoors. 'Well, Gabriel, given that your best business interest is clearly in my death, I'm grateful that you came. And surprised.'

'At the moment, so am I, you sarcastic, supercilious wastrel.' Gabriel shook his head like a wet dog. 'Why do you think you're so superior, Baruch? Why do you think you are so much better than everybody else? There's nothing special about you, believe me.'

Tears came to my eyes. 'Leave me alone, Gabriel. I've had enough. How real is the threat, from the Alvarez brothers?'

'Very real. I'm surprised they aren't here already. I tried to ask that rude landlord of yours if he's seen them, but all I got was complaints about the state of your bed linen. Incidentally, what do you—?'

'I don't want to talk about it. So what should I do, Gabriel? About the Alvarez brothers?'

'You must leave here immediately.'

'Very well. I'll go tomorrow.'

'No, go now. This evening. This minute.'

'Where? Obviously, I can't come back to our house.'

Gabriel nodded. 'That's the first place they'd look.'

'Then...?'

'I have no idea, Baruch. It's your problem. You've brought it on yourself. I've warned you. That's all I can do.'

Gabriel stood to leave. 'Goodbye Baruch. Good luck, my brother.'

I had an idea. 'I've got an idea.'

'Oh no!'

I thought rapidly. Franciscus van den Enden was on his uppers, financially. There were many rooms empty in that large house. Renting out one of them would be manna from heaven to him. I would be near Clara Maria. At close quarters, I would be able to get her to drink a lot, to urinate into a chamber pot, and then, when I had analysed the result, propose marriage to her.

'Gabriel, I could stay somewhere, with people the Alvarez brothers do not know. But the rent might be more than it is here. Will you pay it?'

Gabriel did not hesitate. 'Yes,' he said. 'I've never liked you, Baruch. I hate every minute I have to spend in your company. But I'll do it because you are my brother.'

'Oh, Gabriel...' I stood and we embraced tightly.

'And also, if the Alvarez brothers are caught killing you, and executed, the consortium would be finished.'

Packing my personal possessions was a matter of moments. The only possession of any significance was my new microscope, together with my specimens and my slides. It would be impossible, naturally, to take my lens-grinding machine with me on this flight into the unknown. Gabriel said he would send servants to fetch it later.

I bade farewell to the family bed, the site of so much action, of various kinds. There were no farewells to my landlord as we left, carrying all my worldly goods in three bundles. Teunissen had not yet returned from wherever he was going when he encountered Gabriel.

To my surprise, it became clear that my brother intended to accompany me to the van den Enden household. Wary of emotion, as ever, he gruffly announced that this was because I would be unable to carry everything unaided.

Footsore, we arrived unannounced at the van den Enden place well after dark. Gabriel, naturally, handled the negotiations. To my amazement, these took place in the *sael*, the best room in the house, on the first floor, where I had never set foot before. Van den Enden ordered us shown there, lamps and a fire to be lit, the moment Gabriel announced the reason for our visit.

Van den Enden seemed to hear everything Gabriel said perfectly. He was mainly interested in the amount of rent on offer. After some haggling, they settled on three guilders a week. Van den Enden required a contract. Gabriel agreed, saying he would have his notary draw it up in the morning.

I was then shown to my new home, a room at the back of the house, on the third floor. Though small, it was bigger than my previous room. I did not notice Gabriel leave, let alone bid him any sort of farewell. I lay on my new bed and fell into a dreamless sleep, as black as the night around me.

* * *

Gabriel had dinned into me that the next week, before the *Den Prince* sailed, was the period of maximum danger for me, because the Alvarez brothers had most to gain if they disposed of me in time to reconstruct the consortium. All I could think about, however, was my new-found proximity to Clara Maria. And in this, the change of abode proved a stroke of good-fortune which exceeded my greatest hopes.

Although I did not take meals with the family – my arrangement covering the room only, not food – I quickly attuned to the household's rhythms, so as to engineer meetings with her as she left the dining-room. This seemed not to displease Clara Maria. Sometimes I thought she welcomed our conversations as much as I did. Well, almost as much.

We would repair to the mezzanine room, where she once taught me Latin. There I would talk as I had never talked before. I told her about my early studies for the rabbinate. About how my life had been planned out before me since the age of five. And how I had come to a crossroads in my life because of Moses and Morteira.

I looked into her serious grey eyes and told her that I understood, even before the farce of my barmitzvah, that abandoning the rabbinate meant leaving my family behind, leaving the family firm, leaving everything, travelling alone.

'And leaving Judaism?' she asked, her mouth opening slightly in her efforts to understand.

'I don't believe I thought about it,' I said, thinking about it for the first time. 'But, yes. That was a necessary corollary, naturally.'

'My father, too, has suffered for his beliefs,' Clara Maria said. 'They sent him to prison because he denied the immortality of the soul.'

'I didn't know that,' I said, instantly revising my opinion of a man I had considered an idiot, albeit an erudite idiot.

On other occasions, she spoke about Theodor Kerckrinck, to whom she was indeed informally betrothed. I was prompted to examine the nature of jealousy then, the better to overcome it. I had asked van den Enden for a desk in my room, and my thoughts on the subject were the first I wrote in his household.

On my next meeting with Clara Maria, clutching the paper damply in my hand, I confessed my jealousy of Kerckrinck, which did not appear to displease her, and read her my conclusion on the subject:

'If I imagine that an object beloved by me is united to another person by the same, or by a closer bond of friendship than that by which I myself alone held the object, I shall be affected with hatred towards the beloved object itself, and shall envy that other person.'

I gazed at her, screwing the paper in my hand, tense for her approval. Her laughter rang across our little meeting-room.

'Oh, Bento!' She wiped her eyes with a linen handkerchief, trying and failing to stop laughing. Her hand rested briefly on my forearm, as she saw I was upset. 'You are a kind and good man, are you not? But I have never heard anyone state the obvious at such length.'

Her efforts to hold back her laughter only caused it to redouble. She rocked backwards and forwards in her seat, even slapping her thigh, tears of mirth coursing down her cheeks. I was happy to see her happy. Happy to be the cause of her happiness, though not perhaps in the way I might have wished. I laughed too.

I believe it was during our next conversation, or at any rate soon after I moved in, that she first talked about Kerckrinck at length. From sensitivity, I believe, toward what she knew my feelings to be, she always kept her account of him factual. Kerckrinck was studying under Deijman at the College of Surgeons to be a doctor.

'He is currently studying the heart,' she said, then giggled.

I nodded, indicating polite interest, looking into her eyes.

'There was something he wanted to ask you,' she said carefully, as if leading up to a large announcement, 'at the last rehearsal of the play. But he was too shy.'

'Shy?'

At the last rehearsal of the play he had hit me in the face. What could this shyness have inhibited?

'It's about his studies,' she said, suddenly composed, hands folded in her lap. 'He has no microscope, you see. And he really needs one. It's important for him.'

'Then he must have mine!' I cried.

'Oh, Bento. That would be so good of you. But are you not using it yourself?'

I shrugged. 'Some observations,' I said. 'The results of which will no doubt be laughably obvious to everybody.' She looked abashed. 'No, I can get on with other work. I'll get it now.'

I jumped up.

'No, but—'

I ran helter-skelter for the door, raced up the stairs to my tiny room, grabbed the microscope, complete with half-observed louse on its slide, and ran back down again. I started coughing as I re-entered the room.

'Here,' I wheezed, waving my microscope at Clara Maria, so she could pass it on to her betrothed. 'Here...' Cough cough cough. 'Give...' Cough cough cough. 'Kerckrinck...' Cough cough cough. I doubled over.

Clara Maria took the microscope. 'Oh Bento! Oh, thank you so much.'

Ten

*If we have the kind of knowledge of God that we
have of triangles, then all doubt is removed. And just as
we can arrive at such a knowledge of the triangle, so
we can arrive at such a knowledge of God.*

Spinoza
Treatise on the Emendation of the Intellect

My brother had told me not to leave the van den Enden
household until the *Den Prince* sailed. Actually, his exact
words before he left me that first night under van den Enden's
roof were 'Just keep your head down, you dreamy fool. And for
once in your life think before you speak.'

I ignored Gabriel's instructions. I had to buy food and drink,
for a start, and I had no intention of becoming a hermit. I was
spared this fate by the unlikely figure of Franciscus van den
Enden. My exit to life beyond the household took me through
his shop, on the ground floor of the house. I kept bumping
into him. And we talked. Now that I was a tenant, bringing
in three guilders a week, van den Enden's attitude to me was
transformed, as was his hearing.

For our first few casual conversations, breaking off when
customers came in for etchings, woodcuts or prints, he used
a hearing trumpet. But after a while, he abandoned even that
pretence. It appeared that he could hear when he wanted to.

We were talking about the play. I was trying, for the
umpteenth time, to get the author to cut the bit where I, as

Baucis, am kissed by Philemon, in the unsavoury form of the painter Ruisdael.

And then I had another idea, also about the play. 'I've got an idea,' I said. 'Why don't you get Rembrandt to paint a series of backdrops for each tableau in the drama?'

'What, you mean...?'

'A woodland scene, say, where the Gods are refused hospitality. The poor room where Philemon and Baucis live. Two trees, their branches intertwined, the dead Philemon and Baucis forever.'

'Would Rembrandt do it?'

'I'll ask him if you like.'

* * *

It was van den Enden who first told me the Waterlanders were planning another meeting. I was delighted. I was even more delighted when they sent a message to me – via Gabriel, who sent Ribca rather than come himself – that the Waterlanders wanted me to speak at this meeting.

I had given talks before, about the bible being a collection of fables, and had always enjoyed it. I immediately set about planning a demolition of Calvinism – that should go down well. Calvinism had been the official state religion for only five years, but during that time they had tightened the screws on dissenters like the Waterlanders.

The next bit of good news was van den Enden crying off from attending the meeting, the day before it was due. He said he was close to establishing the exact moment of the Second Coming of the Messiah, by mathematical means. Amsterdam —indeed the whole Republic— was awash with rumours of the Second Coming, as it had been foretold for this year, 1656.

I had seen van den Enden working on his numerical theory. He had a 'Numbers Room' on the second floor. In it, he donned a robe adorned with the Signs of the Zodiac, mystic symbols and magic numbers – 666, that kind of thing. The room was full of every measuring instrument known to man, from protractors to an astrolabe. Van den Enden spent hours measuring and calculating, often following the Jewish kabbalah, which peddles this kind of mumbo-jumbo.

Anyway, when he told me that his work, establishing the arrival-time of the Second Coming, took precedence over the Waterlanders meeting, I feigned great disappointment – unconvincingly, perhaps, as he shot me a suspicious glance. I immediately made my way to Clara Maria's chamber.

It was improper of me to go there. But when I tapped timidly on her door and announced myself she did not look at all put out. Indeed, she seemed quite pleased to see me. She is an extraordinarily bright young woman, and I do believe her daily diet of Latin lessons, in the service of her father's finances, is a chore and a burden to her, which conversation with me relieves.

At any rate, although she did not let me in, which would have been most improper, she favoured me with a bright smile. More importantly, she agreed immediately to come with me and hear me speak to the Waterlanders. We agreed to meet at the corner of the street, it being understood that her father was not to be told.

And so we met at the corner of the street, she the Beatrice to my Dante. I remembered to accommodate my stride to her gait. We set off silently, slowly.

We came to a patch of light from a lantern shining through a large downstairs window of a house and I stopped her with a light touch on her arm. She looked at me questioningly. I shyly presented the poem I had written to her.

'What's this?'

'Please read it, Clara Maria.'

'It's not philosophy, is it? I fear if I laugh at any more of your philosophy, I shall offend you.'

'You could never offend me. I love you.'

As ever, she ignored my declaration. She took the poem, though, and read it aloud. Although my Latin was coming

143

along remarkably well – forgive my lack of modesty, yet another of my faults – I did not yet trust myself to write an ode in that language. Clara Maria did not understand Portuguese or Spanish, so I had composed it in demotic Dutch:

> *Wat Naelt, Penceel en Pen, wat wil, verstant en deught,*
> *In wet- en zeden-konst volwerckten, is t'aensschouwen,*
> *In Clara, die een Baek van Wijsheydt voor de Jeught,*
> *Athenen en Parnas aen d'Amstel sal herbouwen.*

> *A book of song, in pencil and pen! What sense and virtue,*
> *In knowledge and ethics complete, is to be found*
> *In Clara. A beaker of wisdom in the drought,*
> *Where Athens and Parnassus shall rise on the Amstel.*

As she read it aloud, I was a prey to doubt as to whether I had chosen the right theme. Should I have praised her beauty? I have been told – by whom? Gabriel? – that women like praise of their parts and their allure. Perhaps I should have done that, not the 'beaker of wisdom' stuff. I don't know.

Come to think of it, the trouble is, she isn't all that good-looking. She's a slight wisp of a thing, very skinny, small breasts, with a pointy elfin face. Decent eyes, though, I'll give her that.

Even as I thought that, the eyes filled with tears. 'Oh, Bento. It's lovely! I shall keep it and treasure it. May I keep it?'

'Of course! It's for you!'

As we slowly walked on, she tucked the poem into the muff which was keeping her hands warm. 'But... Bento, I am promised to Theodor. You know that. Sometimes I think that you... that you are making hopes for yourself that I cannot fulfil for you.'

It was the first time she had alluded to her betrothal directly. I nodded vigorously, even though we had now reached a part of the street where there were no houses, so it was too dark for her to see me.

'I know! But I will always love you, hoping as little as I can, the while.'

'Oh Bento, that was beautiful!'

I was rather pleased with it myself. I reached the meeting-point floating on a beautiful cloud of hope. The Waterlanders spread the word of the meeting-point immediately before every meeting. Only when those gathered had been scrutinised was the venue made known. This rudimentary device was meant to weed out Calvinist spies, though I know nobody who believed in its efficacy. Still, we went through the motions.

The gathering was at Het Giethuys, not far from the Wester Kerk. When we arrived, a knot of men were already in the looming shadow of the foundry building: I saw Pieter van Rixtel, the poet, in earnest conversation with my friend Lodewijk Mayer. I recognised other friends – Jarig Jelles, Simon de Vries – as well as many I did not know. I estimated the gathering at around twenty, average, or perhaps slightly better for a meeting of the Waterlanders. There was one other female, beside Clara Maria.

I proudly introduced Clara Maria to van Rixtel and Mayer – they knew her father, naturally, but not her. Clara Maria was confident in their company. Jarig Jelles had met her before, at the van den Enden household. He greeted her with an enthusiastic kiss, which aroused my jealous ire.

Fortunately, the evening was mild for the time of year, and clear of rain, so we were comfortable waiting for more Waterlanders to join our gathering. Eventually Simon de Vries announced that he believed the company complete. We were meeting, he sang out, at the home of Jarig Jelles.

'Obvious!' I whispered to Clara Maria. 'His home is the nearest to the foundry, that's why it was chosen as the meeting place.'

Clara Maria nodded, a little uneasily. Several people had looked round, angrily. I realised I had spoken more loudly than I had intended.

The gathering set off for Jelles' house. As they did so, I caught sight of the figure I thought had been following me – not Miguel da Silva, his replacement, the smaller, broader redhead. He stepped out from the shadows around the foundry, then disappeared. But I had no time to follow up these suspicions.

'Just a moment,' I called out loudly to the dispersing Waterlanders. 'I must ask you to walk slowly to the house of Jarig Jelles. My good friend Clara Maria van den Enden is lame, from an attack of the Child-Laming disease. It was that, wasn't it?' I looked at Clara Maria for confirmation, but she didn't answer. Probably shy. 'She drags one leg, as you see,' I called out. 'So can we keep together, please, and walk slowly? Thank you very much!'

There was no reply to this. The Waterlanders walked off, not slowing at all, as I had instructed. 'Oh, look at them!' I said in irritation to Clara Maria. 'That's far too fast! I'll call them all back.'

'No!' she said, in a slightly strangled voice. 'No, please don't!'

I shrugged and tried to take her arm, as I had seen couples do. To my amazement she roughly shook my hand off.

'Oh, sorry,' I said, a bit sarcastically. 'Pardon me!'

'I can't walk like that,' she said, close to tears.

The moon was hidden behind cloud. We quickly lost sight of the others. They were all, despite my injunction, walking at normal pace.

'Fortunately, I know where Jarig Jelles lives,' I said, conversationally, to Clara Maria. 'Otherwise they would have lost their speaker for this evening. And serve them right.'

She made no reply.

'Am I walking too fast for you?'

She made no reply.

'It must have been horrible, that disease, when you were young. Does it bother you now? You're fine sitting down. Nobody would ever know there was anything wrong with you.'

She made no reply.

We had crossed a small footbridge – not wide enough for carts – over the canal in front of the Wester Kerk and had nearly reached t' Blaew Bolwerck, hard by where Jelles lives. We were heading west toward the old city wall, along a track between vegetable gardens. This would eventually lead to one of the many curved canalside streets which form Amsterdam. Jelles had his house near one of them – it did not have a name, as far as I knew. But at any rate we were still between the vegetable gardens when I was attacked.

Mercifully, I heard him coming, I heard the slap of his boots on the hard ground – if there had been rain, and the ground softer, I might not be alive to write this now. I whirled round, immediately recognising the younger of the Alvarez brothers, Abraham. Clara Maria screamed. Alvarez had a knife; it gleamed even in the poor light.

Alvarez was upon me and lunged with the knife. I turned sideways, grabbed his arm enough to deflect the blow and hit him. As you are reading this, you know that I survived, because I will write more of this journal, so you are not yet at the end. But please believe this: as Alvarez turned and raised his dagger I felt sure I was going to die.

To be honest, I did not think of Clara Maria, who had stepped back into a patch of cabbages and was screaming. To be as honest as if honesty itself were under a microscope, I thought of my philosophy, and the loss to mankind if I were unable to complete it.

So I fought as I have never fought before, on mankind's behalf. As luck would have it, I was wearing a ring for the first time in years – a touch of vanity to impress Clara Maria. The ring had been given to me by my late father, and was inscribed with a word I had taken as my motto: *Caute* – caution. So I swung with my ringed fist, the left, and *Caution* gratifyingly opened up Abraham Alvarez's cheek.

But the thug came back at me. He swung once more with the knife, and once more I evaded the curve of his lunge. Then he smote me mightily in the solar-plexus, quite near the part of the body discovered by Dr Tulp. I gasped and bent over. He kicked at my legs and had me down. Then he knelt on my chest, wheezing, and raised the knife on high.

I heard Clara Maria scream 'No!' I slashed at him in vain with the *Caution* ring. All this, naturally, is taking me longer to write than it took to happen. But I was aware of someone calling Alvarez by name: 'Alvarez, you rogue.' Or something of the sort.

It was enough. Alvarez hesitated, at being unmasked. My rescuer kicked out at his knife hand, sending the weapon spinning into the darkness. He then hauled Alvarez off me by his doublet.

'You knave!'

Alvarez broke free and ran for it. My salvation stood over me, panting. He spoke not to me, but to Clara Maria: 'Dear lady, please do not be alarmed. The danger is past.'

Still lying on the ground, I looked up at the wax and resin which made up his mask, at the red hair, which I could now discern was a wig. It had come slightly awry in the fight. But in any case, I had recognised his voice.

'Titus?'

'The very same. Let me help you up, my dear Baruch.'

'Titus! Titus, my dear friend. I thought I'd lost you.'

'Yes, I'm not surprised. I owe you an apology, Baruch.'

'Oh, my dear boy. Forget it.'

'Bento, who is this?' Her voice was a little thinner than usual; she sounded more her real age. But she was brave.

'Excuse me!' I said. 'My social graces are limited at the best of times. Really non-existent, I'm afraid.'

And so, in the middle of a field of cabbages, in near total darkness, I presented Clara Maria van den Enden to Titus van Rijn.

'As Papa has risked ninety per cent of our capital in the D'Espinoza consortium, I thought I'd better protect our investment,' said Titus. He brushed some of the mud off me, with great dexterity, and felt my face and ribs for injuries. 'Nothing broken, it would seem.'

'Thanks to you. You saved my life.'

I saw the faintest movement of Titus's shoulders, a shrug in the gloom. 'The Alvarez brothers will try again. Like all men of their stamp, thwarting them only makes them more determined.'

'Then you are in danger yourself!' I cried out. 'Once they find out who my rescuer was.'

'They know who I am, all right. Come on, let's get moving or you'll miss your own talk.'

That, naturally, led me to ask him how much he knew of the Waterlanders and their present situation. He replied over his shoulder as we walked in single file on the narrow pathway, Titus leading the way, then me, then Clara Maria. As he walked, he removed his disguise. He wouldn't need it for the Waterlanders, many of whom knew his father.

'The Waterlanders are in a parlous situation,' Titus said. 'The Calvinists are skittish about opposition, as these rumours of the Second Coming of the Messiah take hold. Be careful what you say tonight, Baruch. Be circumspect.'

'Naturally! Your father is not coming, I assume. He was not at the foundry, where we met.'

'That farce! Half Amsterdam knows where the meeting is. He's going straight there.'

'How is he?'

'Could be better.'

We turned off the path onto the street, heading for the patches of light from houses. The door to Jarig Jelles's house was open, confirming Titus's low opinion of the Waterlanders' precautions. Heading for the buzz of noise, the three of us made our way to a lighted *sael* where the meeting was to take place.

I paused on the threshold. I hoped my bruised, bloody and torn appearance would occasion some comment. But nobody seemed to notice; everybody was busy with their own affairs.

Looking round, I noticed the unappetising figure of the painter Ruisdael, mouldering quietly in a corner, with nobody near him. He nodded to me, but I looked away. The sight of him reminded me of the kiss he was supposed to give me towards the end of the play. The thought of it was making me feel queasy.

Philemon and Baucis, indeed! Why are the stories which survive down the centuries, sacred and secular, so far-fetched? Do we need them to be nonsense in order to distance ourselves from our humdrum daily lives?

My musings were broken by our host, Jarig Jelles. He approached Clara Maria, ignoring me, and led her to the rows of chairs. In order to do this he took her by the arm, just above the elbow, rather impertinently I thought. I glimpsed the two of them through the throng. He had seated her in the front row, sat himself down next to her and was talking to her, animatedly.

I lost sight of her as Rembrandt approached – same coat and hat. He greeted me with a massive bear-hug, followed by one for Titus, who grinned fondly at him. He followed this up with a short jab to the arm I had fallen on, then another to my injured ribs. This left me doubled over, winded and gasping.

'There's never any bloody beer at these meetings,' Rembrandt boomed. 'Nobody expects food, but they might offer some beer.'

I coughed and retched to indicate agreement. I was expecting to be announced, as speaker, by Jarig Jelles, when he finally managed to tear himself away from Clara Maria. But in the end, all that happened was that he waved me to the front, mouthing something above the hubbub of noise that I think was 'Get going.' Charming!

I stood in front of the rows of various sizes and shapes of chair. The gathering had grown to something like twenty-five. The men were uniformly in black, with soft black hats. Their clothes were workaday and patched, but not dirty or torn –

except for mine, naturally. There were three women by now, including Clara Maria. The other two were middle-aged, wore linen caps and had already adopted dignified blank expressions and respectable poses, sitting with their hands folded in their laps.

I stared at Amsterdam's *libertijnen*, waiting for them to come to order. Behind me, I noticed a school easel, its blacking surface spotted and worn. Evidently, it had been placed at my disposal. There was a piece of chalk and a wooden pointer on the blackboard's wooden ledge. I took the pointer and rapped with it on the easel.

'Come to order, please, ladies and gentlemen. I am about to begin my talk.'

I have a confession to make. Approbation makes me swell like a pig's bladder blown by a ragamuffin. I am prey to the most dreadful hubris, and an audience tends to fill me with it. Roughly speaking, the larger the audience, the larger the hubris. My aches and pains from my beating at the hands of Abraham Alvarez were forgotten, as I swelled. I was out of control before I had even opened my mouth.

'The likes of van der Welde and Witsius,' I announced 'see the whole of Dutch history as the prelude to the creation of the new Jerusalem, here in Amsterdam.' The Jews wanted to create *their* new Israel in Amsterdam as well, but I left that out.

'But I believe in the new Jerusalem here.' I banged my heart, but winced because my whole chest was bruised. The audience, I sensed, was with me. 'I believe that the working of God and obedience to him consists solely in justice and charity or love towards one's neighbour.'

I stopped and looked at my audience. Clara Maria was looking up at me from the front row, her eyes shining. Towards the back, Titus was looking quizzical. Next to him, the painter Rembrandt looked serious. For some reason, I looked for the other painter, Ruisdael, but couldn't see him at all.

'It is only by works that we can judge anyone to be a believer or unbeliever, however much he differ in religious dogma from other believers, whereas if his works are evil, he is an unbeliever, however much he may agree with them verbally.'

This unleashed a storm, a veritable tempest and it was all blowing my way. Two or three men, including Jarig Jelles and Simon de Vries started applauding. There were a couple of cries of 'Hear, hear.' Many fell to chattering with the person next to them, giving examples of religious hypocrites. Some even called out names. The burgomaster, Cornelis de Graeff, was high among the hypocrites cited. There were many mentions of Nikolaes Tulp, too.

I stepped forward until I was almost touching Clara Maria, in the first row. I looked down at her and smiled. She flushed beetroot red, squirming in her seat. I shut my eyes for a second, gathering the Latin I had memorised to impress her:

'*Qui enim justitiam et charitatem amant, eos per hoc solum fideles esse scimus; et qui fideles persequitur, ANTICHRISTUS EST.*' I yelled the last bit, before rendering it in Dutch. 'Those who love justice and charity we know by that very fact to be the faithful. While he who persecutes the faithful IS ANTICHRIST.'

A roar twice the volume of the previous one greeted that, as the hounded and persecuted Waterlanders relieved their feelings. Half a dozen of them stood and applauded. It was all going magnificently. And I hadn't really got started yet.

The meat of the matter was coming now. 'But look what we get from the Calvinists,' I yelled. 'The miserable sods!' That got a laugh. 'Just look at the Calvinist beliefs: Total Depravity.' I wrote that on the board. 'We're all born enslaved to sin, from top to bottom. Rotten to the core! All of us! You!' I pointed. 'You!' They were laughing.

Names would be better. 'Jarig Jelles, rotten to the core. Don't talk to that pretty girl next to you, you sinner!'

They were roaring with laughter. 'Simon de Vries.' I paused dramatically. 'I know what you're thinking!' Simon turned around, playing up to it, pointing to his head, indicating his irredeemably sinful thoughts. The audience had their heads back, slapping their knees with laughter.

'Next Calvinist doctrine: Unconditional Election.' I wrote that on the board. 'You know what that means? It means that those who will be brought to God will be chosen by God. *And there isn't a damn thing you can do about it.* So, Jarig Jelles, you might as well go on having those impure thoughts about Clara Maria van den Enden.' There was an 'Oooh' from the audience. Clara Maria looked horrified.

'No, don't deny it, Jarig! Rembrandt, you might as well carry on drinking.'

One or two people looked serious, Titus among them. He was pointing to someone further along the row where he was sitting. But I shrugged it off. I had never heard a Waterlanders audience convulsed with laughter like this before. My talk would be historic.

'Hang on! Hang on!' I was drunk on the crowd's adulation, waving my arms to quell mirth and approbation only to fan it the more. 'We then get—' I stopped, and seized the chalk. 'Calvinist doctrine number three: Limited Atonement.' I wrote it on the blackboard under the other two doctrines. 'This one's really nuts. Basically, it means that Jesus died on the cross for some us, not all of us, because some of us, you will recall, are damned anyway. Like Jarig. And Simon. And probably Rembrandt. But not Clara Maria because she's an angel, the gorgeous girl.'

There were those resisting the wild mood I was conjuring – farouche and out of control – but not many.

'Now, I've got just one more Calvinist doctrine for you,' I shouted. 'Possibly the maddest of them all, though God knows there's plenty of competition.' That fell a bit flat. 'It's called Preservation of the Saints.' I wrote that on the board, under the others.

'And this one means if you're a saint, that is just a good person – so, someone like Clara Maria, but not like Jarig...' I paused but perhaps the effect was wearing thin. 'If you're a saint,' I repeated, 'you'll stay a saint. You'll never lose faith. How's that?'

One or two people thought I had finished, there was a spurt of applause, but I silenced it with an extravagant wave. 'Wait for it! Wait for it!' I turned to the board, indicating the four Calvinist doctrines. I thickened the first letter of each doctrine with my chalk:

Total depravity

Unconditional election

Limited atonement

Preservation of the saints.

Some of them knew what was coming, between a third and a half, I would guess. I circled the first letter of each word. 'T-U-L-P,' I yelled out. 'What does that spell?'

Some of the audience shouted it back to me. 'Tulp!'

'Yes, Tulp. The very same hidebound Calvinist, who is blocking payments to the greatest painter in Amsterdam. The bastard!' I caught sight of Rembrandt's face. It was a mask. I didn't dare look at Clara Maria. I thought Titus was waving me to stop.

'So that's it,' I finished, bathetically.

There was hearty applause, far more than speakers at Waterlanders gatherings usually received. I am ashamed to admit not only that this pleased me greatly, but that I encouraged the clapping, almost literally fanning it by waving my arms, and then by bowing extravagantly.

Clara Maria and Jarig Jelles were deep in serious conversation in the front row. I wandered toward Titus and Rembrandt, so excited I hardly knew what I was doing. Titus left his place to apprehend me. He gripped me by the arm.

'We've got to get you out of here,' he murmured in my ear.

'Why?' I was unwilling to cut short my evening of glory, as I still saw it.

'You see that man...' Titus whispered. 'About three places down from me.' I looked at the man Titus indicated, a swart fellow with heavy stubble, sitting with his legs wide apart. 'He's Tulp's coachman.'

'Wha—'

'I'm afraid there's no doubt.'

'Oh dear!'

'You might get away with a denunciation from every pulpit in Amsterdam next Sunday, but I doubt it, not in the present fervour.'

'Wha—'

'I think they'll come after you, Baruch. They'll kill you for this.'

'What, them too?'

But even as we were speaking, a second entertainment was starting, at the spot where I had stood just a few seconds ago. The danger to public health that was the painter Ruisdael was standing before the gathering. Two servants were balancing a painting on the ledge in front of the blackboard. The painting was covered by a ragged cloth.

Jarig Jelles left his place beside Clara Maria and addressed the assembly. 'Ladies and gentlemen.' There was immediate quiet. 'The Master Painter Jacob van Ruisdael, once of Haarlem, but now a member of our own Guild of St Luke, here in Amsterdam, wishes to present a painting for our delight and edification.'

The praise provoked the appearance of most of Ruisdael's limited selection of black and brown teeth. He strode to the board and faced us. 'I am the rod of God,' the lunatic informed the gathering, nodding his head vigorously. The information was received with polite silence.

Ruisdael then struggled with the none-too-clean oil-cloth over the painting. Eventually, he managed to remove it. For a moment there was a deep silence, a calm even, in welcome contrast to the mood my talk had engendered.

The painting showed the Jewish cemetery, with the old ruined church, the Oude Kerk, behind it. My father's grave was clearly visible in the foreground. In the background, the very rocks behind which the Alvarez brothers had cudgelled my brother, Gabriel, and myself – my first beating at the hands of Abraham Alvarez.

And then there was heard a collective gasp, pulled from the belly of the audience. I looked at Titus, he at me. I jerked my head toward the front. Clara Maria had turned in her seat and was staring at me.

'Oh no!' I said.

Over the Oude Kerk, the decomposing Ruisdael had painted a rainbow. The sharper of wits were explaining the meaning to the laggards. But in case there was any doubt, Ruisdael suddenly spoke, 'We shall set the truth of Christianity in writing against the error of the Jews, as the light against the shadow, and with the intention and purpose...'

I winced. Here it comes. It was from the second epistle to Timothy. And it duly came, from the fetid mouth of the painter '... and with the intention and purpose that God may grant the Jews a change of heart and show them the truth, and thus they may come to their senses and escape from the devil's snare.'

He screamed the last bit, his meaning unmistakeable: The Second Coming of the Messiah was to be accompanied by the conversion of the Jews. Ruisdael was telling us that the time for the conversion had come. Unfortunately, though, the deal with the Dutch Republic was that the Jews had to stay Jews. Any conversion and they – we – were out.

'The Second Coming is nigh,' Ruisdael called out. 'The conversion of the infidel unbelieving Jews is nigh, before the new Messiah. *And...*' Ruisdael paused and waved at his picture, as dramatically as I had waved at the blackboard. '... the Messiah is already among us.'

Ruisdael appeared to be in some sort of trance, his eyes screwed shut, a trickle of spittle running down his chin. But he suddenly opened his eyes wide, impossibly wide, until they looked as if they might fall out. He pointed, stiff elbowed.

'His name...' He paused. Don't tell me. Let me guess. ' His name...' His voice rose again to a shriek. 'The Messiah who will end Judaism is Benedictus Spinoza!'

Right! Well, it would be, wouldn't it? I mean, who else?

Eleven

*Nobody is bound by natural right
to live as another pleases.*

Spinoza
Theological Political Treatise

The atmosphere in Amsterdam was thickening for the Jews, like moisture gathering in clouds before a storm breaks. The Calvinists, never shy of borrowing from their enemies, took up the verses Ruisdael had quoted from Paul's Epistle to Timothy as their own.

The Sunday after the Waterlanders' meeting, every pulpit in Amsterdam thundered with the chants of denunciation. The Messiah in our midst heralded the conversion of the Jews. The Jews thus were attempting to inveigle themselves fully into Dutch society. I was accused by name in some churches, but not in the majority. It hardly mattered, everybody knew who was meant.

As a corollary, the paintings of Rembrandt were more and more moved from public view – his name being increasingly linked with mine. The plague grew worse, too. More bodies tossed into the gullies in front of houses; the tocsin bell of the plague cart man tolled in every part of the town; the lime pits outside the city walls filled with the tainted dead. A rumour was spreading in step with the disease that the plague would stop when all the Jews left Amsterdam and returned whence they had come.

Gabriel visited me at the van den Enden household with further warnings to disappear from public view. I must adopt the first principle of Jewish survival, adapt and imitate the host culture; camouflage until anonymity became invisibility, bringing with it the mirage of the longed-for safety.

Mind you, a distinctive feature of my own situation was that some, if not most, of the people trying to kill me were Jews themselves. Gabriel will tell you that that was the result of my determination to be different from – oh all right then, 'above' – the multitude in every way.

I was not unhappy, at this time, with this turn of events, neither was I happy. I was indifferent to happiness. I busied myself with philosophy.

I had to discontinue my practical observations, because Kerckrinck had my microscope. At the next rehearsal of van den Enden's play, I had expected thanks for my generosity, with regard to the loan: a change in his attitude toward me. I even harboured the secret and low hope that we might become friends, united in our devotion to Clara Maria. Not a bit of it! He refrained from assaulting me, but this by now unusual omission was mainly due to the lack of any provoking circumstance.

My life, in short, had briefly resumed what I intended to be its unremarkable course, even if only for a few days. I had even continued my quest for a sample of Clara Maria's urine, although a certain shyness on her part prevented her from passing water in my company, so I still had not achieved my aim. This all-too-brief period of tranquillity, this lull before the storm of my woes, was brought to an end by another visit from Gabriel.

Never one to look on the bright side, Gabriel announced 'an utter catastrophe' before he had removed his cloak. The *Den Prince*, the ship on which our Jewish consortium and Rembrandt had placed such hopes and staked such risks, had gone down, Gabriel informed me.

His actual words – striking a dramatic pose, one arm outflung – were: 'Our ship has sunk to the very bottom of the ocean.' This as if some intermediate position were possible, half-way down the ocean perhaps, which Gabriel's unfailing gloom was immediately ruling out.

'How do you know?' I cried, as ever seeking proof, rejecting speculation as much as superstition and hearsay.

We were sitting in my room at the van den Enden's, Gabriel twisting his hat in his hands in anguish.

'How do I know?' Gabriel managed to pack an extraordinary amount of scorn and disbelief into his near echo of my words. 'It's in every newspaper in Amsterdam. Don't you read newspapers?'

'No.'

'No!' Repeating my words in contempt was a trick Gabriel had had since infancy.

'What happened?' I asked. 'Was it the English? Those dastardly pirates. Rabbi Aboab has been there, you know. To England. He said there isn't an ounce of scruple or conscience on the entire island, search as you might. You can't believe a word any of them says.' I nodded, hoping I was pleasing him.

'Will you shut up!' my brother yelled.

'Excuse me! Shan't say another word.'

'That'll be the day. As it happens, the *Den Prince* never got as far as the English pirates. She sank outside Amsterdam harbour from the weight of Rembrandt's bricks. You can see her masts from the quay.'

'Oh dear!'

'Those bricks were your only contribution to the consortium, I seem to remember.'

'You mean it's my fault?'

'It was you who suggested the bricks to Rembrandt, wasn't it?'

'No!'

'On top of everything else, we face a huge bill to remove the ship from its present position. The water is so shallow at that point it's blocking the sea lane.'

'Oh God!'

'Everything is lost. If father could see us now, he would die again from shame. All his hard work, all those years of endeavour, to make us a successful and respected family, and his oldest son, his heir, ruins everything, at a stroke.'

Gabriel sat with head in his hands, his hat a wrecked victim of his anguish.

There was a long silence. 'What are we going to do?' I asked eventually.

'Do? *Do*? There's nothing we can do. We're finished. You've finished us. The lot of us. Me, Ribca, Miriam, Samuel. You've done for the lot of us, Baruch. Ruined us.'

'So...'

'We'll have to sell the house, of course. The family home, our place in the New Israel on the Amstel. Maybe we'll go back to Portugal. Give ourselves up to the Inquisition. At least we'd make an end of it all.'

Gabriel attempted to rend his garments, a Jewish sign of mourning, starting with his shirt. But it was of stout linen and refused to tear. So he pulled his hair, then both cheeks with both hands. What he said next was therefore indistinct – actually, incomprehensible.

'What?' I said. 'Let go of your cheeks and say that again.'

Gabriel let his cheeks go. 'I said there is no further hope for us. Our lives are at an end.'

'Gabriel, why did you come here?'

He looked surprised. 'To tell you about the meeting, obviously.'

I sighed. 'Gabriel, what meeting?'

He waved his arms. 'The meeting of creditors. You dolt. You stupid family shame, you liability, you curse of our enemies made flesh.'

'I see.' I nodded. 'And when is this meeting?'

Gabriel rolled his eyes up into his skull, indicating one tried beyond all previous limits of human forbearance. 'The meeting is now, Baruch. We're late already. You've made us late with all your whining and useless lamentation. Come on!' He stood up. 'It's you they all want. You're the majority shareholder. They want to tear you limb from limb.'

'Will the Alvarez brothers be there?'

'Of course they will! As our consortium partners, you've ruined them, too.'

'But they've already tried to kill me once, or Abraham has.'

'Oh, for heaven's sake! This is a public meeting. They won't try anything there.'

'And afterwards?'

Gabriel shrugged. 'If they kill you, your shares would then pass to me. I'd become the majority shareholder, which, frankly would be better for the company.'

I fetched my cloak and hat. 'Well, in that case we'd better get going.'

* * *

The meeting of creditors was in the Temple of Freedom, as Amsterdammers referred to the new Town Hall. It was the first time I had seen it. It was massive, the largest building I had ever set eyes on. As we rushed up to it, through the seafood market and across Dam Square, it seemed to keep growing, like some bloated whale taking in air. Close up, I noticed it had the same motto painted over the door as the old Town Hall: *God behoed ons* – The Lord will provide for us. 'Don't count on it,' I thought, as we stormed the porticoed doorway.

Our meeting was apparently to take place in a room on the second floor, next door to the Chamber of Magistrates. We ran past a marble statue of Solomon in the vestibule, then quickly past a ghastly *Moses and the Tablets of the Law* by Ferdinand

Bol, on the first floor; up two more flights of stairs, and we made a dramatic entrance, bursting in late.

All the creditors who wished to attend were already there. Gabriel and I passed through their glares on our way to our places on a dais at the front, next to the Alvarez brothers. Adriaen Alvarez, the older of the two, was on the outside, then my would-be assassin, the younger Alvarez, then Gabriel, then me.

All round the walls of the chamber ran a marble bas-relief depicting the *Worship of the Golden Calf*. Facing us was a stained glass window, mainly blue, which blocked out most of the sunlight. It commemorated the Siege of Leiden, the heroic Dutch resistance against the Spanish.

I averted my gaze from the scenes of Dutch stoicism – eating 'the food of affliction' and all the rest of it – and glanced sideways at the Alvarez brothers. Both were dark-haired, broad shouldered, barrel-chested. Both carried belted daggers. Abraham, I noticed with some satisfaction, bore more bruises and scabs from his encounter with Titus and myself than I did.

Turning from our consortium partners – the thugs – I considered our audience of creditors. There were fewer than I had expected – fewer than the ten males needed to start a sabbath service, a *minyan*. The mood also differed from my expectations: it was sullen rather than angry. It was later explained to me – or I worked it out, I can't remember which now – that the few people present represented mini-consortia themselves. As to the mood, it was clear that expectations were low.

There was no sign of Rembrandt, which did not surprise me at all. Titus's disguise was so good that at first I failed to recognise him, sitting at the back. Titus had turned himself into the best spy in Amsterdam. He had enlisted a veritable army of ragamuffins, who, for a few *penningen*, would follow anybody they were set to. They were rendered invisible by the very ubiquity of ragamuffins.

Investing slightly larger sums, Titus also bribed coachmen, footmen and maids, especially those disaffected with their masters, to get information. The Tulp household was particularly rife with such disaffected servants. The household of Cornelis de Graeff, the burgomaster, was also a fruitful source of secret knowledge.

Gabriel crisply embarked on what he described as 'a factual account of our present circumstances.' His gaze fixed on a point of the ceiling above the creditors' heads, he explained that the ship had foundered because of its over-heavy load.

'This load,' he said, speaking confidently and clearly, 'was accepted at the insistence of the majority shareholder, Benedictus D'Espinoza. None of the minority shareholders in the company could have gainsaid him, by virtue of his holding.' Gabriel lowered his gaze from the ceiling, making sure his audience were with him. They were.

'Similarly,' he continued, 'our consortium partners, the Alvarez Brothers,' he indicated the thugs by a gracious wave of the lace at his wrist, 'were not in a position to refuse the extra load of bricks once personal opposition to Benedictus D'Espinoza throughout Amsterdam had resulted in the withdrawal of nearly sixty per cent of consortium members. Resulting, in turn, in the loss of over seventy percent of consortium goods.'

The thugs nodded, sagely and sadly, helpless victims in the face of my skulduggery with the bricks. Adriaen was so moved he vigorously scratched his crotch under the table. Abraham fiddled with the pommel of his dagger.

'There was nothing we could do,' he confirmed, sonorously, to the meeting.

One of the few in the audience I recognised, Jacob Pereira, Rembrandt's neighbour, the original supplier of the bricks, got to his feet. 'I suggest we refer the whole sad matter to the DBK,' he said. 'Let's just rescue from it what we can.'

He sat down again. The DBK – *Desolate Boedelskamer* – dealt with all matters of insolvency, mainly insolvent estates.

The older Pereira, the old fox, was suggesting declaring the D'Espinoza company bankrupt, so he could pick over the carcass.

Gabriel pretended to be weighing this contribution in his mind, but I knew my brother well enough to know he had seen it coming. 'Fortunately,' he said softly, 'I had taken out insurance with the maritime agency. This will by no means cover all of the losses but I have a suggestion to make up the difference.'

Gabriel paused for dramatic effect. I shook my head in admiration – we should give baby brother a part in van den Enden's play.

'What's your idea then, eh?' said the older Alvarez, obviously unable to bear the tension. God, he's thick!

Gabriel adopted a thoughtful pose, chin in his cupped hand, eyes briefly shut. I wondered which artist had associated that slightly ridiculous contortion with thinking.

'Now is the time,' he said softly, 'at a low point in my company's fortunes, to issue new shares in the firm of D'Espinoza' He went on quickly as an understandable murmur of disagreement at the idea ran through the gathering. 'As my brother, Benedictus D'Espinoza, was entirely responsible for the debacle which has caused our present difficulty, I move that we vote to remove his seventy per cent shareholding from him, in its entirety, with no compensation whatsoever.'

This went down well. Approval bubbled along the creditors. There was a time lag while the Alvarez brothers worked out what Gabriel meant, but then their agreement was signalled by a simian grunt from Adriaen and a nod from Abraham.

'This shareholding...' We all knew what was coming, always a comforting feeling. '... will be put on sale now, at this moment. The money raised will be used to salvage the ship *Den Prince*, and even perhaps some of its cargo. We will re-equip a new ship...' Gabriel paused, looked me in the eye and said 'with a balanced load,' in my face. 'The ship will rise again,' Gabriel cried, in defiance of basic hydraulics. 'The company will rise again.' Probably in defiance of basic economics.

It was put to the vote, but the vote was a formality. My connection to the family firm removed, along with my shares, I slipped off the platform and slunk away. Titus left the meeting to accompany and guard me. But the Alvarez brothers were so busy buying up as much as they could of my shareholding, they even forgot to try and kill me.

* * *

Next day, I was in the mezzanine room with Clara Maria van den Enden. We were in the midst of a Latin lesson, I recall. Unfortunately, she had not needed to pass water.

In fact, I believe she suspected my intentions in this regard, sternly abjuring me to stay in my seat whenever she left the room. Also, she once read to me a passage about 'Strange Passions' which she had found in a medical book, Jan van Beverwijck's *Treasures of Health*, I think it was.

I responded with a lecture in praise of the *piskijker* – the quacks whose starting point was the analysis of urine. I was insincere – all right, I was lying my head off.

And she spotted it, cocking her head on one side sceptically, like a puzzled spaniel. I have *never* been able to lie effectively. One of the many ways in which virtue, most irritatingly, has been thrust upon me. (Another is of course celibacy, a lifelong virtuous state I was trying my hardest to be free of.)

'*Cognitio sui*,' Clara Maria called out, in her beautifully-modulated voice. 'Translate please, Bento!'

'Knowledge of the self,' I said promptly.

Footsteps thundered on the stairs leading to the chamber, clearly hostile. Did I, I wondered, have knowledge of myself? To what extent is this a prelude to, or indeed does it impinge on, knowledge of, firstly, other people, secondly that generalized knowledge which people call wisdom?

Clara Maria had turned pale. I heard Kerckrinck's voice, though not what he said. He was clearly, however, leading one or more persons in a boot-thundering charge up the stairs. And what about the relationship between knowledge of the self and knowledge of God? As usual, the very issue would no doubt be regarded as a blasphemy by everyone from the Calvinists to the Jews. And the Catholics.

'He's in here!' Kerckrinck shouted.

As he did so, I recalled that he was a student of surgery – that's why he needed my microscope, which he had kept. It also occurred to me, for the first time, that any student of surgery would certainly knew Dr Nikolaes Tulp. An instant after that, he burst into the chamber, interrupting my Latin lesson and my tentative conclusions as to knowledge of the self.

Behind him, there was a swart semi-shaven figure I recognised from the meeting of the Waterlanders: Tulp's coachman. He was carrying a whip. So was another figure in the same livery.

'Grab him!' shouted Tulp's coachman, raising his whip to me.

As Tulp's two minions and Kerckrinck rushed toward me, Clara Maria moved with astonishing speed. She stood. Holding onto the table, she hauled her lame leg behind her, moving round until she was in front of me.

I was still sitting. "The joy which arises from contemplating ourselves,' I thought, 'is called self-love or self-approval. No doubt Clara Maria would say that was obvious.'

'Theodor!' Clara Maria called out, her voice resonating with a depth I had not heard before.

Tulp's men seized me, breaking my train of thought, hauling me to my feet.

'Theodor! Tell them to let Bento go. If you don't, I will never speak to you again, let alone marry you.' She rounded on the two men holding my arms. One of them had his whip raised. 'And you two ruffians! You are in the house of Franciscus van den Enden. And you will desist! Now!'

My three assailants looked at each other. The whip was lowered.

Kerckrinck held up his hand to Tulp's men. 'Wait...,' he said. The coachmen loosened their hold.

I believe Clara Maria knew that was all she could achieve, at least as far as the ruffians were concerned: 'Bento, run! Run!'

I needed no second bidding. As I have said, I have always been fleet of foot. I tore myself free of the clutching hands and bolted. Kerckrinck's face, a horrified tense oval, was the last image etched on my mind.

I ran and did not stop running until I reached Rembrandt's house.

Twelve

*Man is subject to and slave of the passions. Reason is the
means of his escape to perfect salvation*

Spinoza
Short Treatise on God, Man and His Well-Being

The Wandering Jew. Another new home, my third – fourth
if you count the family house on the Houtgracht. Arriving
breathless, hatless and cloakless at Rembrandt's house, I was
received solicitously by Hendrickje, who insisted on preparing
food for me and insisted that I consume it. Titus was out spying,
but Rembrandt broke off his painting —a rare accolade— to
listen to my story and see me settled.

Hendrickje made ready a box bed for me in the kitchen.
Waiting in the *sael*, I heard one of the Rembrandt maids,
Lysbeth, protesting vigorously at this I gathered she slept
in the bunk below. Eventually she gave in and found herself
somewhere else to sleep.

When Titus returned, he embraced me warmly. On hearing
the tale of my attempted kidnap at the hands of Tulp's ruffians, he
summoned some of his ragamuffins to fetch my belongings from
the van den Enden household. They were quickly brought to the
house in Breestraat, where I was already beginning to feel at home.

* * *

Rembrandt, at this time, was absorbed in a portrait of one
Arnout Tholincx, a worthy with sly eyes and a stiff square beard.

This Tholincx was Tulp's son-in-law. Like Tulp, he was a surgeon. He was of the faction supporting Rembrandt's *Anatomy Lesson of Dr Deijman*, in which I appear, which put him in the opposite camp to Tulp.

Titus told me that Tholincx wanted his portrait painted to spread his name again. Out of political influence for some dozen years, he had just been appointed to the Loans Office. Tholincx was back! The smug, yet threatening look that Rembrandt captured, both in the portrait and the etching, announced that to the world.

Simultaneously, the old master-painter was working on an etching of the lugubrious Pieter Haringh, the auctioneer who helped Rembrandt on the road to ruin by selling him a chandler's empire of artefacts, art and junk. No doubt the etching was being done for nothing, as part of some complex deal sealed in the Keizerskroon auction rooms.

Rembrandt was quieter than I had known him before. His digestion was worsening; volleys of fetid wind exploded from him at both ends. He was also tormented by the toothache, but sensibly, in my view, refused to submit himself to a quack to have the problem teeth pulled.

Every now and then, though, he would roar forth like the Rembrandt of old: 'The trouble with impasto is it's so bloody expensive! You need three times as much paint.'

* * *

A meeting had been called by our enemies. I had this from Titus, who in turn had it from his spies. It was at this point that Titus told me the full story of Rembrandt's painting of Andries de Graeff, the burgomaster's younger brother. He had first mentioned it on that fateful day when Joris Fonteijn had stolen Rembrandt's coat.

Titus now told me that Andries was a good twelve years younger than the burgomaster, Cornelis. He was a wastrel, Andries was, over-conscious of the family's riches and of their leading position in Amsterdam society. Rembrandt had painted him more than fifteen years ago, but such was the impact of the image that it was still stamped on the collective mind of Amsterdam.

Rembrandt had painted Andries as an effeminate fop and a weakling, leaning against a pillar, as if not even strong enough to stand up straight. The studded door in the background was known to any Amsterdammer. It was the door to the *Tugthuis*. Andries had been portrayed just outside prison.

Even more telling were the gloves. Gloves, as anybody who has ever read a painting knows, are a symbol both of strength and cunning (concealment). And guess where Andries' gloves were? On the floor. Dropped. The fop was portrayed as so careless in his affairs that prison beckoned. Rembrandt had always had a mischievous streak, but this painting was audacious to the point of recklessness.

Titus told me that many viewers roared with laughter when they first saw it. It was often compared with the journeyman Pickenoy's portrait of brother Cornelis, which, naturally, flattered the burgomaster.

So when a meeting was called at the New Town Hall to discuss 'what to do' about the heretic Waterlanders, mainly myself and Rembrandt, it was not surprising that the tubby Andries de Graeff played a leading role.

I shall give an account of this meeting now, repeating what Titus told me at the time, supplemented by what I gleaned later. I cannot claim historical accuracy for this account, but then the Bible can't claim historical accuracy either, and that hasn't done too badly.

The meeting took place in burgomaster Cornelis de Graeff's private quarters, not in the administrative offices. There was no amanuensis present. All this gave events a clandestine flavour. Present were three people only, at least at the initial stages. I shall return to this point: the three were Tulp, who had called the meeting, and the brothers Cornelis and Andries de Graeff.

The driving force of Tulp's nature was bitterness. He sought resentment like a dog seeks meat. His successes assuaged the bitterness only as long as meat assuages hunger in the dog. The successes which, judged by anyone else, were considerable, appeared of no moment to him. If he were made burgomaster it would satisfy him briefly before he would wish to be Stadholder. If Stadholder, then King. If King, then King of somewhere bigger.

His constellation of lifetime bitternesses circled round one rather curious sun. Just as I emerged from my mother's womb – when so much was going on, as I have had occasion to point out – the Athenaeum was founded in Amsterdam. Tulp was expecting and expected to be appointed to the professorships of both medicine and botany. He was already rehearsing his acceptance speech when the Athenaeum decided not to establish the posts at all. No rival got them, he was not done down. But Tulp never got over it.

'There is a threat to public order,' the bitter Tulp now said. 'For the greater good, the troublemakers must leave Amsterdam. That has always been our way. We do not kill or torture. We are tolerant people, but those who abuse our tolerance must go.'

'Didn't you try to have Spinoza seized?' The burgomaster leaned back in what was, appropriately, the most comfortable chair in the room. He smiled.

Tulp looked furious. He gripped his goatee beard and pulled, before letting it go to speak. 'How did you hear about that? Oh, never mind. He's living with Rembrandt now. We dare not touch him there. Rembrandt's too well known. Contacts in Venice... links to the Stadholder... He knows Huygens, for God's sake. No, it will have to be legal.'

Andries de Graeff's pudgy face contorted with loathing, making his tiny features disappear into the fat. 'I don't care who Rembrandt knows. I want that provincial boor out of Amsterdam.' He turned in his seat to face his older brother, the burgomaster. 'I want him out *now.*'

'That shouldn't be difficult,' said Cornelis smoothly, in the unctuous tone he adopted for official business.

Tulp stared at him. 'The debts?'

Cornelis nodded. 'The debts. I have taken over Rembrandt's debt to Witsen, my predecessor as burgomaster. The amount, 4,200 guilders, may not be great by our standards, but with the state of Rembrandt's finances it is easily enough to tip him into bankruptcy. I have therefore called in the debt, with immediate effect.'

Andries cackled and shifted around on the padded seat of his chair. 'Good! Good! That's very good, brother.'

'Just a moment, Andries.' Cornelis waved a languid arm, bound in tight black silk. 'I have taken the further precaution of applying at the *Desolate Boedelskamer* for Rembrandt to be declared bankrupt. The application is in the name of the City of Amsterdam.'

Andries threw himself backwards and forwards on his chair, cackling until he was red in the face.

Tulp nodded in weighty judgement. 'Good. But what about Spinoza?'

'Who is this Spinoza?' spluttered Andries, pulling a handkerchief from his sleeve and dabbing at his face. The other two ignored him.

'Bankruptcy is again the route to take,' Cornelis said slowly. 'I have enlisted a significant ally. Matters are in hand, but I would rather not say more until I have placed all the boulders across the stream.'

Tulp nodded. 'That's fine,' he said. 'But the Jews must also disown him. As much for their own sake as ours. The rumour is that he wants the Jews to convert—'

'That's rubbish!' said Cornelis, sharply.

'Nevertheless, it is what people believe. And what people believe is stronger than the truth. We must stop all talk of the Jews converting. It would mean their expulsion from Amsterdam. And they would take all our trade with Portugal, Spain and Brazil with them.'

Cornelis had been nodding all the time Tulp was speaking, to indicate that all this was known to him, as indeed it was. 'I have been enlisting allies among the Jews. They can best deal with their own. I can see that I shall now have to show you my hand.' He rang a bell on a side table and a footman appeared instantly. 'Show them in,' he said.

* * *

As I have said, my source for the above account of the meeting was Titus and his spies – Cornelis de Graeff's footman was one of them, I think. But Titus never told me the part I am about to set down here. I believe that is because he wished to spare me pain.

No, my source for what follows was my sister, Ribca, my main – my only – ally in the family. She had visited me a few times during my stay with van den Enden, often bringing me food and beer in a basket. Shortly after my removal to Rembrandt's house, she appeared again, diffidently tapping at the door of the great master-painter.

Close to tears, she sat on a wooden stool in Rembrandt's kitchen while I stretched out in the box-bed newly vacated by the maid.

'Rabbi Morteira is working against you,' Ribca said, in a voice tremulous with sorrow.

'In what way?'

'He was summoned to the Town Hall. The maid Esther heard this from the burgomaster's maid.'

'And?'

'Oh, Baruch! Your expulsion from the Jewish community is being sought.'

'I've already been expelled. Thrown out of the synagogue. We no longer pay dues. Remember?'

'Oh, Baruch! Listen to me! They want you out of Judaism, altogether. They want you out of Amsterdam.' She began to cry, loudly, snuffling, streaming from her nose as well as her eyes.

I got off the box-bed, found a chair and went and sat next to her. The kitchen was warm and smelt of fish. I put my arm round her shoulders. 'It doesn't matter,' I said softly. 'I am only a Jew because I am seen as a Jew.'

'Only!' she cried, hoarsely.

'Inside, I am a part of nature like everything else. And as to leaving Amsterdam, nothing could be easier! My work is portable. I carry it in my head. I will take the next coach or the next barge out to wherever they want me to go.'

'And live alone?'

'Yes.'

'I will come with you.'

'No, Ribca.'

'Why not?'

'Because I don't need you.'

The pain which came into her face will stay with me until my dying day. 'Ribca, I'm sorry. I... Oh, I am so bad with people. I prefer ideas. I can control them. The universe is so much simpler to me than any person in it. I—'

'Baruch, I have not told you the worst.'

'No? What then?' I still had my arm round her.

'It was not only Chacham Morteira who spoke with your enemies. Gabriel was there, too.'

I slowly took my arm from around her shoulder. 'I see,' I said.

* * *

Titus wanted to talk to us – Rembrandt, Hendrickje and me. We met in the tiny ante-room off the *sydelkaemer*, where Titus and Hendrickje had first asked me to restrain Rembrandt's expenditure – a task in which I had so lamentably failed.

Rabbi Chacham Saul Levi Morteira was there, too. He stared down at us from the wall, in the form of Rembrandt's fifty-guilder portrait. Every aspect of the man was there: the intellect, the cunning – all embodied in eyes and hands, in the body illuminated by the mind.

'What's that doing here?' I said, nodding at the portrait, as we sat round the table. 'Why hasn't Morteira got it?'

175

Titus looked apprehensive, but Rembrandt bellowed laughter; back to something like his old full-throated, barrel-bellied self.

But surprisingly it was Hendrickje who answered: 'Rabbi Morteira feels that Rembrandt has not captured a good likeness,' she said, softly. 'The – what are they? – Jewish elders or whatever, have refused to pay for the painting or take delivery of it.'

'Absolute rubbish!' I yelled, loud enough to make the candelabrum on a side table shake. 'Look!' I shouted. 'I've known Morteira since I was a child. I know him better than his mother. I know him better than God. And Rembrandt, what you have represented there,' I waved at the painting 'is the Ashkenaz Saul Levi Morteira; his body, his mind, his soul, in all their painful nakedness. I tell you, Rembrandt, some people just don't know what they look like. It's as simple as that.'

'That may be,' Titus said, softly. 'But it's also possible that Morteira was never interested in the picture, but just wanted an excuse to spy on us. And make mischief.'

'I hadn't thought of that,' I said.

Hendrickje smiled gently at me. 'You really must eat more,' she said to me. 'You're not eating enough.'

'Can we get down to business?' Titus said, with just a touch of impatience.

'Of course,' I said, adopting an expression I hoped was businesslike.

Hendrickje burst into giggles.

'What are you laughing at?'

'Your face! Oh, you're so funny!'

'Business?' Titus said. He passed documents round to me and Rembrandt. Hendrickje looked at Rembrandt's copy, even though she couldn't read.

'We all know who our enemies are,' Titus said. 'And their tactics are clear enough. They are singling out you, Baruch, and you, Papa, as the focus of their attack on the Waterlanders. They want you both out of Amsterdam.'

'I'll go,' I said. 'I'll go now, if you like.'

'It's not that simple, Baruch. And anyway *we're* not going anywhere. Amsterdam is the main art market. Leaving really would ruin Papa.'

For some reason we all looked at Rembrandt, but he said nothing. His face had dropped into a sagging mask.

'As you can see,' Titus said, nodding at a document curling up on the table, 'the bankruptcy people have been in touch. A petition has been made on behalf of the city. De Graeff is behind it of course, but they have roped in Christopher Thijs who owns the mortgage on the house.'

'That bastard!' Rembrandt muttered.

Titus gave a small sigh. 'Actually, he's been pretty patient up to now. But they've got at him. The petition will be heard on 26th July.'

'Less than a month away,' Hendrickje murmured.

'The *Desolate Boedelskamer* has ordered an inventory of all Papa's goods on 25th and 26th. Everything is to be sold.'

Rembrandt went pale but said nothing.

'Everything?' Hendrickje said.

Titus nodded. 'Every single thing.'

Hendrickje swallowed hard. Her beautiful brown eyes were full of tears. She looked at Rembrandt, then at Titus. 'Can anything be done?'

Titus nodded again. 'I believe so. We can't stop this procedure. It's gone too far. But there's a device called *cessio bonorum*. We can use it because Papa's money was lost in the shipwreck of the *Den Prince*.' Titus shot Rembrandt a wry glance. 'This device is often used after shipwrecks. It means, in effect, that the debtor's financial problems aren't his fault. It allows the state to take over all the debts. The creditors then claim what they can from the state. They are off our backs.'

Hendrickje was close to tears. 'Titus. We can't live here with... nothing.'

Titus nodded. 'We will rent a smaller, furnished place. In Amsterdam.'

'My paintings?' Rembrandt said.

'I'm sorry, Papa, but they are possessions like any other. The materials you use for painting and drawing are safe. So is the etching machine. Once we move, I will start a new company, with Hendrickje. You will be our employee. That way they cannot touch you any more.'

'So I can paint?' Rembrandt asked his son.

'Yes, Papa. You can paint.'

'That'll do.' Rembrandt shrugged his massive, sagging shoulders. 'As long as I can work. But, Titus...?'

'I know what you're going to say. What about the rest of my money, from Mama? Mama's family, the Uylenburghs, have blocked your access. They say you're not a fit person after—'

Rembrandt laughed. 'Yes, all right, all right.'

Titus smiled. 'I've been down to the *Weeskamer*. I was practically brought up there.'

'What, in the Orphans' Chamber?' I was laughing.

'Yes!' Titus laughed, too. 'They used to hold auctions there. Papa used to take me, from when I was what? About six?'

'Younger than that,' Rembrandt said. 'About three, I think.'

'Just think. My first memories are of auctions. Anyway, I've had to declare myself an orphan, now. So I'm independent of you, Papa. Otherwise they could get any money I protect back from you.'

Titus nodded at another document, rich with red wax stamps, curling up on the table. Next to it, I noticed an apparently identical document. It had my name on it.

I nodded at it. 'What's that?'

Titus cleared his throat. 'That? Ah, now it gets a bit complicated. I've had you made an orphan, too.'

'What?'

'How old are you?' Titus said.

'How old do I look?'

Titus gave a faint sigh. 'Baruch... Please?'

'I'm twenty-four. Bit old to be an orphan.'

'Not according to the Orphans' Chamber. They say you have to be under twenty-five. Sign that please.'

'What's the point of me being an orphan?'

'I dug up a rather wonderful idea known as *Herstelling*. It means that any disadvantageous deal done by a minor, caused by his lack of maturity, is null and void.'

'So everything I've ever done, doesn't count?'

'That's about the size of it. Because you were too immature.'

'I'm absolved?'

'Correct.'

'Of everything?'

'Correct.'

'Positively Catholic. Show me where to sign.' I signed. 'Right, I'm an orphan. Now what?'

'Everything you signed before is now null and void. That will protect your fortune.'

'What fortune?'

'You gave away all your shares in the family company, for a start. At that meeting in the new Town Hall.'

'Oh yes, so I did. I had to. Gabriel insisted.'

'Quite,' Titus said. 'I was there. You've got them back now. You were too immature to make the decision to give them away.'

'Oh... Good.'

'But I'm afraid there's something else, Baruch. The Jewish authorities have been prevailed on to institute a... excuse my pronunciation... a herem, is it? Against you.'

'A *cherem*! Oh, don't make me laugh!'

'What is it?' Hendrickje said.

'The word *cherem* means separation. You are cast out from the community. No longer a Jew. It's rare and usually temporary.'

'Not in your case it won't be,' Titus said.

'No?'

'Why do they do it?' Hendrickje said. 'Oh Baruch, will it horrible like what the church authorities did to me?'

I squared my shoulders. 'It's sometimes done for non-payment of synagogue dues,' I said. 'Or in any financial dispute – providing it's between two Jews. Technically, you can get a *cherem* for masturbation...'

I blurted this out without thinking, then felt myself blushing. I looked aghast at Hendrickje. She and Rembrandt were rolling with laughter.

'Technically!' Rembrandt roared. 'Oh that's good. Technically!'

I cleared my throat, then coughed, rallying. 'There have been *cherems* for heresy,' I added. 'And no, it won't be pleasant. When I was a kid they did it to somebody called Uriel da Costa. They made him lie down on the steps of the synagogue while the entire congregation walked over him.'

'That's horrible!' Hendrickje said.

'It made a point,' I said, with studied nonchalance. 'Then all the kids stoned him. I did myself; I was only eight. It was fun. They say he committed suicide in the end, but I don't believe it. He was stabbed to death, murdered.'

'Your *cherem* procedure was fixed for the day after Papa's inventory. 27th July. That cannot be a coincidence,' Titus said.

'No!'

'They want you both out.' Titus hesitated. 'If... if you are expelled from the community, Baruch, I have learned—'

For once, I was ahead of him. 'Anyone under *cherem* is forbidden to buy and sell. Gabriel would take over. Take everything. '

'That's what he was after. The orphan device will protect you against that.'

'Right, well, thank you for arranging it, then.'

There was a polite knock on the door. The maid, Lysbeth, entered with a letter for me. It was from Clara Maria.

Thirteen

*A free man thinks of death least of all things; and
his wisdom is a meditation not of death but of life.*

Spinoza
Ethics

Hendrickje had wanted me to read my letter aloud, at
our meeting in the little chamber off the *sydelkaemer.*
Her currant-bun of a face caught the light from a window of
coloured glass, high in the outside wall. She was gleaming with
animation and mischief. But I excused myself from the business
of business, dashing to my home in the corner of the kitchen,
clutching my precious letter. I realised that I had not even
excused myself properly, after all Titus's efforts to help me. I
felt remorse at that.

The cook and the maids were at their posts, churning butter,
salting herrings, making pies, chattering the while. They fell
silent when I came in. The letter was from her all right, even
though only my name was written. I knew her hand well enough.

Impatient of Franciscus van den Enden's pompous red seal,
I shut my eyes and tore at the letter. I ripped it. The seal held.
Groaning in frustration I held the torn bits together. Lysbeth,
the maid whose sleeping place I had usurped, was looking at
me curiously. The other two women pretended to ignore me.

'Got a letter then?' the pert Lysbeth said. 'From a lover, is it?' she added. All the women started to laugh. I shot them a ferocious glance, then head-down devoured the words.

Dear Bento,

I blush for shame that you were obliged to leave my father's house in the manner that you were. My father, too, regrets it Huh! That sporadically deaf old coot regrets the loss of three guilders a week rent. That's all! *I have spoken to Theodor most severely* I'd love to have heard that! *and he now understands the error of his ways. He assures me he means you no further harm.* Say you've broken off the engagement! Go on. Say it! *My father is anxious that the performance of his play should not be affected by the unfortunate incident, consigned to the past.* Well, yes. If you accept that duration is indefinite continuation, then time becomes not exactly irrelevant but unimportant. *The next rehearsal is this afternoon at the Theatre, the Schouwburg, where the final performance of my father's work is due to be held. We are expecting to see you there.* Oh are you, now? Oh, all right.

It was signed. *Your Latin teacher, Clara Maria Margarethe Valpurgis van den Enden.*

Across the bottom was a stamp: 'The van den Enden Art Emporium: The Finest Art in Amsterdam at Affordable Prices. Never Knowingly Bested on Price For Prints, Engravings and Woodcuts.'

A love letter! I had received my first ever love letter! My heart soared in the manner of lovers. Clara Maria loved me! I had seen off the unworthy Kerckrinck!

Pausing only to write some thoughts on the nature of will – that it is not a free cause but can only be called necessary – I set off for the Schouwburg. I passed Titus in the vestibule on the way out. He started to say something, but I cut across him 'No time now, Titus! Urgent business. See you later.'

On the way to the theatre, on the Keizersgracht towpath, I was harangued by a lunatic.

Dressed in rags, with a lolling tongue, waving scarecrow arms, the wretch looked even worse than the painter Ruisdael, and one does not see that too often.

'You are the Antichrist,' the lunatic screamed at me.

'Go away!'

The lunatic attempted to grab my arm. I shook myself free and walked on. The lunatic gambolled behind me, with the strange loping half-crouch of his kind. The simian nature of his movements was emphasised by the curve of his arms and the slope of his back.

'The conversion of the Jews is a false dawn,' he screamed.

'Glad to hear it.'

'It is not the will of God.'

I quickened my pace, speaking over my shoulder. 'There are two assumptions underlying your proposition: one is that God exists; the second is that He shares knowledge of what is and what is not His will with a lunatic on an Amsterdam towpath. If you cannot justify both assumptions, your proposition falls. Good day to you, sir.'

The lunatic screamed. 'The Jews are responsible for all the ills of the world,' he opined.

I slowed my pace. 'You are far from being the only lunatic who thinks so.'

The man wiped his forearm across his mouth and nose. 'I hate you,' he said. 'You killed my mother.'

I stopped. I felt a powerful urge to confess to the murder of the lunatic's mother. Why?

Just, in some inchoate way, to get it over with. I wasn't even sure what the 'it' was that I wanted to get over with. I walked on.

'How on earth did you know?' I called over my shoulder. 'Mind you, your mother was a very irritating woman.'

'That's true.'

The lunatic and I were getting along famously, united in our condemnation of the lunatic's mother. However, our new-found friendship was to be short-lived. The lunatic grabbed my arm from behind. Impatient at the possible delay to my meeting with Clara Maria, I lashed out without looking.

The lunatic fell backwards into the canal, drowning surprisingly rapidly. I had killed him. I felt no remorse, thinking only of my appointment at the theatre. I made a mental note to elevate the incident into a possible philosophical doctrine, something to do with the futility of existence and the primacy of death. But when I considered it later, I found it a threadbare and stupid idea, too trivial to pursue, so I abandoned it.

Just as the lunatic breathed his last, I was grabbed from behind by at least two men and had a cloak thrown over my head. I was then lifted bodily by even more men, carried along like a rolled-up carpet, before being unceremoniously and painfully thrown into a cart. My assailants then climbed up into the cart with me, someone shouted to the coachman, the coachman whipped the horse and we set off, I knew not where.

On the cart, a hood was put over my face. I was wrapped even more tightly into what I had taken to be a cloak, but judging by the smell it might have been a horse blanket. Two leather straps were put round the bundle that was now me. They were buckled tight.

My two, possibly three, assailants held me down, but I made no attempt to struggle. For one thing, their pressing of me into the struts of the cart reduced the amount I was thrown about.

I was scared of suffocating, though. My nose was pressed against the slats. From the smell of hops, this was clearly a dray cart, usually used for transporting barrels of beer. It started to rain, which made the smell stronger.

I felt us jolt over a bridge, but by that time I knew where we were going. Miguel da Silva, Morteira's man, had said something in ungrammatical Dutch, with that unmistakeable lisping voice. He was probably the one with a fist in the small of my back, pressing my nose down into the boards of the cart.

When we arrived and the cart stopped, I was unloaded. You could hear the rushing sluice-water from outside Morteira's house. It was a sound from my childhood, when our disputations were still friendly. Were they going to kill me because we had fallen out over theology?

I expected them to carry me up to Morteira's study. This hope was naïve. I was hauled over two sets of shoulders, still bound like an Egyptian mummy, still hooded like a tethered hawk. With difficulty, I was taken through the entrance hall, which I recognised even trussed up, and then down some flagstone stairs. One of the oafs carrying me kept cursing – he was the one going first, so bearing all the weight.

Miguel da Silva lispingly directed operations, not carrying me himself. The door which clanged shut behind me sounded like a prison door, or at least a cellar. Were they going to flood the place and keep me in water until I did their bidding? Or perhaps just let me drown. No, not that. They could have drowned me in the canal, saving themselves the trouble of my transportation.

No, Morteira wanted to talk. Morteira always wanted to talk, ever since I have known him. Talk. But you had to agree. I was quite ready to agree now.

'Untie him.' The voice was unmistakeable, even the tone of slight disdain, as if the words themselves were made of over-ripe cheese.

I gasped as they pulled the hood off, sucking in a lungful of air. Then, none too gently, they pulled my covers off – it *was* a horse-blanket – without untying the leather straps.

'Now tie his wrists together behind his back. He thinks he is a free man. He is here to learn that no Jew is free. We are bound to each other.'

'Good afternoon, Chacham Morteira. My rabbi, my teacher, my learned one.'

This was not defiance; it did not even sound like it. It was certainly not bravery. I was so frightened I had soiled my breeches. But I wanted to assert something of sarcasm; I wanted to say something quintessentially me; I wanted still to exist and be felt to exist. I both wanted and strongly needed that.

As the minions were tying my wrists together behind my back with thin leather thongs, my eyes swivelled round the cellar. Against the walls were barrels of wine from Portugal. I realised we had been speaking Portuguese, Morteira and I. There were also a couple of barrels of salted herring, some sea chests – possibly containing valuables – some bales of cloth, some tools.

And there was a contraption that reminded me of Rembrandt's machine for printing off his etchings. It had a wooden frame and rollers. Although it also had ropes running through the rollers, which Rembrandt's device did not.

I knew enough of my father's past in Portugal to glance up to the ceiling, above the device. Sure enough there was a thick rope, slung through a pulley. The pulley device was a strappado. The one that looked like Rembrandt's etching-machine was a rack.

They were often used in conjunction – for torture.

The minions had been waved away. They left. But Miguel da Silva stayed at Morteira's side. The sound of wooden shoes clattering on the flagstone steps announced a third figure joining them. He was a massively broad man in a leather apron, with shoulders which did not stop until they reached his wrists. His face was hidden by a black mask with holes cut for the eyes.

'Ah, Morteira's cousin, the butcher,' I cried out. 'The lousiest butcher in Amsterdam, purveyor of meat full of gristle.'

The masked figure glanced at Morteira. Morteira smiled. Miguel da Silva slapped me backhanded across the face. The butcher, unmasked, took his mask off.

'Do you know what the word "Inquisition" means?' Morteira said to me. 'It means an inquiry into heresy. I declare this inquiry open. Do you know who Fernão Martins Mascarenhas was?'

'No.'

'Mascarenhas was called the laughing bishop, he used to run the Inquisition in the Algarve, then the whole of Portugal. You see Miguel, here? His family knew Mascarenhas well.'

Miguel da Silva and I stared at each other.

'Miguel tell him what happened to your family.'

Without taking his eyes off me, da Silva shook his head. A faint movement of a surprisingly beautiful hand indicated that he wanted Morteira to do it.

'Miguel's family had successfully hidden their Judaism for years, worshipping in secret, pretending to be good Catholic converts. And then one day, Miguel's little sister brought a friend home, a Catholic girl. She found olive oil in the kitchen. It was enough.'

The thongs were biting into my hands. I tried to look as if I knew all this, just to stop Morteira dominating me, but in truth it was new. My father never spoke of these things. Suffering and shame were understood. We didn't need the details.

'All the family were made to wear the *sanbenito*. It's a yellow bell-shaped dress that is designed to make you look a fool. That's just when you are accused. When they parade you through the street to the *auto da fé* you also wear a cardboard hat that makes you look even more stupid. You go barefoot and you carry a candle. What was your father's occupation, Miguel?'

'He was a surgeon.'

'A surgeon. Yes. So, he and his wife and his two daughters were marched to the *auto da fé* dressed like clowns. Miguel himself had got wind of the arrests and escaped. He was in the crowd. He was hoping to rescue them, but could do nothing. Right, Miguel?'

Miguel's face was blank. He nodded yes.

'He became a helpless onlooker, a watcher at the feast. The *auto-da-fé* is a party, Baruch. It's a celebration. Everybody gets the day off. There are tables laden with food and drink. Bands play music. There is dancing. The accused have already confessed, because they have used *these* things...' Morteira waved at the strappado and the rack.

'There is only *one* decision left.'

Morteira stroked his beard. Then, almost absent-mindedly, he reached over and pinched my cheek between his thumb and forefinger.

'Each – person...' Morteira was speaking very slowly. 'Each – accused – person is asked if they want to die a Catholic. If the answer is Yes, they are tied to a post and garrotted from behind. Quick. Like that.' Morteira mimed garrotting, round his own throat.

'How many of your family agreed to die quickly, Miguel? When you were watching in the crowd?'

Da Silva was silent.

'None. Right? None of them.'

Da Silva nodded agreement.

'Did you eat any food, Miguel, there in the sunny square, where you were watching your tortured family, dressed like clowns, being laughed at? You know why I ask? I imagine the scene, and I tell myself, if this Miguel da Silva does not join in, if he does not pretend to enjoy himself, someone might smell a rat. Someone might say, this is a Jew watching his family die in pain and mockery. So did you eat anything, Miguel?'

I could no longer look at da Silva. I looked at Morteira's cousin, the butcher. He was crying. Miguel said nothing.

'Miguel, I asked you a question,' Morteira said, mildly. 'I asked you if you ate anything.'

·'Yes,' Miguel said. 'For the reason you said.'

'You partook of the feast? Of course you did. What?'

'Salted fish, sardines, sweetmeats.'

'And if drink could numb the feelings, who could blame you, with the wine flowing...'

'Yes! Yes!'

Morteira seemed to suddenly forget da Silva was even there. He has always had this tendency to enter one person at a time. 'So, anyway, Baruch. People who refuse to say they are dying a Catholic, let's call them Jews, shall we? Just for the sake of argument. Proper Jews. You may have heard of them. Have you?'

'Saul...' I had never called him that before.

'Silence, Baruch, there's a good boy. You have made your decision. So these Jews, Baruch,' His voice was hypnotic. 'These Jews are taken to a stake that is higher than the one where the good Catholics were garrotted. They are led up a ladder to a platform, attached to the post – is that right, Miguel? I don't know, first hand. I'm just an ignorant old Ashkenaz. That right, Miguel? About the post?'

Miguel shut his eyes for a second. He nodded, silently.

'So there they are on the platform, Miguel's family. You get the picture? Wood at the foot of the pyre. The crowd are drunk by now. But there's one more bit of entertainment to come.'

'No!' I screamed. 'Chacham Morteira! Please! Who is being tortured here?' I tried to move my head to indicate Miguel. The thongs were biting deeper into my wrists. It was surprisingly painful.

Morteira shrugged. 'I'm torturing Jews. That's what everybody does, isn't it? Why should I be any different? Because I'm a Jew? No, think it through, Baruch. Think it through. And anyway, you don't mind, do you? You don't mind about the Jews.'

'Of course I do!' I howled.

'Do you? Do you really? Now there's a thing... Where was I?' Do you want to finish this story, Miguel?'

'Saul...' It was the butcher, but the faint protest died in his throat.

'Baruch, there was just one more thing this good party needed. This party out in the sunshine.'

Miguel da Silva gave a faint retching cough, Morteira ignored it.

'A bit of fun, you know, a competitive element. But first the executioners and torturers got their bonus. They shaved the heads of the da Silva family. Although, come to think of it, at least that means they got rid of those ridiculous cardboard hats, eh Miguel? There's always a bright side. But to do that, they had to get quite close, didn't they? Close to your family? For the shaving?'

'No!' Miguel said. 'Stop it! How did you know?'

Morteira smiled. 'Educated guess. The shaving wasn't just of their heads, was it? Your sisters were, what, one sixteen and the other how old?'

Da Silva was silent.

'How old was your older sister, Miguel? Rachel, the pretty one. How old?'

'She was twenty-two.'

'And your mother. Would you say she was an attractive woman?'

I screamed. 'Morteira! For God's sake! Stop! Please!'

'Sorry, Baruch? I think I must have misheard you. In whose name did you cry out for me to stop?'

'Rabbi... Chacham. Tell me what you want of me. I will try... I am not your enemy. Please just tell me what it is that you want of me. Please. I beg you.'

'In a minute,' the rabbi said, so softly I hardly heard him.

'Could you see, Miguel? From where you were? They were all naked by then, weren't they? Your family? Could you see... the hairs, for example? The places where they were shaved? Could you?'

'Yes.'

'And the next time you took a woman...'

'No!' The butcher advanced on his cousin. 'You say that and I will strike your mouth bloody, learned rabbi or not.'

Miguel was retching, bent over double.

Morteira nodded, very slowly, as if to himself. 'There was something else they did, after the shaving. Remember it was a carnival – no work done that day. They held a lottery. Did you enter Miguel? No, you could have avoided that. You couldn't really leave the square, that would have got you noticed. But no lottery for you. The winner got... what was it now?'

Miguel straightened. But he waved an arm at Morteira, unmistakeably beckoning him to continue.

'The winner got a long brand dipped in tar. You see, the victim, the Jew, had been tied to the post by the neck. It was not possible to move the head very much. So the lucky winner lit the long brand from the fire at the foot of the pyre, then he lifted it aloft and slowly roasted off the victim's face. Who did they do first, Miguel? That genuinely interests me.'

This time Miguel answered. 'My sisters first. Then my father, then my mother.'

Morteira said nothing. There was complete silence in the room. Eventually the rabbi spoke again: 'Baruch, I am going to show you a document. Look at the date on it.'

He fetched a parchment from a shelf. The date was just above the seal. He held it in front of me, as I sat with my hands bound.

'What is the date, Baruch?'

'Last week,' I said, obediently.

'Good. Good. Good boy. The document is from the Council of the Provinces of West Holland and Friesland. Now read where I point to you, with my finger. Read aloud.'

I saw where his finger was and read, like a child, without reading ahead. '*After mature deliberation and consultation upon the subject, we consider it necessary to take care by any proper means that the true Theology and Holy Scripture should not be offended through liberty of philosophising or by any abuse of it.*'

'Do you know what means, Baruch? Hmmm? Do you understand it?'

'I believe so. Yes.'

'It means, boy, that they are losing patience with the Jews. We Jews who, since the decline in trade because of the war, do not bring in as much money as we used to. They are threatening to throw us out if we – or one of us – makes any waves. They will take us, lock stock and barrel, the three hundred Jewish families of Amsterdam, and they will send us back to Portugal. Do you understand?'

'Yes.'

'Don't just say yes, in that insolent manner.'

'Yes Chacham Morteira. I understand.'

'And are you suffering, Baruch, at this moment? Or shall we string you up on the strappado?'

'I am suffering, Chacham Morteira.'

'Good, my boy. Good. You are suffering. So now, Baruch, now you are a proper Jew. Aren't you?'

'Yes.'

'Good boy. And you will stay a Jew and not make trouble. Won't you, Baruch?'

Fourteen

... a man is bad only in respect to one who is better

Spinoza
Short Treatise on God, Man and His Well-Being

I walked back, round the corner, to Rembrandt's house. My wrists were still sore from the leather thongs, my mind still bruised by the pictures stamped on it. I had recanted. As they hoisted me up to the strappado, I had promised Morteira all manner of things to avoid pain. So they let me go.

Morteira's voice was resounding in my mind: 'It is better not to make a vow at all than to vow and not fulfil it.'

I know, Chacham Morteira. I know.

Back at the vestibule of the Breestraat house a hubbub was boiling. Titus was in the same mask and wig he had donned when he rescued me on the way to the Waterlanders meeting, but this time he wore an old fashioned doublet and baggy breeches. He was surrounded by five or six ragamuffins of assorted shapes, sizes and ages. The youngest cannot have been above ten years of age.

'Baruch!' Titus looked amazed to see me. 'Baruch, we were just coming to get you.'

Curious ragamuffins pressed round me. 'Hello mister!' one of them said.

'Hello.' I smiled at the ragamuffin. Then spoke to Titus. 'Coming to get me?'

'Yes. We heard from one of Morteira's maids that he was planning to kidnap you. He has some rather strange contraptions down in his cellar apparently. That's what I was going to tell you when you went out, but you rushed past and ignored me.'

'Oh... sorry...'

'Don't worry! I'll send the gang home. I'm just glad you're OK.'

At that moment, I fainted.

* * *

I awoke in my bed in Rembrandt's kitchen, dressed in a nightshirt. I was hot as a volcano. Both my body and the nightshirt were drenched in sweat. I gave a couple of coughs, to see if I was still alive.

'He is returning to us,' Hendrickje said calmly, to the maids.

There was no discernible reaction from them. They went about their business.

Hendrickje dabbed my forehead with a poultice of herbs. 'Here. That should make you feel better.'

'Thank you.'

The fever did not abate. My cough returned to plague me, especially at night. I was a prey to nightmares with a cast of rabbis, Latin-speaking playwrights, younger brothers and proofs and corollaries which came alive, then refused to stay in the places I had assigned them.

Rembrandt visited, booming at me and punching my aching joints encouragingly. He took meals in front of me, now and again, notwithstanding that cheese, herring and beer were revolting to me. Titus came for frequent but brief visits. He was still watching over my affairs and his father's, both openly and clandestinely – using his spies and ragamuffins.

But my mainstay was Hendrickje. She fed me a sort of porridge with rose hips in it. It was the only food that did not provoke immediate vomiting. Titus decided to summon a doctor.

I knew the man, he had attended the family – Georg Hermann Schuller. He was a grey fellow – grey hair, grey face – who habitually wore a ridiculously high black hat, as if that gave him extra authority. He had attended my father on his deathbed. In fact, if it hadn't been for Schuller, it might not have been his deathbed. It was the mercury Schuller administered which killed Papa, not the disease it was prescribed for.

Anyway, the entire household gathered round my sickbed to watch Schuller go through his paces. He started by swilling my urine round in a pisspot, a procedure which always makes me think of Clara Maria. He examined my waste judiciously, then he sniffed and tasted it.

He shook his head, sorrowfully. 'There is albumen in the deposit. Not good. Not good at all.' The doctor turned to Rembrandt. 'A seton for this patient will cost twelve *stuivers*.'

'We'll pay,' Titus said.

Schuller took a scalpel from his case. I shut my eyes. He made an incision in my upper arm, causing me to scream with pain. Hendrickje held my hand – the other one.

'That will let the bad humours escape,' Schuller informed his audience. 'I am not one of those fools who believes the blood goes round and round, so you need do this only once. But keep the wound open.'

'Yes, sir,' Hendrickje said, her eyes wide.

'You must replace this herb poultice you have been using.' He looked sternly at Hendrickje, who dropped her eyes. 'I will have one made up of hellebore. And a tincture for the stomach. I will order you some Cream of Tartar.'

'Will he live?' boomed Rembrandt, scratching under the brim of his hat.

'No, sir. I do not believe he will. I will do what I can for him, but I am a doctor, not a miracle worker. Furthermore, the patient is stubborn, unpleasant and un-cooperative.'

I hadn't said a word! I tried to point this out, but had a coughing fit. The ulcer he had made in my arm hurt worse than anything yet done to me.

'That coughing is most unpleasant,' said the doctor. 'And irritating. Given the trouble the fellow has caused in the community, I think death may be the best outcome for all concerned.'

Rembrandt nodded, sadly. 'Thank you anyway for your trouble, doctor,' he said, respectfully. 'Titus will see you out.'

* * *

I had more visitors ill than I ever had well. Ribca came. Ribca wept. In John 11:35 the Bible tells us Jesus wept, but he had nothing on Ribca. She sat on a low stool by my box-bed for the best part of a day, saying not a single solitary word. Not a syllable, even. She just wept.

She wept into a handkerchief. She wept silent tears down her cheeks. She sat up and wept, she leaned back and wept. She leaned over me and wept. Her tears splashed into my midday porridge, into my ulcerous seton, down onto my fevered brow. She was absolutely no help at all.

More surprisingly, my other sister, Miriam, also appeared, towing the husband, Samuel de Caseres. Miriam had evolved a Sickness Visiting Protocol worthy of the Court of Spain in its complexity.

For a start, they had both dressed up. Miriam was wearing a strange bonnet which clung tight to both ears and pushed forward over her cheeks like the wings of a visor.

She also sported a long cape. I had not seen this garment before; it gave her the look of a Jewish nun. She had a patch on one cheek, which she kept touching.

Samuel was wearing a violet cassock. It looked new, despite being bespattered with food stains. His black velvet hat, obviously bought for the occasion, kept slipping down over his eyes. A plague charm dangled prominently at his neck; he kept touching it.

As they came in, Samuel presented me with a bowl of medlars, as if he were an ambassador presenting a chalice at a foreign court. I can't stand fruit, it gives me diarrhoea, especially medlars. I balanced them on the far side of my sick bed, ready to throw them away when the visitors had gone.

Miriam summoned a maid and demanded a foot-warmer. When this was brought, Samuel demanded one for himself. Feet warmed, they both leaned back, as far as they could, away from me. This, I understood, was to distance themselves from possible contagion.

They also – both of them – spoke stiltedly in high voices. I am not at all clear what the reason was for that.

'All the family send greetings to you, our brother,' Miriam piped, in the new Dialect For The Sick.

'We send greetings,' echoed Samuel de Caseres, falsetto, his hand in front of his mouth.

As usual, Samuel was imitating and echoing the strongest presence. In the absence of Gabriel, he echoed his wife.

'Arrangements have been made for your funeral,' Miriam said. 'But we need to discuss them with you, O my brother.'

I sat up in bed. 'My funeral?'

'We need to discuss the arrangements,' clarified Samuel de Caseres, helpfully.

'Don't you think that's a bit premature?' I said.

'Don't take that tone with me, Baruch,' snapped Miriam, back to her waspish best, forgetting the diplomatic protocol she – or somebody – had invented. 'There's no helping you, is there? You were always so aggressive, even as a little boy.'

'You *are* aggressive, Baruch.'

'Oh belt up, Samuel. You dopey milksop.'

'There, see what I mean.' Samuel waved his hand in front of his mouth to ward off contagion, simultaneously appealing to his leader, who gave him a tight nod of support.

'You are to be buried in the family vault, next to father,' Miriam said, in the manner of an ambassador magnanimously ceding land. 'Are you going to eat those medlars, we brought you? You're rolling around on them. You're going to squash them in a minute.'

I seized the bowl of medlars and shoved them at her. The movement jolted the arm the doctor had wounded and made me cry out in pain. 'Ow! Here, take the bloody medlars. I don't like them anyway.'

Miriam shook her head sorrowfully at her husband. 'See? So aggressive.'

'Aggressive.' Samuel pronounced his finding.

I screamed. I had a fever. My arm was giving me agonizing pain. I was racked with coughing, drenched with sweat, I hadn't slept well since my ordeal at Morteira's house and when I did sleep I had nightmares. I had had enough of my family.

'Will you stop calling me bloody aggressive!'

Samuel and Miriam looked at each other. Miriam had to turn her shoulders to achieve this, as otherwise she could not see round the bonnet.

'Aggressive,' Samuel de Caseres murmured.

'There were other matters we wanted to discuss with you,' Miriam said, standing, kicking the foot-warmer out of the way. 'Matters to do with the difficulties you have created for the family – yet again – with your latest selfish financial machinations.'

I tried to sit up, but succeeded only in jolting the wounded arm. 'Ow! What the hell are you talking about? What financial...?'

Miriam wagged a finger at me, bending toward me, her indignation overcoming her fear of contagion. 'You liar!' The Diplomatic Protocol seems to have gone by the board, then. 'You liar and you cheat!'

'Liar and cheat.' Samuel de Caseres stood, looking at Miriam, as open to instruction as a finger puppet.

'You're trying to deny it, aren't you?'

'Yes! Well, I would if I knew what it was.'

'You know the trouble with you, Baruch?'

'Look, Miriam...'

'You think you're so much cleverer than everybody else. We're all stupid, aren't we Baruch, compared to you? Everybody's stupid.'

O the wicked-imp urge to agree. 'Not everybody. No. You are. Samuel certainly is.'

'Aggressive,' said Samuel. Case proved.

'Samuel you've already repeated that.'

Samuel looked at Miriam for clarification.

Miriam wagged the finger all the way from her shoulder. 'My brother the clever philosopher, surrounded by fools like us. You've declared yourself an orphan, haven't you? Admit it! An orphan, indeed! Mama and Papa would turn in their graves!'

'Look, why don't you just...' I struggled up onto one elbow, tearing my thin nightshirt in the process.

'Everything this family thought we'd achieved has been thrown into doubt! Everything's been undone, because of you. We don't know whether we're coming or going, in the firm. You've brought *Bento y Gabriel D'Espinoza* to its knees! And I hope you're proud of that. You arrogant wastrel, you!'

'Arrogant wastrel,' Samuel confirmed, apparently more in sorrow than anger.

Then they walked out. At least they took the medlars away with them.

* * *

A couple of days later, Clara Maria came. As I awoke one morning, she was there, at my bedside, eating my porridge.

'Oh Bento, you're waking up! I was just having a spoonful of your food. I hope you don't mind.'

'No! No, not at all. Eat all of it if you like. I don't want it.'

She bolted the porridge, shovelling it into her mouth with the wooden spoon they had left in it. 'I'm starving! Lord alone knows why. I had breakfast. I get like that sometimes. Papa says it's a growth spurt.'

'How is your father?'

'He's well. Thank the Lord. He's all I've got since Mama died. He said to tell you that leaving your room without notice, as you did, has caused him financial loss. So he intends to sue you.'

'Oh,' I said. 'I'm sorry, Clara Maria.'

She nodded. 'That's all right. I'll tell Papa you apologised. I expect he'll still sue you, though.'

I rose up on one arm.

She gasped, put the bowl down and put one hand to her mouth. 'Bento!'

'What?'

Her eyes were enormous. 'Bento!' She pointed at me. 'Blood! There's blood on your arm.'

'Oh that!' I attempted to look brave and nonchalant. 'That's nothing!' I glanced down at the seton, which was indeed bleeding profusely.

'Bento!' The lovely eyes filled with tears. This was going rather well! 'Bento,' She leaned forward in her chair and whispered. 'Did they, did they... torture you?'

'Well, when you say "torture"...'

'Oh Bento! They had wicked instruments down there in that dungeon, didn't they? Titus told me.'

'Yes. Yes, they did.'

She nodded, seriously. 'I have heard of such things, Bento. Wicked instruments. The Inquisition uses them. O Bento you must have been so brave.'

I shrugged modestly. 'I told them nothing,' I said.

Clara Maria picked the bowl up again, wolfing the last of the porridge. 'What did they want to know?' she asked, as she chewed.

'Oh. Well. You know... The situation, at the moment...'

'With the Jews. Yes, I know. It's a disgrace! Those Calvinists have no right to agitate against the Jews. They shame Amsterdam.'

The sheer simple decency of her siding with the Jews had me close to tears.

She went on. 'There is even talk of the Jews being told to leave. And they are calling you the Messiah. You aren't, are you?'

'Absolutely not. No. Case of mistaken identity.'

'Good. Anyway, Papa's as incensed as I am. He's already started writing a pamphlet defending the Jews. He's letting me help.'

'Good for you!'

'Yes. I'm doing research. And I even suggest some phrases.'

And to think I called van den Enden an evil, venal deaf old bastard. Goes to show, there's good in everyone. Even evil, venal deaf old bastards.

Clara Maria had finished the porridge. She was looking round, evidently for more food.

'Are you still hungry?'

'Mmmm.' She nodded hard, hands now folded in her lap.

'Lysbeth!'

Lysbeth was helping the other maid at the far end of the kitchen. 'What is it? Can't you see I'm busy?'

'Lysbeth can you get my guest some food, please?'

'This isn't a tavern.'

'Please...'

Lysbeth came over. 'What can I get you, *Vrouw* van den Enden?'

'Some cheese, if you'd be so kind.'

Lysbeth walked off, returning quickly with a hunk of Leiden cheese the size of a cannonball. She handed it to Clara Maria, who tore at the rind, then bit at the cheese, without breaking it first.

'Bento, I bring you a message from Papa,' Clara Maria said indistinctly, though a mouth full of cheese.

'I know. You said. He's going to sue me.'

'No...' She swallowed a huge mouthful of cheese. 'No, another message.'

She bit off more cheese. The sight of the half-masticated food in her mouth was distinctly unpleasant, but I banished the unworthy thought as soon as it formed.

'Papa says—' she broke off what she was saying to swallow. 'This is exceedingly good cheese.' She turned in her chair to shout to the other end of the kitchen. 'Lysbeth, this cheese is excellent, thank you.'

Cutting vegetables at a long marble-topped table, Lysbeth paused to curtsey. 'You're very welcome, young lady. Let me know if you want anything else,' she called back.

Clara Maria looked me in the eye, her demeanour suddenly serious. 'Papa says he hopes you can resume rehearsals soon. For now, he's been playing the part of Baucis himself. But he wants you properly rehearsed, he says, because you are the weakest member of the cast. The one with the least natural aptitude, the poorest speaker, the least vivid actor—'

'Yes, all right.'

'There's a rehearsal tonight, at the theatre. You missed the last one.'

'Sorry, but I was kidnapped and...'

'You *can* come to that, can't you? You can always go back to bed again afterwards.'

'Did your father look for a replacement for me?'

She tore off some more cheese from the main hunk with her teeth, then swallowed it.

'Oh yes! He's looked high and low. Asked hundreds of people. But nobody will do it. Nobody wants to dress up in women's clothes, you see. Papa says you have no pride and no dignity, so you are the only man in Amsterdam willing to do it. That's why we need you.'

'All right. I'll be there.'

She stood. 'So, that's tonight at the theatre for rehearsal. And the performance is on the evening of July 27th.'

'That's the day I am due to be expelled from the Jewish people.'

'Oh Bento!' She stamped her little foot – the good one. 'You'll just have to rearrange your expulsion from the Jewish people. The theatre is booked. Bento, this is very important to Papa. It's mean of you to cause problems like this.'

'I'm sorry.' I sighed. 'What time is the performance?'

'In the early evening. There will be braziers, with lanterns lit all round the stage.'

'That should be all right. My expulsion from the Jewish people is in the late afternoon. I'll ask them to keep it brief, so I can get to the theatre in time.'

Clara Maria prepared to leave, swallowing the last of the cheese. 'Good! If it drags on, just tell them you have another appointment.'

'Yes. That should go down well.'

'See you this evening, then. Make sure you know your part. You'll look lovely in your dress, as Baucis. We can have a fitting this evening, too.'

* * *

About an hour later, Gabriel turned up. Like Miriam and Samuel, he had adopted a special manner for the occasion. But in a sense, his was the converse of theirs. Whereas they had started the visit, at least, in a curious formal mode, Gabriel had cloaked himself in a ghastly mateyness.

He strode manfully into the kitchen, just as I had dozed off, yelling 'Hello, brother. Hello!' The cook and the maids stared at him, curiously.

I had seen him like this before. He adopted this mode when he wanted something very badly, and was being duplicitous to get it. When he was very little – well, he's still very little, I mean when he was very young – he used to laugh whenever he lied. He's no longer that obvious. But almost.

'Hello Gabriel,' I said, wearily, as I struggled out of sleep.

Gabriel grabbed the chair recently vacated by Clara Maria, vigorously brushing bits of cheese off it with his palm. He looked as if a barber had recently trimmed his hair and wig, as well as oiling and stiffening his beard.

'Hey big brother! I've come to see you!' Broad grin.

'In philosophy, that statement is known as a redundancy.'

Gabriel roared with laughter, slapping his knee at my shaft of wit. 'Oh Baruch! You're priceless! You always were.'

'To people like you, nothing is priceless.'

'Nothing is priceless!' More roars of laughter. 'That's... price... Well, Baruch, I can't stay here all afternoon, much as I'd like to.' He'd been here under thirty seconds. 'Just popped in to tell you about those old rogues Abraham and Adriaen Alvarez...'

'Up to no good are they?' I enquired, innocently.

'Up to no good!' he repeated, helpless with mirthless laughter. 'Oh that's a good one, brother. The Alvarez brothers, up to no good!'

I waited patiently. The false laughter stopped as suddenly as it started.

'No, the thing is... Might be best to leave Amsterdam. Soon as possible. Not go through with this *cherem* business. Just a thought.'

'Why?'

'Oh, the Alvarez brothers... You know how touchy they can get. They make threats...'

'What's happened now?'

Gabriel twisted his body on the stool. His hands were gripping each other in his lap. 'It's all this stuff with the Orphans' Chamber. I know you hate business, Baruch, so I won't give you chapter and verse.' He stood to leave. 'I've warned you, that's all I can do.'

I made a guess. 'The Orphans' Chamber have given me back my shares in the company, haven't they?'

Gabriel looked furious. 'Yes!' He ground out. 'Yes! We tried to fight it, but the Orphans Chamber said it was clearest example of a decision made because of immaturity they had ever seen. The Alvarez brothers had bought about half your shares, using every *penning* they had. There's been no compensation. They're ruined now.'

'I feel terrible.'

'Oh, don't be so bloody sarcastic!' The friendliness fell away; Gabriel straightened up.

'The Alvarez boys have gone bankrupt. They're both working as stevedores on the docks.'

'And, knowing them, their reaction would be...?'

'They want to kill you.'

'Again?'

'If they knew you were here, you'd be dead by now.'

A thought occurred. 'Who bought the other half of the shares, Gabriel?'

Gabriel's little face was contorted with rage. 'Who do you think?' he said. And stalked out.

I struggled out of bed. I had to attend the rehearsal at the theatre.

I called to Lysbeth to fetch my clothes.

'Fetch them yourself. I'm not your skivvy. I'm not handling your mucky drawers.'

The other maids shrieked with laughter. Eventually, I prevailed on her to fetch Hendrickje, who brought my clothes and helped me dress. I felt weak and dizzy and my arm ached abominably. But one must suffer for art. And one must suffer for love.

Wrapped in my brown cloak, I was just leaving the kitchen when I bumped into Titus coming in. He was in his disguise, one of his ragamuffins with him.

'Ah, Baruch!' Titus looked concerned at the sight of me. 'I heard you were going to the theatre. Is that wise?'

I shrugged. 'I have to,' I said, bravely.

Titus smiled. 'All right, but be careful. Pieter here,' Titus indicated the ragamuffin, 'has just brought us some intelligence from our informant in the Morteira household. It seems that Morteira has hired an assassin from outside the city.'

'Don't tell me. He intends to kill me? '

'Precisely,' Titus said. 'But you'll be fine if you recant. At the *cherem* ceremony, all you have to do is embrace Judaism. Just tell them you believe in it all. Then they'll call the *cherem* off. But if you don't play ball, they won't let you leave the Houtgracht alive.'

Fifteen

A table strives to be and remain a table in that
its atoms strive to stay in that position

Spinoza
Ethics

The theatre is a splendid wood and brick structure on the Kaizersgracht. As soon as I went inside, Clara Maria appeared, pulling Kerckrinck like a skiff tied to a cargo ship.

'Theodor has something he wants to say to you.'

Kerckrinck was red in the face, but he spoke sincerely enough, 'Spinoza, my betrayal of you to Tulp's men was hardly the act of a gentleman. Especially as you were Clara Maria's pupil, under van den Enden's roof. I offer you an apology, sir. And I hope you will accept it.'

A huge hand was thrust at me. I took it and pumped the attached arm. 'Handsomely said, Kerckrinck. I am not one to nurse grudges. Apology accepted.'

'There's no need to make such a bloody meal of it!' Kerckrinck yelled at me, jerking his hand free. 'He's got horrible sweaty hands,' he complained to Clara Maria.

'Good!' Clara Maria beamed. 'Now you two are friends.'

'Have you finished with my microscope?' I asked my new friend. 'I'd rather like it back. If that's all right with you...'

Kerckrinck's face contorted with fury. 'Of course I haven't finished with it!' he shouted, spraying me with indignant spit. 'I'm engaged in advanced medical studies. I dunno. I declare a truce and you try to take advantage. No wonder people say the Jews are untrustworthy.'

Clara Maria had gone off to fetch my dress. She now appeared with it folded over one arm. 'Good to see you boys getting on so well,' she beamed. 'But I'm going to have to tear you away from Theodor, Bento.'

'No! Oh please, we were having such fun!'

'That's as may be. But you've got to have your fitting. Come on! Be a good boy.'

Clara Maria led me up some stairs, which she negotiated with difficulty, onto the large wooden apron. We made our way to the back, where the stage narrowed. Here, on a table, Clara Maria had laid what she described as my things.

This turned out to be my set of women's attire, plus make-up – rouge for my cheeks, with pink-face for the rest of the face and neck. Clara Maria also proudly presented me with two soft woollen bags stuffed with rice, to represent Baucis's breasts. While I was struggling into the guise of Baucis, with my beloved's giggling help, van den Enden appeared.

'Spinoza! At last! What a broken reed you turned out to be. At one blow, I lose a tenant and you jeopardise the entire artistic endeavour. Then you swan around Amsterdam pretending to be the Messiah. It's erratic behaviour, sir. Unsteady. What have you got to say for yourself?'

Clara Maria was inserting a bag of rice down the front of my dress.

'My leaving your establishment was against my will.'

'You're damn right there'll be a bill!' Van den Enden had evidently gone deaf again. 'You'll be presented with a demand until the end of the month. You would expect no less, I'm sure.'

Rehearsals were about to start when I caught sight of the painter Ruisdael decaying in the distance, in his costume as my husband, Philemon. Hitching up my Baucis dress, I made my way off the stage and across to him. He appeared not to recognise me. Was my disguise as Baucis so convincing, or was the painter, as I had long suspected, totally deranged?

'Ruisdael, it's me. Spinoza.'

'What?'

'The philosopher, Spinoza? I'm playing your wife, Baucis, in this production of van den Enden's play. Also, you may recall announcing at the Waterlanders' that I am the Messiah, presaging the conversion of the Jews. Is any of this ringing any bells, you malodorous madman?'

'Oh yes! Spinoza! Yes. How are you?'

'How am I? How *am* I? Look, do you still think I'm the Messiah?'

'No.'

'Aha! Progress!'

'I don't *think* it. I'm quite sure of it. I get visions, you see. And in these visions you are the Messiah. There's no doubt at all about that.'

'Visions? But you're a Waterlander, not a Catholic. You're in the wrong bloody religion to have visions, you idiot!'

'I used to be a Catholic, actually. I converted. The visions didn't stop, though.'

'Great!'

'I say, Spinoza. You know that scene where Philemon and Baucis kiss, just before they both become different types of tree? Do you think we could rehearse that?'

'No!'

'Oh go on. Please! Just one little kiss... ' Ruisdael treated me to a view of his appalling mouth. His tongue and gums seemed to have gone black since the last time I saw him.

'You wouldn't mind kissing the Messiah, then?'

'Oh no! Not at all.'

'Very broad-minded of you!'

At that moment, van den Enden called us to order, sending us back up on the stage. Rehearsals began. Fresh from my sick-bed, still boiling with the fever, I had forgotten my lines so completely that I stumbled even when given the script to read. The entire cast of the play – plus, sadly, Clara Maria – abused me for being so ill-prepared.

* * *

Shortly before Rembrandt was to be declared bankrupt – his house to be returned to the mortgager, his possessions to be taken by the city of Amsterdam and sold – Titus and Hendrickje found the little family a new place to live. They rented it, in the Rozengracht, further out from the centre of Amsterdam than the old three-storey house. Rembrandt refused to go and look at the place.

None of us who loved him – Titus, Hendrickje, myself – were sure if Rembrandt was sound in mind and body or not. Outwardly, he was his old self, working every daylight hour, and on by candlelight, on two paintings and several etchings at the same time. He was perhaps a little more subdued, a little slower than of old, but the laugh still boomed out, the beer still swilled the herring down, the friendly punches still battered my person.

So what was strange? It was a refusal to discuss, mention, even acknowledge the coming changes. Titus asked him time and again to give him a list of objects and paintings to be saved before the fateful day, July 26th, when the bankruptcy people from the *Desolate Boedelskamer* would come to take everything. But Rembrandt not only refused to name any paintings or objects, he would not reply at all when questioned on the subject.

Hendrickje invited me to the new home, more than once, so that I could describe it to Rembrandt, and perhaps awaken his interest that way. But the device failed. When I started to praise the charms of the Rozengracht cottage – and they were real enough, although the place was of necessity small – Rembrandt walked out of the room.

Never a great one for the physical care of his person, he now stopped cleansing himself at all. He wore the same outfit day in day out, including the hat I had first seen him in and the coat that had cost poor Joris Fonteijn his life. His teeth continued to pain him, but he would not admit it. Hendrickje and Titus and I held many a meeting and hatched many a plan to make him happier, but nothing worked.

I was able to return to my philosophy, jotting notes for my proofs as to the workings of life. The Latin lessons resumed at the van den Enden place, concentrating on the lines for my part in the play. Titus continued his drawing lessons; Hendrickje continued to run the house. It seemed that all of us had found a degree of peace and contentment, except our beloved Rembrandt.

And that is how matters stood when the bailiffs from the *Desolate Boedelskamer* knocked on the door, early on the morning of July 26th.

It is an unsettling experience meeting someone when one has seen a Rembrandt painting of them. On the morning of July 26th 1656, when the painter was to be stripped of all his possessions, the day before my *cherem* at the synagogue, I was to have this experience twice.

I had last seen Pieter Haringh in his capacity as auctioneer at the Keizerskroon Inn. He was here today as bailiff for the *Desolate Boedelskamer*. He had a gang of bailiff's men in leather aprons behind him, five or six of them. Titus and I met the knot of officials in the *voorhuys*.

'I'm sorry about this,' Haringh murmured to Titus. 'We'll be as quick as we can. We've got three carts outside. It's just a question of getting everything inventoried and then loaded up.'

'Where are you taking it all?' Titus asked.

Haringh hesitated. 'Bonded warehouse at the East Dock,' he muttered into Titus's ear. 'It has a *DB* shield at the window. If there's anything he particularly treasures, tell me and we'll leave it near the door.'

Titus nodded and squeezed Haringh's arm.

The cook and all the maids had been released except one, Lysbeth, who was already at the new place in Rozengracht.

She was caring for the baby, Cornelia – Hendrickje's child by Rembrandt.

The rest of the household was to remove to the new place as soon as the bailiffs had cleared all the possessions from the Breestraat house. Titus had not wanted Hendrickje to be there while the house was cleared, but she had refused to leave Rembrandt. There was no sign of her at the moment. The painter had locked himself in the big north-facing room where he painted and refused to come out. As far as we knew, he was painting.

Without a word, one of the bailiffs took two chairs from the *voorhuys*, and carried them outside. Through the open door I saw him load them onto the first of three carts. I could see the driver, idly flicking flies away from the chestnut horse with his whip. The rest of the bailiffs, including Haringh himself, glided past us, making their way to the top of the house.

Titus and I looked at each other. 'We'll have to get him out,' Titus said. 'Haringh will break the door down otherwise. He will have no choice.'

We made our way up to the top of the house, the agile Titus taking the tight stairs three at a time. Hendrickje stood outside the *grote schilderkamer* in her outdoor clothes. She looked pasty, tense and helpless, wringing her ungloved raw hands. Obviously relieved to see Titus, she spread her arms wide.

'He's in there all right, but I can't even get him to speak to me. He's bolted the door.'

Titus tried the door, finding this to be true. Next door to the *grote schilderkamer* was the smaller *kunstkaemer*. Two of the bailiffs were in there, gathering up armfuls of art books, a globe and some items of armour. Fortunately, they both set off down the stairs, fully laden, at the same time.

Titus called out 'Papa, papa!' When this was ignored, he spoke urgently at the door, before the two bailiffs came back. 'Papa, Haringh has offered to put items you most treasure where we can reach them, to save them. We cannot reclaim too much, or we will get him into trouble. But you must tell me what you want now. Now, Papa. Or you lose the lot.'

We heard the bolts being drawn back. The door swung open. As the three of us entered, Rembrandt was walking back to his easel, paint brush and a tube of paint in hand. His coat was grubby. He was covered in paint.

'Papa!' Titus sounded really angry.

Rembrandt sighed. 'Save the drawings by Raphael first. Then my own drawings, especially those of Hendrickje.' She went over to him; he touched her hand. 'After that... There's a book of portraits. You'll see the Mierevelts first but the book contains some Titians. I need that. I always need Titian near me.'

'All right,' Titus said. 'Papa, let us take you to our new home now. There is no need for you to witness this.'

Rembrandt gave a heavy shrug. 'Nah! I've got work to do.' There was a long pause. 'I'll come this evening.' It was his first acknowledgement of the events.

'Very well,' Titus said, with heavy judiciousness. Yet again, I had to remind myself that the youth was not yet twenty. 'But, Papa you are not to lock the door again. Is that clear? You are making Hendrickje unhappy, in her worry for you. And I will not have that, Papa. I simply will not tolerate it. Is that clear?'

Rembrandt was silent, but looked contrite. I glanced at the easel. He was working on the portrait of Arnout Tholincx, Tulp's son in law, having completed the engraving. My eyes were irresistibly drawn to it, even as I listened to Titus becoming the father of his father.

'Papa!' Titus was shouting now. 'An undertaking from you, please.'

Rembrandt gave a huge sigh. 'I will not lock the door again, my boy. And before you say it, no I will not obstruct Haringh and his men. They can take all my objects. It doesn't matter. I can replace them easily enough.'

'Let me make you something to eat, my dear,' Hendrickje said. 'You have not eaten.'

Rembrandt smiled. 'Very well.' He had laid his brush down along the palette and resumed his pose in front of the painting. Not only was he squinting badly, he suddenly cupped both hands against the side of his head, channelling his vision. Titus told me later that this artifice reduces the depth of the field, but I had never seen Rembrandt do it before. Just as I thought that, he dropped his hands back to his sides, as if the burden of them had become too heavy. His old eyes grew rheumy.

'I am lucky to have you.' He rumbled this from his belly, so indistinctly I only just made it out. 'Hendrickje, Titus, and you too, Baruch. I have been blessed in my sadness, as old Tobit was blessed by Anna and by his angel.'

Hendrickje disappeared to the kitchen, to make food and drink for Rembrandt. Titus saw no profit in watching while the family home was despoiled. He said he was going to the East Dock to wait for the items Rembrandt wanted to arrive there.

I said I would go with him. He shot me a grateful glance. I realised that my concern for the painter had caused me to overlook what Titus must be feeling. It was his home, too. The only one he had known. He had been born here.

Outside, in the sunshine, a knot of neighbours and passers-by had gathered to watch Rembrandt's house being emptied of everything he owned. Rembrandt had been declared *bankroet* – bankrupt with blame, not the other version *faillissement* – faultless bankruptcy. And there were enough superstitious folk around who still thought bankrupts were abandoned by God.

Among those rejoicing in the painter's misfortune I recognised Samuel and Jacob Pereira, looking gleeful. Rembrandt and the Pereira brothers were in dispute over payments to builders to stop the subsidence in the party wall they shared. The brothers' faces bore looks of ill-concealed glee.

The bailiffs were working quickly. Despite the huge number of artefacts Rembrandt had acquired, one cart had already set off and another was almost completely loaded. Haringh, whose unhappiness made him humble, was fetching and carrying just as hard as his men. As we stood on the threshold of the fast diminishing home, he passed us, bearing statues of a lion and a bull, which occasioned much mirth from the gleeful onlookers.

When he had loaded the statues on the cart, Titus waved him over – with that natural authority that some are born with. Haringh stood at his disposal.

'How much will all this fetch, do you think? The whole lot.'

Haringh the auctioneer, in preparing us for bad news, looked even more like a bloodhound who has lost the scent than usual. 'I doubt you'll make much more than one thousand five hundred for the lot.'

Titus nodded. 'Hardly a dent in the total debt.'

Haringh gave a brief nod. Titus told him the items Rembrandt valued most. Haringh said he would fetch them next, take them to the warehouse straight away and leave them by the door. He then went back into the house for another load.

Titus led me to a field behind the house, where he had tethered a horse near a dog cart.

He fixed the horse between the shafts, and we set off to the East Dock. Once there, we left the dog-cart and horse in a field and concealed ourselves in the ditch. Haringh appeared soon, with one of his bailiffs. They unloaded a cartful of Rembrandt's possessions. True to his word, Haringh left Rembrandt's most cherished items near the warehouse door. We took them to the house in Rozengracht, then returned to what had once been the family home in Breestraat.

Later in the afternoon, on the same day, I had my second experience of seeing in life a man Rembrandt had painted. And again the shock was profound. Titus and I were having a beer in the kitchen of Rembrandt's rapidly denuding house when we heard a rap on the door. As the bailiffs felt no need to knock – and neither did the curious neighbours – we both went to investigate. Arnout Tholincx stood on the threshold.

'I am here to convey my most heartfelt sympathies, young sir,' the pompous surgeon said to Titus, completely ignoring me.

'I have been made bankrupt myself. It is not pleasant. No, not at all. But, as you see, it is possible to rise like a Phoenix from the ashes. I am fully restored to my former glory.'

'Good,' I muttered, *sotto voce*, 'I'd been worried about that.'

Not *sotto voce* enough, apparently. Tholincx drew himself up to his full insignificant height, sticking out his little chest like a caged parakeet. 'There is no need for sarcasm, sir,' he bristled. 'No need at all.'

'Right, I'll bear that in mind in the future. I'm a changed man.'

'Who *is* this?' Tholincx said indignantly to Titus.

Titus was laughing. 'Benedictus de Espinoza, the philosopher,' he introduced. 'Please meet the magistrate Arnout Tholincx.'

'Spinoza!' Tholincx said, recoiling. 'That Jew everybody hates? The one about to be thrown out of Amsterdam? The Messiah, reviled and scorned even by his own people?'

'That's me,' I said. 'Pleased to meet you.'

I extended a hand. Tholincx grew red in the face, stuck out his beard at me and spluttered. 'I shall not shake your hand, sir.'

'A disappointment I shall carry with me to my grave.'

Tholincx endeavoured to turn his back on me and at the same time speak to Titus. As Titus was standing next to me, this was only partly achievable. Tholincx turned, then turned back again. 'I have come here to warn you, sir,' the windbag spluttered. 'My father-in-law, Dr Nikolaes Tulp, is on his way here.'

'Have you any idea why?' Titus said, suddenly grave.

'I'm not sure. I suspect his purpose is to witness Rembrandt's discomfiture and mock it, under the guise of quoting Holy Scripture, of course.'

'That sounds like Tulp,' I said.

Both of them ignored me.

'He may have some deeper design,' Tholincx added.

There was a silence. Tholincx and I were looking to Titus for a lead.

'Are you warning us?' Titus asked, his eyes never leaving Tholincx's face.

'Yes! The man may be my wife's father, but that doesn't mean I don't detest him. The fellow is insufferable. He was instrumental in my own bankruptcy.'

'Baruch,' Titus said. 'Please accompany our guest to the *grote schilderkamer*, even though he knows the way.' Titus then turned to Tholincx. 'My apologies, sir, that we are so ill-equipped to offer hospitality at the moment. But my father will certainly wish to see you and thank you for your warning, even as he works on your portrait.'

This pleased the little windbag, who again puffed himself up. I led the pompous dough-ball back up the stairs to the top floor. Titus hurried off.

A while later, Tulp's magnificent carriage drew to a spectacular halt outside Rembrandt's house, as the four splendid greys were, with difficulty, reined in by one of the two coachmen. The crest on the carriage door was still immaculate after the ride – a single tulip set on an azure ground, with a star in the upper left corner. Below the crest, the motto – *Tollitur arte malum* – art drives out evil.

Tulp threw open the door. The coachman who had spied on the Waterlanders meeting, the swart fellow, the one who had attacked me at van den Enden's house, hurriedly placed the steps for his master to descend. Tulp, in regal black, duly did so, admired by the knot of neighbours, passers-by, ne'er-do-wells and vultures of all sorts who had gathered at Rembrandt's door.

I myself was standing at the open front door at this point. Tholincx had gone. Rembrandt was still upstairs, painting. Hendrickje had gone to prepare the new home. Titus had not returned, though I was rather wishing he would.

'You!' Tulp cried, recognising me.

'Yes, me!' I riposted, matching the redundancy of his greeting. 'What do you want here, Tulp?'

Tulp bridled at the manner of my address. Instinctively, showman that he was, he glanced round at the appreciative audience gathered outside Rembrandt's house. 'What do I want?' Tulp echoed. 'You have the cheek of the devil, Spinoza. I'll grant you that. And devil you surely are. I'll tell you what I want. Some of Rembrandt's daubs are a blasphemy, others are a sin. These come within the responsibility of the city. They must be destroyed. Now!'

Tulp nodded to his coachman, the swart one, and a second, who looked no less sinister. Both fetched their whips. They followed their master the short distance to Rembrandt's house.

But at that point I discovered where Titus had gone. He arose from the ditch in front of the house. And so did a good half-dozen of his ragamuffins, led by the one I had met, the one Titus had addressed as Pieter. Titus was serious, firm in his purpose, but most of the ragamuffins were grinning as they advanced in a phalanx on the surgeon and his two men.

Tulp rounded furiously on the swart coachman. 'Rembrandt's son has the best intelligence in Amsterdam,' he yelled at the coachman. 'Everybody knows he does it by bribing servants. It was you, wasn't it?'

'No, sir!' the hapless coachman said.

But Tulp was not listening. His mind was set, he was accepting no denials, no protestations. He seized the coachman's whip. To the yelling delight of the watching crowd, he belaboured his own coachman with it, lashing him across the shoulders.

The coachman roared, threw up his arms, then ran off in the direction of the bridge. Tulp threw a glance at Titus's ragamuffin band, who were still closing. 'Come on!' he yelled to his remaining coachman. 'To your seat! I will away from here.'

The surviving coachman hastily climbed back up. In his haste to whip up the four horses he forgot the steps that had been placed for Tulp to alight. Indeed, Tulp himself barely made it back into his own coach before it was away, the laughter of the crowd pursuing it down Breestraat.

Later that day, toward evening, Rembrandt finally took leave of his home for the last time. He insisted on carrying his palette, maul stick and many of his paints himself. Titus carried his unfinished painting of Tholincx, shrewdly talking away in his father's ear about how it would be finished in their new home. I myself bore some of the great man's tubes of paints, some of the rags he used in his art and assorted jars of materials. I felt honoured to carry them.

But there was to be a final visitor, before we cleared the portals for the last time. This was a gentleman dressed from feathered hat to buckled shoes in nothing but the finest, as if his well-made frame deserved no less. He was of late middle-age, to be sure, some would have said old. But his fineness of form and face cocked a snook at age.

Rembrandt could not keep the pleasure from his voice as he cried his name. 'Lievens! Jan Lievens! The playmate of my youth!'

'Rembrandt!' Lievens grasped Rembrandt by the shoulders in a gesture both tough and tender, then hugged him. This necessitated everything Rembrandt carried being rapidly passed to Titus before it was dropped.

'Lievens, we are going to our new home...' Rembrandt said. He could have been a decade older than Lievens, not a contemporary, he was so worn by life. 'Jan. Jan. What are you doing here?'

'I have heard all about it,' Jan Lievens said, his voice breaking with emotion. 'I have been away. But I am back now. Back, to find this city of ingrates using you so cruelly.'

'Ah, Jan.'

'Come old friend. *You* do not carry loads.' Lievens gently took all the art materials from Titus, who understood and let him do it. Even I was relieved of my small burdens. 'You... You are Rembrandt van Rijn, the towering genius of our age. And I, I am the workaday fellow who can reach a likeness. I am the painter lucky enough to have embraced the shoulder of greatness, when we were boys in Leiden. Come, my old friend. You do not carry the apparatus of art. I carry it for you. And I walk behind you.'

'You will come to my new home, Jan?'

Jan Lievens smiled. 'Yes. If you will do me the honour of admitting me. Yes, indeed.'

Sixteen

They cannot imagine an infinite fly, but they can imagine an infinite soul... This is madness.

Spinoza
Treatise on the Emendation of the Intellect

C *herem* time! Roll up, roll up. Let's all come and see the heretic expelled from the Jewish people.

You know what is engraved in stone over the entrance to the synagogue? 'In the greatness of your mercy I will come into your house' – *Be'-shanat ve'ani berov chasdecha abo beitecha lifek*, in Hebrew. But I wasn't really expecting much mercy. If any.

I stood in the synagogue on the sixth day of the holy month of Av, in the year 5416. The Jews are an ancient people; their – our – calendar is longer than anybody else's, so we had reached 5416 while the Gentiles were still lagging behind back in 1656.

The month of Av is holy for the usual reason that holiness is holy – because it is sad. In three days time it will be *Tisha B'Av*, the ninth of Av – the commemoration of the destruction of the Temple in Jerusalem. This was the day the Jews became a people without a place, a race forever teetering on exclusion and expulsion, forever being ejected – or worse.

The *Mishnah* says that on *Tisha B'Av* there were five calamities – which is a lot of calamities on one day, even for Jews. And my *cherem*, my excommunication from the Jewish people, was due to take effect – guess when? Yup! On *Tisha B'Av*. In three days time, I was due to become the sixth calamity.

The three day gap, for the procedurally minded, was because the *parnassim* had to ratify the *cherem*, which only they could actually issue, once Morteira had proclaimed it.

Not that it was all inevitable, cut and dried. Far from it. I knew Morteira still hoped I would recant, take the easy path. That's what he would have done; a politician to his fingertips, Morteira. He had to be.

If I publicly confessed my errors and sins, pretty much any errors and sins, and reaffirmed my Judaism, then any problem I posed would be an internal matter for the Jews. The Jews would have kept their part of the bargain and stayed Jews.

If I publicly re-entered the fold, in this way, I would not be excommunicated on *Tisha B'Av*. I would not go down in Jewish history as Baruch The Sixth Calamity. And – a bonus this – I would not be quietly murdered thereafter.

I would be free to resume my philosophy, in secret. Nods and winks. Do not antagonise... well, anyone. That was all it would take. A public confession of my errors and sins.

* * *

The synagogue on the Houtgracht was the second largest building I had ever been in, after the new Town Hall. I felt its size even more because I had shrunk to my childhood dimensions. I was five – and small for five; I grew tall at puberty. I was a child looking up at Morteira, who had remained physically unchanged over the years to an astonishing extent.

I stood on the *bimah* – the raised dais in the middle of the synagogue – in my least stained white linen collar, washed and starched by Hendrickje. Other than that I was all in black, including my leather waistcoat, except for my best camel hair cloak and tan gloves. I looked good, though I say it myself. I must have been the best-dressed heretic they had ever had.

The holy place still felt new and smelt new. The pervasive smell was the spruce wood from the *bimah*, the balcony and the area behind the ark and the rafters. And it *was* new, I suppose, by the standards of an ancient race. This synagogue had been built just seventeen years ago, when the original three synagogues amalgamated, amid much politicking. Morteira, naturally, came out on top; one of his rival rabbis decamped for Brazil, never to be seen again.

My eye kept flickering to the tombstone-like monument set into the brick wall. Gold lettering in Hebrew proclaimed great uncle Abraham to be one of the founders. I had imagined great uncle Abraham's arrival here – at the new Jerusalem on the Amstel – so often it was stamped into my mind. Even though great uncle Abraham had died years before I was born.

The Calvinists, of course, thought Amsterdam was the New Jerusalem, too. I wonder who thought of it first? The Jews probably. The Jews were always first. First to come up with the bizarre idea of a non-corporeal, invisible God, outside nature. Who would have thought that would catch on the way it has? How strange we creatures are…

But anyway… the congregation was packed like salt fish in a barrel. I hadn't seen so many people in one place since poor old Joris Fonteijn was dissected and his brain passed round the multitude. It dawned on me that people had turned out again to see the equivalent of what had happened to Joris. I was to be taken apart, in argument, and the bits scattered far and wide.

Up in the balcony, the women's section, I saw Morteira's wife and daughter having a good old chat. My sisters were next to them. Ribca was in deepest mourning; she always was well-prepared.

Miriam's husband, Samuel de Caseres, was squashed against a pillar downstairs, clutching at his hat, which kept falling off, waiting for someone to tell him what to think.

There was no sign of Gabriel.

The Alvarez brothers, presumably armed, were paying one of their rare visits to the synagogue. The last time they had appeared was at a fund-raising event. They had turned up with bodyguards and a bag of gold. The gold was literally dumped in

Morteira's lap with a low threatening 'That's from the Alvarez brothers. All right?' Then they lumbered off, bodyguards in tow.

And Morteira? Rabbi Chacham Saul Levi Morteira was standing in one of the pulpits, the one directly in front of the Ark of the Covenant, in which reposed the five Books of Moses, the *Torah* he was defending from the heretic. The Ark was always built facing east. So while the Ark faced Jerusalem, facing the lost Temple, facing the calamities, *I* was facing... O, I don't know. Oblivion?

Although I was on the raised *bimah*, Morteira was even higher, as curved stairs led to the pulpit. We were a good twenty feet from each other, so would have to shout, even if the congregation kept quiet – something Jewish congregations tend not to do. We were late starting, as usual and the congregation were making a racket.

How was Morteira going to start? Jewish ceremonies normally started with a prayer. But even in the extensive Jewish lore, I wasn't sure there was a prayer for the exclusion of heretics. In the event, he opened, low-key, with some questions designed to establish to what extent I was a Jew.

'*Mijnheer* Spinoza, do you keep the dietary laws?' he said, mildly, without preamble, as if we were chatting in his study. 'You are *nefesh ha-yafah*, are you not?'

The Talmudic phrase, meaning one who eats anything, was not meant as a compliment.

'Yes, I am *nefesh ha-yafah*.' If it doesn't actively fight back, I'll eat it. Pigs. Crabs. Dogs. 'It is irrelevant if we eat pork, and all the rest of it. Ritual acts as social glue. It is custom, Chacham Morteira, not divine decree.'

My lecture to the rabbi on God's meaning drew a gasp and indignant muttering from the onlookers.

'Do you attend the synagogue on the sabbath and on High Days and Holy Days?'

'How can I? I've been thrown out.'

'Answer!'

'No!'

'Did you before your exclusion from the synagogue?'

'No!'

I was getting bored. I hadn't prepared specifically for my cross-examination, I had been working on my philosophy; but I hoped Morteira would come in at a deeper level soon – make it more interesting. He did.

'Maimonides lists in the *Mishnah Torah* three types of those who say that the Law is not true.' Morteira indicated the law, in scrolls of the five books behind him, each sheathed in blue velvet cloth. 'There are those who say the *Torah* is not of divine origin. There are those who say Moses said it of himself. There are those who deny its interpretation, that is the oral law – the *Mishnah*. All three are cut off by their great wickedness and sinfulness, and are condemned for ever and ever. Which type are you?'

I sighed, somewhat theatrically, I'll admit. 'Those categories are not discrete.' Typical medieval thinking. Really woolly. Incidentally, do you know what Maimonides' book is called? *A Guide to the Perplexed*. I mean, what a lousy title!

'That is typical medieval thinking. Really—'

'Which?' Morteira screamed, pointing like Moses. The congregation were baying. I glanced up at the women. Morteira's daughter was crying.

'All three.'

'So you are not a Jew!' Morteira thundered.

'Not necessarily.' I had spoken without thinking.

'So you *are* a Jew?'

'Yes.' Morteira had outsmarted me; the teacher had bested the child. I had just re-entered Judaism.

'Why? If you deny the *Torah*?'

I shouted. 'Because I am a Jew in the eyes of my enemies.'

I was a Jew again. Re-Jewed. Foreskin re-peeled. Morteira thought he was home and dry. I caught that smug look, even at this distance, as his lips quivered under all that hair. He would now keep talking until we all got bored, then declare me a Jew. No *cherem*. No trouble. Everybody please go home.

'All Jews are sureties for each other, all of them like a single person with many limbs and organs. We may learn from the analogy of the body. We may learn a lesson from nature.' O very clever! You old goat! 'All the limbs and peripheral organs help to their utmost ability the inner organs, especially the heart, even if they may be damaged by doing so.'

'Just wait a minute—'

'For example, a person instinctively raises his hand and places it in front of the head to save it from injury. That is why my son, Baruch – I venture to call you my son.' You cunning old goat! 'We need you in the community just as you need us. A member of the community, my son. That is what you are, and should be.' Well, it was you who threw me out.

Morteira was positively radiating geniality. 'You are no Messiah, my boy! And I no Elijah!' That's *that* out of the way then.

'I never claimed to be a Messiah, Chacham.' It was that rat-infested painter, Ruisdael.

Morteira ignored me. 'Now, it often happens that because of the weakness of human reason,' Oy! 'a person will utter insolent words out of the anguish that he cannot bear and say things that are not right.'

'The soul dies along with the body,' I said.

I said it quietly, not everybody in the congregation heard me say it. And to this day I have no idea why I said it. Did I wish to hurt Morteira, as a man?

I went on: 'Whenever scripture speaks of the soul, the word soul is used simply to express life, or anything that is living. It would be useless to search for any passage in support of its immortality. As for the contrary view, it may be seen in a hundred places, and nothing is so easy as to prove it.'

Was I trying to kill Judaism? For centuries the immortality of the soul had become intertwined with two other beliefs, the truth of the *Torah* and the existence of God, until the three formed a solid rod to which the people held, as the *chachanim* – the wise men – led them blindly through life.

I went on: 'God exists only philosophically. The *Torah* is not true, not of divine origin and can be questioned. The soul is not immortal.'

Moses had laid down his life for these ideas. Maimonides, in the *Mishnah Torah*, had given them 'commentary' status since medieval times. Morteira's own life's work, accompanying his book on Moses, was a treatise passionately arguing the immortality of the soul. It was the heartbeat of his belief, and his belief was the heartbeat of his being, both as a public and private man. I had stabbed him in the heart, I knew I had. I was sorry for it.

Outwardly he did not change. 'He breathed into his nostrils a living soul,' he intoned.

That's the standard pro immortal soul quote, weak though it is. Genesis 2:7

'As Genesis tells us,' he said, hastily, before I could show off and give him the source. 'But as for the *minim* – ' That's heretics, in Hebrew. '– and the *aprikosim*,' scoffers, Greek. He yelled: 'They will go down to Gehinnom and be punished there for all generations.'

Morteira glanced at one of the *parnassim*, Joseph de Azevedo, who was taking notes. It was his last despairing hope. Azevedo shrugged and gave a half-apologetic nod at what he had written. What I had said had been recorded. It was among The Words.

The greatest heresy and simultaneously the greatest threat to Jews everywhere: I had said the soul dies with the body; everybody's soul, everybody's body. Jewish souls, Jewish bodies, along with everybody else. Just like everybody else.

One more word emerged from Morteira, almost a howl: 'Why?'

* * *

Of course there was a rearguard action. Morteira was a fighter to the core; he had fought with his fists in the Venice ghetto of his childhood. He had had to.

'We cannot return to the lands of idolatry,' he said, as if speaking to a child. He meant Spain and Portugal. 'This, the New Jerusalem, is our home now. We cannot be expelled again. Exile – *galut* – is a kind of death. But the danger is that, owing to the length of time in exile, we would forget our early history, our precious pedigree, our noble character—' (That's *meyuhas*, in Hebrew. A word meaning noble but applied uniquely to the Jewish people.) Morteira was playing to the gallery, literally: most of the women were now in tears.

'—and above all, our exalted God. In this way, false beliefs could be rampant among our people. They might deny their *Torah* by doubting their origins and many other similar errors that they would learn from Gentiles, in whose midst they were exiled. And so I shall remove the spirit of impurity from the land.'

'Zechariah 13:2, that last bit,' I said.

Morteira muttered something under his breath. It sounded like 'clever little devil'.

Preparations had obviously been made in advance. *Parnass* Joseph de Azevedo, no longer required to take notes, dramatically drew back the velvet curtains of the Ark of the Covenant and opened the spruce-wood doors. The five books of the *Torah*, each scroll in its velvet jacket with silver breastplate, ornate bells and pointer, appeared in silent reproach at my rejection of them.

Ushers were already distributing black candles among the congregation. There was a pause while they were lit. I looked round at every person there. Not one of them met my gaze. The huge place was silent.

And Morteira... Morteira was apotheosised. The congregation hushed on an intake of breath as he raised his arms, seeming to grow to twice his previous size, more than ever an incarnation of the outraged Moses, whose engraved instructions from above had been so wantonly disregarded. He fixed me with flaming wounded eyes. My own eyes fell from his gaze in mute apology.

But then I raised my head again. 'Do you want me to help you with the form of the *cherem*, Chacham Morteira?' I called out, brightly.

His look could have smitten a whole tribe of sinners 'The Lords of the *Ma'amad*—' thundered the sage. The *Ma'amad* is six *parnassim* plus the *gabbai* or treasurer. '—having long known the evil opinions of Baruch de Spinoza, have endeavoured by various means and promises, to turn him from his evil ways.'

True! True! Nobody can say you didn't try. Let's see... There was bribery, expulsion from the synagogue, kidnapping and mental torture. You gave it a go, Rabbi Morteira. You really did.

'But having failed to make him mend his wicked ways, having daily received more and more serious information about his abominable heresies and monstrous deeds...'

Oh, look I'm not all that bad! Come on! Ribca likes me. And... There must be somebody else? Yes, Rembrandt and Titus and Hendrickje. And Clara Maria.

I'd missed a bit, wool-gathering.

'By the decree of the angels.' Oh, don't make me laugh! 'and by the command of the holy men, we excommunicate, expel, curse and damn Baruch de Espinoza. Cursed be he by day and cursed be he by night; cursed be he when he lies down and cursed be he when he rises up. Cursed be he when he goes out and cursed be he when he comes in. The Lord shall not spare him.'

Fair enough.

'No one shall communicate with him, neither in writing nor accord him any favour nor stay with him under the same roof nor within four cubits in his vicinity; nor shall be read any treatise composed or written by him.' Morteira glared at me. 'Have you anything to say?'

That was a mistake. 'Since you want it that way,' I said. 'I enter gladly on the path that is opened to me, with the consolation that my departure will be more innocent than was the exodus of the early Hebrews from Egypt.'

Uproar. The place exploded. Everybody was shouting and screaming. Cushions were thrown at me, books were thrown at me. I dodged them all easily enough.

I was no longer a Jew. Un-Jewed? De-Jewed? At any rate, I was an ex Jew. I felt excitement prick the pit of my stomach. If I was no longer a Jew, I could marry Clara Maria.

Cast out from the outcasts, excluded by the excluded, excoriated by the most reviled people the world has ever seen. And how did I feel? The word ecstasy comes from the Greek, to stand outside of. I'll tell you how I felt. Ecstatic.

I made my way in a blind daze from the synagogue. Fortunately, the congregation made no attempt to lay me on the floor and tread on me, as they had with Uriel de Costa, my immediate predecessor in exclusion by *cherem*. But then da Costa was barking mad – I was merely a threat to the Jewish nation's survival in the New Jerusalem.

I stepped out into the sunshine on the Houtgracht, the most familiar street in the world to me, the street where I had been born. My head was empty at that moment – a rarity for me. My body and soul were blank, ready for the rest of my life as a non-Jew. A man without a religion is like a man without a country, a citizen of time and space.

I swear to you I had completely forgotten the threats to my life both from the Alvarez brothers and from Morteira, via this unknown foreign assassin. That is until I was seized from behind and a cloth thrown over me.

As you will perhaps recall, I am no stranger to this experience: I relaxed my body to minimise bruising, something I had picked up the last time I was seized from behind and a cloth thrown over me.

The cloth was wound round me, which must have made me look like one of the scrolls of the *Torah* I had just rejected. I heard a familiar voice. It belonged, I was pretty certain, to Pieter, the only one of Titus's ragamuffins I knew by name.

No doubt the ragamuffins had been instructed to keep me safe until the play performance this evening. I could think of more comfortable ways of accomplishing this, but then one's destiny is a thing of patterns, is it not? I am sure you can recall incidents and types of circumstance that have recurred in your life. Well, with me it's having a cloth thrown over my head and being bundled onto a cart.

Anyway, this time there was a variant. No sooner was I wrapped in a light linen cloth – suitable for the summer? – and swung off my feet than I was dropped painfully on the Houtgracht again. There were loud voices around me, clearly a ruckus.

With some difficulty, I sat up and began to struggle out of my cloth. I realised that the cloth I was removing was a plague shroud. I found myself sitting between the front wheels of one of the parish biers the city had taken to using for removing the bodies of plague victims. They had no sides at all, consisting merely of slats over the frame of the cart, the better to toss bodies on with ease.

As I registered this, I also became aware of a vigorous fight going on around me, with my person the *causus belli*. Pieter was accompanied by only two of the band of ragamuffins, albeit a pair of older and brawnier specimens. Clearly three people had been thought sufficient – or perhaps standard – for tossing bound ex-Jewish heretics onto carts. Anyway, three there were; and no sign of Titus.

There were, fortunately (I nearly wrote 'Thank God' but having got into all this trouble for, in effect, denying His existence, to take His name in vain would be rather adding insult to injury.) Where was I? Oh yes, there were fortunately only two Alvarez brothers, but they were experienced and ruthless fighters. Moreover, they were armed; they had daggers. The ragamuffins had no weapons at all.

However, they were nothing if not resourceful. Pieter had seized a branch from somewhere, presumably from the ditch. Calling to one of his companions to come with him, he circled behind the two Alvarez brothers, while the third ragamuffin faced them. By this means the ragamuffins took maximum advantage of their extra man.

Adriaen Alvarez, the older one, launched himself at the isolated ragamuffin, managing to slash his arm with his dagger. The ragamuffin screamed. But Pieter smashed the branch against the younger Alvarez's head, while the other ragamuffin seized his knife arm. As the younger Alvarez staggered, Pieter pressed home his advantage, seizing the dagger and turning it on Abraham Alvarez, who fell, wounded in the stomach.

The older Alvarez was faring better against the lone ragamuffin, inflicting another slash to the arm and a punch in the face before the ragamuffin's two allies came to his assistance. By now, I had staggered to my feet and proffered help: 'Er, is there anything I can do?' I said. The older Alvarez had his back to me. After some thought, I decided to kick him up the backside. This distracted and annoyed him long enough for the two unwounded ragamuffins to set about him with their fists.

Adriaen Alvarez backed away, making extravagant passes with his dagger. He stood over the motionless body of his younger brother, lying bleeding on the ground.

Pieter was wheezing and breathless. 'Come on,' he gasped. 'Out of here.'

The other two helped the wounded ragamuffin up onto the bier first. Then they picked up my shroud and started to put me in it.

'Is this entirely necessary?' I protested. 'I'll just get up on the bier. And then—'

Pieter shook his head. 'Nobody is to know where you are,' he said, still breathing heavily. 'We don't want Morteira's assassin to see you.'

I was therefore re-wrapped in the plague shroud and thrown up onto the plague bier, where I landed painfully on the wounded ragamuffin, making us both scream. Adriaen Alvarez, meanwhile, was kneeling over the still motionless form of his younger brother, yelling imprecations at me.

'I'll get you, Spinoza,' he shouted. 'Consider yourself dead!'

That was the last I heard before the bier set off, pulled by a solitary spavined nag, whose fate at the Vlooien Island glue works was surely only days away. The crude bier, moreover, had no springs, being merely slats on an oak frame. The ride was unbelievably bumpy, throwing me into the air, then painfully down, as we hit ruts and cobblestones. The groaning ragamuffin, naturally, was faring no better.

For some reason, Pieter and his companion had not only bound me tight in my plague shroud, they had tied me with rope, too. Eventually, I managed to push my face free to gasp in some air, or I may well have suffocated. However, such was the continuing steep rise and fall of the ride, that I vomited copiously all over my shroud, liberally splashing my companion, the semi-conscious wounded ragamuffin.

The groaning ragamuffin and myself, both liberally soaked in my vomit, were finally unloaded at Rembrandt's new abode in the Rozengracht. But even as we stood shakily upright, holding onto the struts of the plague bier, a further complication ensued. My estimation of the spavined nag's life span before the final journey to the glue factory had proved over-optimistic: it died between the shafts with a windy sigh, lying splayed out dead on the ground.

Fortunately, Titus appeared at the door of the attractive, though tiny, stone cottage. At a glance, he took in a scene comprising expired spavined nag; slashed and bleeding ragamuffin covered in vomit; reviled heretic philosopher struggling free of a plague shroud, likewise liberally anointed with sick.

Titus, naturally, took charge. Within minutes I found myself naked in a tub of hot water in the kitchen, while Hendrickje tenderly soaped me with a sponge. I must report, in all truth, that this was among the most pleasurable experiences ever to have befallen me. I never did find out what happened to the wounded ragamuffin, the dead horse or the shroud and plague bier. And frankly, I did not care.

Rembrandt, I was told, was already painting in a small but light and north-facing room, earmarked as his studio. He appeared briefly, paintbrush in hand. He greeted me, scooping suds from the surface of the tub to make my tumescent state obvious to Hendrickje and Titus. He then roared with laughter, clapped me painfully on the shoulder and left again. Titus gave a brief smile at his father's performance, before resuming his earnest attempts to dissuade me from appearing in the play later that evening.

'A hothead like Adriaen Alvarez will undoubtedly try and kill you, in revenge for what's happened to his brother.'

'He was trying to kill me anyway.'

'And then there's Morteira's assassin.'

'Keep still!' This from Hendrickje. 'Would you like me to wash between your legs?'

'I... er... um. Oh, you're laughing at me!'

'Just a little!' She kissed the top of my head.

'We think Morteira's assassin will try and kill you tonight. Before you have a chance to leave Amsterdam. You *are* leaving, aren't you?'

'Oh yes. I have lodgings arranged. In a place called Rijnsburg, in the house of a painter by the name of van der Spyk.'

'You're being very brave, Baruch.'

'No, not really.' I tilted my head back. 'Hendrickje, that offer to wash between my legs... That is, if you don't mind.' Titus and Hendrickje laughed. Hendrickje obliged. 'I have to go tonight, Titus. The play. I can't let them down.'

'You mean you want to see Clara,' Hendrickje said.

I looked up at her. 'Yes. I shall ask her to marry me and come and live with me in Rijnsburg. Well, I shall ask her if she is pure first, or whether Theodor Kerckrinck's account of her is true. I mean about her being his whore, and mad for sex with him.'

'Baruch,' Hendrickje said. 'If I may give some advice: if I were you, I'd just do the proposal. Not the other bit.'

'You think so?'

'Most definitely!'

Seventeen

*I do not differentiate between God and Nature, in the way all
those known to me have done... Man, as long as he is part of
Nature, must follow the laws of Nature. That is true religion.*

Spinoza
Theological Political Treatise

The Schouwburg was packed for the performance of the
play. Every seat was sold; standing groundlings swelled the
space at the back and the aisles. Titus was out there somewhere,
and a goodly sprinkling of his ragamuffins, too. But I wasn't
thinking of them, or of death at the hands of those trying to kill
me. I was concerned about fluffing my lines and quaking about
my imminent proposal of marriage to Clara Maria.

My future wife was applying my make-up: the pink-face to
my features, then rouge. Then my blonde wig of coarse horse
hair, upon which rested my bonnet. Finally, the bags of rice were
dropped into pockets created for them in the shift. And a fine
and buxom peasant lady I made, too!

And so, with the Rembrandt triptych as my backdrop, I
finally seized Baucis's besom broom and stepped out onto the
stage. By the light of the lanterns placed in rows as footlights
and the burning torches in sconces on the walls, I could see the
audience more clearly than I had expected to.

I saw Titus, in his disguise. I thought I caught a glimpse of
Pieter, the senior ragamuffin, standing at the back. Rembrandt
and Hendrickje had stayed at home with my blessing, having

only just moved into their new cottage. And anyway, Titus had warned them of the dangers, saying he didn't want too many people to protect.

And then I began. My first lines, as an actor! I loved it out there, as Baucis. The packed crowd were all yelling, fighting, drinking, carousing... Having a high old time. The reaction to my entrance intensified the din, adding whistles and bawdy remarks and invitations. I swished my skirt, waved my broom, pouted at them, played to the gallery, just as Morteira had during my *cherem*. I remembered the Purim plays I had seen as a child. I always imagined I was playing Haman. I love theatre.

I yelled my opening speech boldly into the darkness, proud of my command of Latin, with Clara Maria's help. This, in translation, is what van den Enden had written for me to say:

Here we dwell, in this forest, in this house. (I waved at Rembrandt's painting of the cottage)

I, ancient Baucis: (I pointed to myself)

Philemon, my even more ancient spouse. (The malodorous painter took a bow)

He tills the soil (The smelly object mimed tilling)

I sweep the floor. (I vigorously swept at the stage with my besom broom, to rapturous applause)

But hark! (I cupped a hand to my ear) *What's that?* (Off stage van den Enden rapped on a panel of wood with his knuckles, but then panicked in case nobody could hear it above the din. He brought the panel on to the stage, and kicked at it. This brought even more rapturous applause and some catcalls. Van den Enden went off again.)

A knock at the door!

Our audience was enthralled thereafter by the unfolding tale – the visit of the gods, the miracle of the replenishing food. But then came the time for Ruisdael and I to be turned into trees. At this point, Ruisdael was supposed to kiss me.

I could see his evil designs in his mad gleaming eyes. At first I tried to hide behind the gods – van den Enden and Kerckrinck.

But when he flushed me out from there, I darted behind the table.

Ruisdael prowled after me. At some stage I had dropped my broom. The audience, quickly seeing what was afoot, howled their pleasure and started cheering, most of them for Ruisdael, wishing him to have his wicked way, but a few for me. I distinctly saw money change hands, as some enterprising groundlings started taking bets on whether Ruisdael would defile me or not.

I was sure, with hindsight, that I could have evaded Ruisdael, had van den Enden, apparently in the interests of the purity of his script, not come to the painter's aid.

'Spinoza! Keep still, you slippery Jew!'

Van den Enden circled the table after me, with Ruisdael coming from the other direction. With the crowd on their feet, roaring one or other of us on, I hitched up my skirts, feinted to dodge toward Ruisdael but went the other way, pushing van den Enden off balance.

Van den Enden fell against the table, knocking some of the miraculous meal onto the floor, breaking the clay pot which was supposed to contain the food for the Gods. 'Grab him!' our author and stage-manager shouted as he slithered to the floor. 'Kerckrinck! Seize him! Hold him! That kiss is in the script!'

Mercury, the descendant of Atlas, bore down on me.

I lost my head, I admit it. 'You've still got my microscope, you bastard!' I yelled at the top of my voice at Mercury, the descendant of Atlas. Then I kicked him in the shins.

Those at the front of the audience were delightedly repeating my aside to those behind, who had missed it. Ripples of laughter spread among the general din as more and more people were told of it.

After that, events moved rather quickly. Ruisdael seized me from behind and with surprising force, no doubt born of powerful suppressed desire – though of what exactly I shudder to think – he spun me round.

Catching me by the shoulders, he pulled me forward into the kiss he so fervently wished. His fetid breath assailed me, his mouth closed over mine, his rotting dental configuration was at one with my mouth. The audience was convulsed with stamping cheering pleasure, excepting only those who had bet on my escaping Philemon's clutches. Some of these were gloomily paying up on their losing bets.

As I retched and heaved in this foul embrace, Ruisdael broke his hold, jumping back with a scream of alarm. My wig was askew; the lunatic appeared to recognise me for the first time.

'That's the Jew Spinoza!' he screamed. 'I saw him in a vision! But he is not the Messiah!'

'I never said I—'

'I was deceived! He is the False Messiah ! He is the Antichrist! Seize him!'

The audience reacted to this by baying for my blood. I glimpsed Clara Maria at the back of the theatre. She was making her way to the door, with a dreamy intense expression on her face – an expression I knew well.

Some of the groundlings were on the stage, coming after me – the Antichrist. Hatred was in their hearts; they were bent on religious revenge. Pushing Ruisdael aside, I evaded my pursuers, jumped down from the stage, pushed my wig back on, and battled my way through the audience in pursuit of my beloved.

I had seen what she had in her hand – a small, shaped china chamber pot. She had withdrawn it from her hand-muff; the light gleamed on it briefly, as she left the auditorium and went outside.

As I pushed my way through, many of the screaming crowd grabbed at me. At the back, I caught a glimpse of Adriaen Alvarez, heaving his way toward me. I could see the dagger at his belt. I ignored him, continuing to elbow and thrust my way through the multitude, my eyes on the door through which Clara Maria had disappeared.

Leaning against the wall, near the door, shrouded in the gloom, I glimpsed a well-made, sinister figure in a short cloak, with buckles on his shoes. At his waist, clearly visible, was a poignard with a jewelled hilt. The last time I had seen him, I was eight years old.

He was Jacob Monsanto, greying a little now at the temples. Jacob Monsanto, who was brought in from Portugal whenever Morteira needed dirty work doing. He had last appeared after the *cherem* against Uriel da Costa. They had put it about that da Costa had committed suicide, but I knew better.

'Are you looking for Baruch Spinoza?' I said, in Portuguese.

Monsanto looked startled, as well he might. My blonde wig was awry, my pink-face was running down my cheeks, my bags-of-rice breasts were lopsided. Even so, I guessed from the strength of his amazement that he had just come in. He had not seen the play.

He hesitated, then said 'Yes,' also in Portuguese.

'Do you know what Spinoza looks like?'

Monsanto hesitated again. 'I was told that he was tall and dark, olive skinned.'

I nodded, relieved I was in my disguise. 'Dark,' I said urgently, still in Portuguese. 'But not so very tall. Come with me. I will point him out to you.'

Monsanto nodded and followed me. As we reached the door, I caught a glimpse of Titus and Pieter, furiously trying to barge their way through the thickest of the crowd. The audience was by now in an ugly mood at the interruption to the play; fights were breaking out everywhere.

Titus and Pieter were caught up in the fighting. Above the din, remarkably piercing, I could still hear the mad painter Ruisdael denouncing the Jews, and me in particular, for the suffering and death of Christ. I lost sight of Monsanto.

I finally flung open the door and was out into the night air. There were some bushes near the side of the building. I heard a stirring. I rushed behind the bushes, aware of chasing footsteps behind me.

Clara Maria was squatting, the pisspot obviously being utilised, as I could clearly hear. I called her name. She screamed.

'Do not be alarmed, my darling,' I called. 'I have studied the subject intensely. I need only the smallest sample, for analysis, then we can be married and go to Rijnsburg together.'

I gently took her by both elbows and tried to lift her. She screamed again. 'Stop it! Stop it! I haven't finished!'

'Never mind,' I said, lovingly, seizing the pisspot. 'Oh dear! No, you hadn't finished, had you?'

'Are you mad! How dare you? What are you doing?'

Clara Maria furiously smoothed her skirts down.

'Be calm my darling!'

'Be calm? I'm soaked!'

I swilled the liquid in the pot, for all the world like an experienced *piskijker*. Fortunately, there was a full moon. I had a good view of the suspension, the surface scum, the deposits. None of the changes described by Tulp which occur after loss of virtue were present. I didn't really need to taste Clara Maria's urine, but I did, with a happy heart.

Clara Mara screamed again. 'Bento! What are you doing?'

'Clara Maria, will you marry me?'

At that moment, I was felled by a blow to the jaw, knocking the pisspot from my hands, all over Clara Maria

I was unconscious for a second, but came round to find Kerckrinck, every inch the martial Mercury, his armour glinting in the moonlight, standing over me. He began to beat me with the rod of Hermes. It was as if I had offended the ancient gods, too. Was there no belief or creed I was not to fall foul of? My future wife, I noticed with a touch of bitterness, made no attempt to stop Mercury lambasting me.

'You foul unnatural creature,' Kerckrinck yelled.

I rolled clear and stood, uncertainly, only to be felled again by another punch to the jaw, very close to the last one. As I went down, I noticed Adriaen Alvarez, standing over me.

'My brother's at death's door,' Alvarez shouted. 'And it's all your fault. Stand up. Stand up like a man, so I can kill you.'

Clara Maria screamed. Kerckrinck looked uncertain. I staggered to my feet. Alvarez drew his dagger.

I pointed to Alvarez with finger extended at the end of a shaking arm. 'In the name of Chacham Morteira and the Jewish people of Amsterdam,' I yelled. 'I declare that the heretic Baruch Spinoza must die!'

I must say, I still had no idea where Monsanto was at this point. I was just hoping for the best. I caught a glimpse of Kerckrinck with his arm round Clara Maria, comforting her. Then he started kissing her, his mouth locked on hers as firmly as Ruisdael's had been on mine. They were oblivious to the world, certainly oblivious to me. Kerckrinck turned her round; he now had his back to me.

My speech demanding my own death had confused Alvarez, who was none too bright at the best of times. His jawed dropped, he stared at me.

'Hang on!' he said, perspicaciously. '*You* are—'

'Spinoza!' I yelled, pointing accusingly at him. 'There, you admit it!'

The assassin finally appeared, having no doubt fought his way through the crowd in the theatre. He pushed aside his absurd short cloak, grasping his poignard.

'There he is!' I bellowed, making it as clear as I possibly could. 'SPIN-O-ZA!'

Monsanto finally got the message, running Adriaen Alvarez through with one smooth stroke to the heart. I do believe he was dead before he hit the ground. That's what you pay for, I suppose, in a professional assassin. Quality. A thoroughly neat job. At any rate, Monsanto was gone in a flash, melting away into the bushes. I bent over my sometime consortium partner, the thug Alvarez, confirming to myself that he was dead.

As I did so, Kerckrinck finally desisted from his ministrations on Clara Maria's person and turned round. His attentions had left her upper clothing somewhat disarranged. Kerckrinck had clearly bested me in love. Well then, I was more determined than ever to get my microscope back.

'Kerckrinck!' My challenge rang out, Mercury-descendant-of-Atlas or no Mercury-descendant-of-bloody-Atlas. 'You will give me my microscope back forthwith.'

Kerckrinck, rather rudely I thought, completely ignored what I had said and pointed to Alvarez lying dead in a pool of blood on the grass.

'You have murdered him!' Kerckrinck cried.

'If that's your level of observational skill,' I riposted, 'you can definitely give me my microscope back. It's wasted on you.'

Kerckrinck took a step back. 'Spinoza has murdered a man!' he cried. He ran back toward the theatre door, shouting 'Spinoza has murdered a man, come and see. Outside on the grass.'

Clara Maria limped after him, hastily doing up the rather fetching little pearl buttons down the front of her dress. I shook my head at the follies of mankind. Following slowly in order to explain Kerckrinck's mistake, based on poor initial observational data, I was knocked unconscious by another blow to the point of the jaw.

I came round to find Tulp's coachman standing over me. This was the ugly swart one. The one who had spied on the Waterlanders. The one who tried to whip me at van den Enden's. The one who had been involved in Tulp's attempt to destroy some of Rembrandt's paintings, when Titus and the ragamuffins had beaten him off.

'You are the ugly swart coachman,' I informed him. I admit an element of redundancy in this, but then I *had* just been hit on the point of the jaw for the third time. 'What do you want?'

'What do I want?' The ugly swart coachman threw my words back at me bitterly. 'What do I want?'

'The issue does not become any clearer by meaningless repetition,' I said a shade testily, getting to my feet. 'I suggest you— '

'Shut up! I lost my job because of you. Tulp sacked me. He thinks I betrayed him for money. I never did. I was the most loyal servant any man ever had.'

'You have my—'

'Shut up! It's all your fault.'

'*My* fault?'

'You people come here from Portugal and we all lose our jobs.'

'What?'

'Do you know what percentage of philosophers are Jews? Forty-five percent. Tulp himself told me. It's gone too far. There ought to be a quota. Decent Christian philosophers are being driven out.'

'But you're not a philosopher. You're a coachman.'

'Same thing.'

'That is a highly contentious statement. One sits on a coachbox with—'

'Shut up! I mean it's the same principle, you idiot. Enough of your Jew casuistry.'

'Are you sure you are using that term—'

'Shut up! I've come here to kill you and I can't get a bloody word in edgeways.'

Tulp's coachman pulled a knife.

'Here we go again.'

'Die Jew!'

As he lunged at me, a wave of sound spilled from the suddenly-opened door to the theatre. Titus flew out and threw himself full length at the coachman, knocking him off his feet. Pieter was not far behind. He seized the knife from where it had fallen in the grass and waved it at the coachman. The coachman picked himself up and ran off into the darkness.

People were pouring out of the theatre. The entire audience, it appeared, was on the move and coming after me. I realised that one of my bags of rice had come adrift altogether. It was on the grass. I fished the other one out of my shift and, after a second's hesitation, threw it at the mob as they ran toward me.

I could hear screams of 'Murderer! Murderer!'

Someone shouted out a recommendation to get me away from the corpse before I drank its blood. I heard one voice in the crowd accuse me of swindling him out of two *penningen* when I bought beer in his tavern. Another was screaming that I had killed Christ. Another that I was pretending to *be* Christ.

Van den Enden, now suddenly clear again, bawled out that I had deliberately sabotaged his play, as part of a Jewish plot against the state. Kerckrinck bellowed that the lens in the microscope I had lent him was scratched. Also that I was a pervert, attempting to defile Christian women. There was a mention of poisoning wells, and I'm sure eating Christian children on unleavened bread was referred to as well.

Just one voice was shouting 'Leave him alone!' I will always love Clara Maria for that.

'Kill him! Kill him! Kill the Jew!'

I turned to face them. 'Actually, I haven't been a Jew for nearly—'

'Come on!' Titus yelled.

He and Pieter seized me and ran along with me to a gate in the wall of the grounds. There, the rest of the ragamuffins were waiting, with a cart. Pieter and Titus threw a cloth over me and threw me on the back of the cart. Then they ran to the front, jumped up, whipped up the horse and drove away, leaving the crowd baying for blood in our wake.

Later I asked Titus why he had stopped to throw the cloth over my head.

'Force of habit,' he said

Eighteen

*Love (amor) is pleasure accompanied
by the idea of an external cause.*

Spinoza
Ethics

Nobody knew where Rembrandt had moved to, or if they
did, they decided to leave us alone. When Titus and Pieter
brought me in, undamaged but just a little weary from being
repeatedly knocked to the ground, Rembrandt insisted on an
impromptu party. Beer appeared, and of course herring and
Leiden cheese. Pieter plucked away on the *vihuela*; Hendrickje
taught me to dance.

Titus asked me who else I wanted at what he was calling my
'farewell to Amsterdam.'

I asked for Ribca, who had always loved me.

'Leave it to me,' Titus said.

He had stripped off his disguise, seeming indefatigable.
Before he left, he and some of his ragamuffins checked the
area outside, proclaiming it 'safe for now, at least.' But Titus
remained concerned that Morteira's assassin might discover his
mistake. He gently insisted I was not safe. We must make an
early start away from Amsterdam in the morning. Titus and
his guard of ragamuffins were to drive me to Rijnsburg, where
I would continue writing my philosophy.

Hendrickje and Rembrandt and I were dancing and drinking
away when Titus returned, leading Ribca in. Ribca cried. He

then went outside again, saying 'I have another guest for you, Baruch.'

Clara Maria, looking pale, in the same dress she had worn in the theatre, came shyly into the room.

I broke off dancing. 'Oh! Does this mean…?'

'No, Bento,' she said, with that familiar firmness. 'Titus has told me what you want of me, and it is more than I can give. But you are the most remarkable man I have ever met.' She smiled, but she was crying a little, too. 'I want us to be friends, Bento. Will you… allow?'

'Yes! Yes, of course!'

'Will you write to me from Rijnsburg? Titus has explained your plans to me, you see.'

'I would love to. I will outline my ideas! I will tell you of my days! I will ask for your news!'

'I would like that very much. And there is one thing more I have to tell you.'

'Yes, my—. Yes, Clara Maria.'

'I have broken my engagement to Theodor.' She took a handkerchief from her sleeve and dabbed at her eyes. 'Know this, Bento,' she said, the firmness back. 'I do love you, in my way.'

'As does everyone in this room,' Rembrandt roared.

'Yes,' Clara Maria said. 'And I cannot contemplate marriage with a man who could use you in the way he has.'

'I just want you to be happy,' I said.

'I know you do. I have brought you a gift.'

One of the ragamuffins had been holding it, I now noticed. He handed it to Clara Maria, who passed it to me. It was my microscope.

I took it from her reverently. 'Thank you. Thank you my dear Clara Maria. I shall make every endeavour to do good work with this microscope. To see better, as my dear friend Rembrandt does, in his way.' Rembrandt bowed. 'And what I see, what I discover, is dedicated to you, Clara Maria, because no man can walk his path alone.'

Clara Maria nodded solemnly. 'Thank you, Bento.'

As I was about to take her hand – it would have been the first time I had touched her skin – there was a thunderous knock at the door. I jumped back. We all looked at each other, in watchful silence.

'I'll go,' said Jan Lievens, Rembrandt's old friend from Leiden. I hadn't noticed he was there.

'No, let me,' Titus said, grimly. He motioned Pieter and another ragamuffin to go with him. A moment later we heard the door opening, then a rumbling noise, like thunder on a distant hill.

'What's this then? All the heretics together? The small heretic Rembrandt; the big heretic Spinoza.'

Rabbi Chacham Saul Levi Morteira had not so much entered the room as picked it up and put it round him, as if it were an alternative rabbinical gown. Titus and the ragamuffins came in behind him, but after that nobody moved. Nobody breathed, such was the utter dominance of Saul Levi Morteira. It was as if God Himself had dropped in unannounced. Although unlike God, in any scripture known to me, he was carrying a rectangular parcel wrapped in mort cloth – usually used for burials – done up with string.

Morteira underlined his power with a massive pause, while we all waited for him to continue. He peered round the room, a room which mysteriously looked smaller than he did, even though he was in it.

Finally, a boom: 'Rembrandt van Rijn! I owe you fifty guilders for the portrait you painted of me. I ask your forgiveness for my tardiness in paying.' Putting the parcel down on a side-table, the rabbi cast aside some of the folds of his gown, like Moses parting the Red Sea while up to his waist in it. He drew out a leather purse with a drawstring, holding it out to the painter. 'The money's in there. All of it. Count it.'

Rembrandt didn't move, ignoring the proffered purse. Even he looked frail beside Morteira. 'I no longer have the—'

'I know you no longer have the painting. I have it. I obtained it from the *Desolate Boedelskamer.*'

'You said it was not a good likeness.' Rembrandt spoke bitterly.

'I have to say all sorts of things, in line with the policy of the day. But policies change.'

I met Titus's gaze, both of us giving faint shrugs of incomprehension at this enigmatic statement, both looking forward to an eventual decoding. Morteira forced the purse into Rembrandt's hand. Rembrandt did not resist.

'Right!' Morteira rubbed his hands together as if rinsing them clean in a running stream. 'Small heretic dealt with, now the big heretic.'

I stepped forward. Just as Morteira started to speak, I seized both his cheeks in two pincer grips with crab-claws made of my middle and index fingers. Morteira gasped.

'Ugh! Ugh!' He tried to say my name, but with both cheeks in a vice, an experience I remembered well from my childhood, all he could bring out was 'Brooch. Brooch.'

The gathering was laughing, especially Titus, the ragamuffins and Jan Lievens.

Rembrandt raised a smile, as did Clara Maria. Hendrickje looked scared.

'You tried to have me killed. You bastard.'

Morteira spluttered and waved his arms, fluttering his rabbinic gown. I let go of his cheeks, so he could reply. 'No, I didn't,' he finally brought out, pausing to rub his bruised face. 'You are quite right not to rely on empirical evidence, as the starting point of your philosophy,' he said huffily, recovering somewhat. 'The evidence of the senses often deceives. Especially what uneducated maids hear, when they listen at the door.'

'Explain,' Titus said softly, at this impugning of his intelligence gathering.

Morteira stared only at me. 'There was a discussion, at my house, about having you killed.'

'As you did with the last heretic, Uriel da Costa '

'No! He committed suicide.'

'So Jacob Monsanto didn't stab him?'

'No! Where did you get that from? Monsanto may have been over here at the time. He's a member of a dance troupe. They give performances all over the world.'

'A dance troupe? He's a professional assassin!'

'The two are not mutually exclusive!' Morteira shouted, putting his face close to mine. 'Who said assassins can't dance? Do I have to lecture you about categorisation theory? You're the logician, *Mijnheer Spinozie*. I'm just an ill-educated mystic Ashkenazi rabbi!'

'But you brought Monsanto over this—'

'Will you shut up, boy!' For some reason the whole room was laughing, including Hendrickje now. 'Will you just shut up for two minutes, and I'll tell you what happened.'

'Let him talk, Baruch.' Titus spoke through his laughter.

'I shan't say another word.' I put my hand over my mouth, like a child.

'Keep it there!' Morteira nodded at my hand. 'I argued against bringing Monsanto over to have you killed. I fought it tooth and nail. I even thought I had won. But they deceived me, pretended to agree with me, went behind my back.'

'You mean, *you*—' I spoke through my hand.

'Shut up, Baruch! I found out only this evening that Monsanto was in Amsterdam. I went to the theatre, but the place was in uproar. I... made some arrangements, then came here, trying to find you. Monsanto is on his way home. Back to Portugal. He thinks he has killed you. You are safe now.'

'I believe you,' I said. 'But if you didn't hire Monsanto to kill me, who did?'

Morteira shrugged heavily, not meeting my gaze. 'It doesn't matter.'

I took a deep breath. 'It was Gabriel, wasn't it?'

Morteira hesitated, then: 'Yes.'

Ribca howled in anguish. Clara Maria moved softly next to me and held my hand. It was the act of kindness that has meant the most to me in my life to date.

I was breathing heavily. 'Oh well... I blame the Bible, you know. That Cain and Abel story. It's done nothing at all for family harmony.'

Rembrandt came to stand the other side of me. He delivered a massive lovingly-consolatory wallop to my ribcage, which doubled me up. I straightened, coughing, to find Morteira had taken his parcel from the side-table and was offering it to me.

'What is it?' But of course I knew.

'Open it.'

I tore the string and mort cloth away. The manuscript of my *Ethics Demonstrated in Geometrical Order*, which Morteira had had Miguel da Silva steal from my room, stared up at me.

'Why?'

Morteira shrugged. 'Why not? You could replicate it anyway. And you are leaving Amsterdam, which means you will be forgotten. And...'

'And?'

'A son is always a son, no matter what he does. Only a fool tries to change love.'

I passed the manuscript to one of the ragamuffins, launching myself at Saul Levi Morteira, throwing my arms round him. 'I've always loved you. I'm so sorry I couldn't...'

'I love you, too, Baruch. I love you, too.'

He was stroking the back of my head; I was clasping him as hard as I could.

'These Jews!' Rembrandt shouted. 'So emotional! Floods of it! It's wonderful. You put a dam on it in one place, it breaks out in another! If it's not floods, it's fire! Raw elements, the lot of them.'

I felt Morteira shaking in my arms. 'Are you crying, you moth-eaten old Ashkenaz?' I held him at arm's length. Then I could see he wasn't crying. He was roaring, shaking, trembling, heaving with laughter.

I started laughing, too, uncontrollably. Clara Mara, still at my side, clinging on to me, was also laughing. Rembrandt boomed laughter; Titus in a higher key; Jan Lievens; Ribca added laughter to her crying. All laughing. The ragamuffins, laughing.

'Now,' Morteira controlled his heaving, wheezing, dribbling laughter long enough to speak. 'See, now, finally Baruch... Now, you are a proper Jew, after all. I won!'

'What, you mean...?' I couldn't speak for laughing.

'Yes. Bugger the theology!'

'Well said, rabbi.'

'You are a Jew because you are laughing at what has happened to you. Whatever they do to us, Baruch, we Jews – those of us who survive – will go on laughing. And when a Jew laughs in the face of his enemies, he wins.'

Author's Note

History follows the paper. Historical novelists have a bit more freedom. I have changed the chronology of real events, the character of characters, and I have invented incidents, happenings and a painting – Rembrandt's backdrop to the theatre production. Here are a couple of examples of changes: Miriam, Spinoza's sister, died in 1650; Rembrandt did not leave his house on Breestraat until two years after the inventory was taken.

That said, the inventory of Rembrandt's possessions, as part of the bankruptcy proceedings, really was taken one day before Spinoza's *cherem*. At least one historian has made a connection (though not the one I invented in the novel). Odette Vlessing writes: 'The question now is whether it was a coincidence that the *Mahamad* took the most drastic measures available against Spinoza on 27 July 1656, one day after an inventory of Rembrandt's assets had been drawn up. It seems unlikely.' (Odette Vlessing *The Excommunication of Baruch Spinoza: The Birth of a Philosopher* p155 in *Dutch Jewry: Its History and Secular Culture 1500-2000* Israel & Salverda eds Brill 2002)

The following is definite: Rembrandt and Spinoza did live round the corner from each other. They really did know the same people, both from the Jewish community and the *libertijnen*. They had the same lawyer. Spinoza and Rembrandt's son, Titus, as in the novel, both used the device of having themselves declared orphans.

So, did the real Rembrandt and the real Spinoza meet? Historians, following the paper, tend to say they didn't. They didn't write to each other. My own gut feeling is that, in the small world of Amsterdam's artistic and intellectual milieu, it would be remarkable if they hadn't.

The following characters are real and there is some evidence for the personalities I have given them: Dr Nikolaes Tulp (strong evidence), Hendrickje Stoffels (quite strong evidence), Rembrandt (some evidence), Spinoza (some evidence. The sarcasm is attested, the intellectual brilliance is evident, and he really did offer to help Morteira with the wording of the *cherem*.)

The following characters are real, but there is no evidence for the personalities I have given them: Jacob van Ruisdael (I can only apologise...), Franciscus van den Enden (and again...), Clara Maria van den Enden, Theodor Kerckrinck, Pieter Haringh the auctioneer, Gabriel, Ribca and Miriam Spinoza, Samuel de Caseres, the Alvarez (or Alvares) brothers, Arnout Tholincx, Jan Lievens, Dr Deijman, Abraham de hondecoeter and the other surgeons, all of the Waterlanders *(libertijnen)*, the de Graeff brothers.

In the case of Rabbi Saul Levi Morteira, the views attributed to him are largely from his own writings. However, his personality is invented.

One final note for anybody interested in what really happened: Kerckrinck and Clara Maria were married, eventually. Baruch Spinoza left Amsterdam and went on to write thoughts which paved the way for the Enlightenment; making him one of the most influential philosophers of all time.

* * *

The poem in Dutch in praise of Clara Maria van den Enden is from Meinsma, Spinoza en Zijn Kring page 141. Meinsma says the original authorship is uncertain. The (rather free) rendering into English is mine.

Thanks to Karen Haddock, whose stimulating lectures on Dutch art, as part of the Colchester WEA programme, were helpful to me with the Rembrandt sections of the novel. Karen also loaned me *De anatomische les van Dr Deijman*, without which I would have been unable to write the fictionalised section on the Deijman anatomy lesson. Needless to say, any errors or infelicities in that or other parts of the novel are mine, not hers.

* * *

Sincere thanks to Kevin Duffy, publisher of Bluemoose Books, for his warm support of *THORN*. Thanks also to the Bluemoose editorial team: Lin Webb, Leonora Rustamova and Hetha Duffy.

Books read or consulted while the
novel was being written

Alpers S, *Rembrandt's Enterprise: The Studio and the Market*
Chicago University Press 1988

Bomford, D *Art in the Making: Rembrandt* (National Gallery
Publications) Yale University Press 2006.

Cook, H *Matters of Exchange: Commerce Medicine and
Science in the Dutch Golden Age* Yale University Press
2007

Crenshaw, P *Rembrandt's Bankruptcy* Cambridge University
Press 2006

Curley, E M (trans) *The Collected Works of Spinoza* Princeton
University Press 1985

Damasio, A *Looking for Spinoza: Joy Sorrow and the Feeling
Brain* Heinemann 2003

Elves, R H M *Correspondence of Benedict de Spinoza* Wilder
Publications 2007

van Eeghen I (transcription) *Seven Letters By Rembrandt*
Boucher, 1961

Garret, D (ed) *The Cambridge Companion to Spinoza*
Cambridge University Press, 1996

Goldstein, R *Betraying Spinoza: The Renegade Jew Who Gave
Us Modernity* Jewish Encounters series Schocken 2006

Gullan-Whur, M *Within Reason: A Life of Spinoza* Pimlico
2000

Herculano, A *History of the Origin and Establishment of the Inquisition in Portugal,* New York 1972

J Israel and R Salverda (eds) *Dutch Jewry: It's History and Secular Culture (1500-2000)* Brill 2002 especially *Philosophy, Commerce and the Synagogue: Spinoza's Expulsion from the Amsterdam Portuguese Jewish Community in 1656* Jonathan Israel and *The Excommunication of Baruch Spinoza: The Birth of a Philosopher* Odette Vlessing

Johnson, P *A History of the Jews* Phoenix 1993

Meinsma, K O *Spinoza en zijn Kring: over Hollandse Vrijgeesten* HES Utrecht 1980

Middelkoop, N *De anatomische les van Dr Deijman* Amsterdams Historisch Museum 1994

Nadler, S *Rembrandt's Jews* University of Chicago Press 2003

Nadler, S *Spinoza: A Life* Cambridge University Press 1999

Nadler, S *Spinoza's Heresy: immortality and the Jewish mind* Oxford University Press 2001

North, M *Art and Commerce in the Dutch Golden Age* Yale University Press 1990

Pollock, *Spinoza* Duckworth Great Lives, 1935

Rickets, M *Rembrandt* Clearway Logistics 2006

Saperstein, M *Exile in Amsterdam: Saul Levi Morteira's Sermons to a Congregation of New Jews* Hebrew Union College Press 2005

Schama, S *Rembrandt's Eyes* Penguin, 1999

Schama, S *An Embarrassment of Riches: An Interpretation of Dutch Culture in the Golden Age* Fontana Press 1991

Schapelhouman, M *Rembrandt and the Art of Drawing*
Waanders Publishers Rijksmuseum Amsterdam, 2006

Schwarz, G *Rembrandt: His life, his paintings* Penguin 1985

Valentiner, W R *Rembrandt and Spinoza: A Study of the Spiritual Conflicts in Seventeenth Century Holland* Phaidon Press 1957

van der Wetering, E *Rembrandt: The Painter at Work* Amsterdam University Press 2000

Yovel, Y *Spinoza and Other Heretics: The Marrano of Reason* Princeton University Press 1989

Yovel, Y *Spinoza and Other Heretics: The Adventures of Immanence* Princeton University Press 1989

Zumthor, P *Daily Life in Rembrandt's Holland* Weidenfeld and Nicolson 1962